The Guns of Bull Run

A Story of the Civil War's Eve

Volume 1 of the Civil War Series

by JOSEPH A. ALTSHELER

RYAN K ENGLUND, editor and illustrator

Volumes in the Civil War Series

1. **The Guns of Bull Run**
2. The Guns of Shiloh
3. The Scouts of Stonewall
4. The Sword of Antietam
5. The Star of Gettysburg
6. The Rock of Chickamauga
7. The Shades of The Wilderness
8. The Tree of Appomattox

ISBN 978-0-9910491-4-1

To Mrs. Ferris, a great teacher

Front cover: Painting of Thomas Jonathan Jackson at the First Battle of Bull Run, also called First Manassas by Confederate troops. General Jackson received the nickname "Stonewall" at this battle[1]

Back Cover: President Abraham Lincoln; copy of a photograph taken by Mathew Brady 16 May 1861[2]

CONTENTS

Introduction.......... ii

1. NEWS FROM CHARLESTON 1

2. A COURIER TO THE SOUTH 21

3. THE HEART OF REBELLION 39

4. THE FIRST CAPITAL 61

5. THE NEW PRESIDENT 79

6. SUMTER 95

7. THE HOMECOMING 109

8. THE FIGHT FOR A STATE 129

9. THE RIVER JOURNEY 148

10. OVER THE MOUNTAINS 164

11. IN VIRGINIA 184

12. THE FIGHT FOR THE FORT 201

13. THE SEEKER FOR HELP 225

14. IN WASHINGTON 243

15. BATTLE'S EVE 262

16. BULL RUN 277

Endnotes 296

INTRODUCTION

"He could have lived all through American history; he makes it so true. You couldn't do better than to read his books."

Such was the speech of a boy of seventeen to friends gathered in at the New York Public Library on the day after the publication of Joseph A. Altsheler's obituary. "Altsheler is dead," they had said. "Let's go around to the library."

Joseph Alexander Altsheler was born 29 April 1862 in Three Springs, Hart, KY. From 1885 to 1892 he was on the staff of the *Louisville Courier-Journal*. He then joined the staff of the *New York World* and, after a period of political reporting, became editor of the *Thrice-A-Week* edition of the *World*, where he served until his death on 5 June 1919. He authored at least 90 works of fiction—novels and short stories. As a boy, he knew many veterans of the Civil War, including both Union and Confederate generals. The U.S. Civil War is the subject of one of his six series.

According to his 6 June 1919 obituary in the *New York Times*, Altsheler had been named in a recent poll of librarians the most popular writer on boy's books in the nation.

See Moore, Annie Carroll; "Joseph A. Altsheler and American History" (*The Bookman.* New York: 1919), available online from archive.org. Another article, available online at filsonhistorical.org, is by Altsheler's niece: Slater, Lucy Brent; "Kentucky's Most Prolific Author, Joseph A. Altsheler" (*The Filson Club History Quarterly*, Vol. 62, No. 3, July, 1988, pp. 380-388). Also see Altsheler's entry in *The Encyclopedia of Louisville*, John E. Kebler, ed. page 27, available online at Google Books.

Joseph A. Altsheler's (1862-1919) eight-volume Civil War Series alternates between the perspectives of two Kentucky-born cousins whose families selected opposing sides in the War: Henry Kenton (Confederate) and Dick Mason (Union).

The Guns of Bull Run, published in 1914, covers the period from December 1860 through the Battle of Fort Sumter (12-14 April 1861) and the First Battle of Bull Run (21 July 1861). This battle was also known as First Manassas by Confederate forces. Harry Kenton, who chose the Confederate side, is the main character.

Unless otherwise indicated, illustrations for this edition are derived from images created during the U.S. Civil War period (1861-1865) and are in the public domain, according to the rights advisory for each image derived from the website of the Library of Congress. Sources are provided in Endnotes.

Of particular interest is the Morgan collection of Civil War drawings, depicting camp life, marches, and battles by artists such as Alfred R. Waud, William Waud, and Edwin Forbes, who worked on assignments from northern pictorial newspapers, primarily *Harper's Weekly* and *Frank Leslie's Illustrated Newspaper.* For more information, please see http://www.loc.gov/pictures/item/2003691200/

The editor also expresses appreciation for the Liljenquist Family collection of Civil War ambrotypes and tintypes at the Library of Congress, from which were obtained portraits of unidentified Civil War soldiers that appear at the beginning of each chapter. For more information, please refer to http://www.loc.gov/pictures/item/2010650519/

Unidentified Confederate Soldier[3]

1. NEWS FROM CHARLESTON

It would soon be Christmas and Harry Kenton, at his desk in the Pendleton Academy, saw the snow falling heavily outside. The school stood on the skirt of the town, and the forest came down to the edge of the playing field. The great trees, oak and ash and elm, were clothed in white, and they stood out a vast and glittering tracery against the somber sky.

The desk was of the old kind, intended for two, and Harry's comrade in it was his cousin, Dick Mason, of his own years and size. They would graduate in June, and both were large and powerful for their age. There was a strong family resemblance and yet a difference. Harry's face was the more sensitive and at times the blood leaped like quicksilver in his veins. Dick's features indicated a quieter and more stubborn temper. They were equal favorites with teachers and pupils.

Dick's eyes followed Harry's, and he, too, looked at the falling snow and the white forest. Both were thinking of Christmas and the holiday season so near at hand. It was a rich section of Kentucky, and they were the sons of prosperous parents. The snow was fitting at such a time, and many joyous hours would be passed before they returned to school.

The clouds darkened and the snow fell faster. A wind rose and drove it against the panes. The boys heard the blast roaring outside and the comfort of the warm room was heightened by the contrast. Harry's eyes turned reluctantly back to his Tacitus and the customs and manners of the ancient Germans. The curriculum of the Pendleton Academy was simple, like most others at that time. After the primary grades it consisted chiefly of the classics and mathematics. Harry led in the classics and Dick in the mathematics.

Bob Turner, the free colored man, who was janitor of the academy, brought in the morning mail, a dozen letters and three or four newspapers, gave it to Dr. Russell and withdrew on silent feet.

The Doctor was principal of Pendleton Academy, and he always presided over the room in which sat the larger boys, nearly fifty in number. His desk and chair were on a low dais and he sat facing the pupils. He was a large man, with a ruddy face, and thick hair as white as the snow that was falling outside. He had been a teacher fifty years, and three generations in Pendleton owed to him most of the learning that is obtained from books. He opened his letters one by one, and read them slowly.

Harry moved far away into the German forest with old Tacitus. He was proud of his Latin and he did not mean to lose his place as first in the class. The other boys also were absorbed in their books. It was seldom that all were studious at the same time, but this was one of the rare moments. There was no shuffling of feet, and fifty heads were bent over their desks.

It was a full half hour before Harry looked up from his Tacitus. His first glance was at the window. The snow was driving hard, and the forest had become a white blur. He looked next at the Doctor and he saw that the ruddy face had turned white. The old man was gazing intently at an open letter in his hand. Two or three others had fallen to the floor. He read the letter again, folded it carefully, and put it in his pocket. Then he broke the wrapper on one of the newspapers and rapidly read its columns. The whiteness of his face deepened into pallor.

The slight tearing sound caused most of the boys to look up, and they noticed the change in the principal's face. They had never seen him look like that before. It was as if he had received some sudden and deadly stroke. Yet he sat stiffly upright and there was no sound in the room but the rustling of the newspaper as he turned its pages.

Harry became conscious of some strange and subtle influence that had crept into the very air, and his pulse began to leap. The others felt it, too. There was a tense feeling in the room and they became so still that the soft beat of the snow on the windows could be heard.

Not a single eye was turned to a book now. All were intent upon the Doctor, who still read the newspaper, his face without a trace of color, and his strong white hands trembling. He folded the paper presently, but still held it in his hand. As he looked up, he became conscious of the silence in the room, and of the concentrated gaze of fifty pairs of eyes bent upon him. A little color returned to his cheeks, and his hands ceased to tremble. He stood up, took the letter from his pocket, and opened it again.

Dr. Russell was a striking figure, belonging to a classic type found at its best in the border states. A tall man, he held himself erect, despite his years, and the color continued to flow back into the face, which was shaped in a fine strong mold.

"Boys," he said, in a firm, full voice, although it showed emotion, "I have received news which I must announce to you. As I tell it, I beg that you will restrain yourselves, and make little comment here. Its character is such that you are not likely ever to hear anything of more importance."

No one spoke, but a thrill of excitement ran through the room. Harry became conscious that the strange and subtle influence had increased. The pulses in both temples were beating hard. He and Dick leaned forward, their elbows upon the desk, their lips parted a little in attention.

"You know," continued Dr. Russell in the full voice that trembled slightly, "of the troubles that have arisen between the states, North and South, troubles that the best Americans, with our own great Henry Clay at the head, have striven to avert. You know of the election of Lincoln, and how this beloved state of ours, seeking peace, voted for neither Lincoln nor Breckinridge, both of whom are its sons."

The trembling of his voice increased and he paused again. It was obvious that he was stirred by deep emotion and it communicated itself to the boys. Harry was conscious that the thrill, longer and stronger than before, ran again through the room.

"I have just received a letter from an old friend in Charleston," continued Dr. Russell in a shaking voice, "and he tells me that on the twentieth, three days ago, the state of South Carolina seceded from the Union. He also sends me copies of two of the Charleston newspapers of the day following. In both of these papers all dispatches from the other states are put under the head, 'Foreign News.' With the Abolitionists of New England pouring abuse upon all who do not agree with them, and the hot heads of South Carolina rushing into violence, God alone knows what will happen to this distracted country that all of us love so well."

A slave auction at the south, Harpers 13 July 1861

He turned anew to his correspondence. But Harry saw that he was trembling all over. An excited murmur arose. The boys began to talk about the news, and the principal, his thoughts far away, did not call them to order.

"I suppose since South Carolina has gone out that other southern states will do the same," said Harry to his cousin, "and that two republics will stand where but one stood before."

"I don't know that the second result will follow the first," replied Dick Mason.

Harry glanced at him. He was conscious of a certain cold tenacity in Dick's voice. He felt that a veil of antagonism had suddenly been drawn between these two who were the sons of sisters and who had been close comrades all their lives. His heart swelled suddenly. As if by inspiration, he saw ahead long and terrible years. He said no more, but gazed again at the pages of his Tacitus, although the letters only swam before his eyes.

The great buzz subsided at last, although there was not one among the boys who was not still thinking of the secession of South Carolina. They had shared in the excitement of the previous year. A few had studied the causes, but most were swayed by propinquity and kinship, which with youth are more potent factors than logic.

The afternoon passed slowly. Dr. Russell, who always heard the recitations of the seniors in Latin, did not call the class. Harry was so much absorbed in other thoughts that he did not notice the fact. Outside, the clouds still gathered and the soft beat of the snow on the window panes never ceased. The hour of dismissal came at last and the older boys, putting on their overcoats, went silently out. Harry did not dream that he had passed the doors of Pendleton Academy for the last time, as a student.

While the seniors were quiet, there was no lack of noise from the younger lads. Snowballs flew and the ends of red comforters, dancing in the wind, touched the white world with glowing bits of color. Harry looked at them with a sort of pity. The magnified emotions of youth had suddenly made him feel very old and very responsible. When a snowball struck him under the ear he paid no attention to it, a mark of great abstraction in him.

He and his cousin walked gravely on, and left the shouting crowd behind them. Three or four hundred yards further, they came upon the main street of Pendleton, a town of fifteen hundred people, important in its section as a market, and as a financial and political center. It had two banks as solid as stone, and it was the proud boast of its inhabitants that, excepting Louisville and Lexington, its bar was of unequalled talent in the state. Other towns made the same claim, but no matter. Pendleton knew that they were wrong. Lawyers stood very high, especially when they were fluent speakers.

It was a singular fact that the two boys, usually full of talk, after the manner of youth, did not speak until they came to the parting of their ways. Then Harry, the more emotional of the two, and conscious that the veil of antagonism was still between them, thrust out his hand suddenly and said:

"Whatever happens, Dick, you and I must not quarrel over it. Let's pledge our word here and now that, being of the same blood and having grown up together, we will always be friends."

The color in the cheeks of the other boy deepened. A slight moisture appeared in his eyes. He was, on the whole, more reserved than Harry, but he, too, was stirred. He took the outstretched hand and gave it a strong clasp.

"Always, Harry," he replied. "We don't think alike, maybe, about the things that are coming, but you and I can't quarrel."

He released the hand quickly, because he hated any show of emotion, and hurried down a side street to his home. Harry walked on into the heart of the town, as he lived farther away on the other side. He soon had plenty of evidence that the news of South Carolina's secession had preceded him here. There had been no such stir in Pendleton since they heard of Buena Vista, where fifty of her sons fought and half of them fell.

Despite the snow, the streets about the central square were full of people. Many of the men were reading newspapers. It was fifteen miles to the nearest railroad station, and the mail had come in at noon, bringing the first printed accounts of South Carolina's action. In this border state, which was a divided house from first to last, men still guarded their speech. They had grown up together, and they were all of blood kin, near or remote.

"What will it mean?" said Harry to old Judge Kendrick.

"War, perhaps, my son," replied the old man sadly. "The violence of New England in speech and the violence of South Carolina in action may start a flood. But Kentucky must keep out of it. I shall raise my voice against the fury of both factions, and thank God, our people have never refused to hear me."

He spoke in a somewhat rhetorical fashion, natural to time and place, but he was in great earnest. Harry went on, and entered the office of the *Pendleton News*, the little weekly newspaper which dispensed the news, mostly personal, within a radius of fifty miles. He knew that the *News* would appear on the following day, and he was anxious to learn what Mr. Gardner, the editor, a friend of his, would have to say in his columns.

He walked up the dusty stairway and entered the room, where the editor sat amid piles of newspapers. Mr. Gardner was a youngish man, high-colored and with longish hair. He was absorbed so deeply in a copy of the *Louisville Journal* that he did not hear Harry's step or notice his coming until the boy stood beside him. Then he looked up and said dryly:

"Too many sparks make a blaze at last. If people keep on quarreling there's bound to be a fight some time or other. I suppose you've heard that South Carolina has seceded."

"Dr. Russell announced it at the school. Are you telling, Mr. Gardner, what the *News* will have to say about it?"

"I don't mind," replied the editor, who was fond of Harry, and who liked his alert mind. "If it comes to a breach, I'm going with my people. It's hard to tell what's right or wrong, but my ancestors belonged to the South and so do I."

"That's just the way I feel!" exclaimed Harry vehemently.

The editor smiled.

"But I don't intend to say so in the *News* tomorrow," he continued. "I shall try to pour oil upon the waters, although I won't be able to hide my Southern leanings. The Colonel, your father, Harry, will not seek to conceal his."

"No," said Harry. "He will not. What was that?"

The sound of a shot came from the street. The two ran hurriedly down the stairway. Three men were holding a fourth who struggled with them violently. One had wrenched from his hand a pistol still smoking at the muzzle. About twenty feet away was another man standing between two who held him tightly, although he made no effort to release himself.

Harry looked at the two captives. They made a striking contrast. The one who fought was of powerful build, and

4

dressed roughly. His whole appearance indicated the primitive human being, and Harry knew immediately that he was one of the mountaineers who came long distances to trade or carouse in Pendleton.

The man who faced the mountaineer, standing quietly between those who held him, was young and slender, though tall. His longish black hair was brushed carefully. The natural dead whiteness of his face was accentuated by his black mustache, which turned up at the ends like that of a duelist. He was dressed in black broadcloth, the long coat buttoned closely about his body, but revealing a full and ruffled shirt bosom as white as snow. His face expressed no emotion, but the mountaineer cursed violently.

"I can read the story at once," said the editor, shrugging his shoulders. "I know the mountaineer. He's Bill Skelly, a rough man, prone to reach for the trigger, especially when he's full of bad whiskey as he is now, and the other, Arthur Travers, is no stranger to you. Skelly is for the abolition of slavery. All the mountaineers are. Maybe it's because they have no slaves themselves and hate the more prosperous and more civilized lowlanders who do have them. Harry, my boy, as you grow older you'll find that reason and logic seldom control men's lives."

"Skelly was excited over the news from South Carolina," said Harry, continuing the story, which he, too, had read, as an Indian reads a trail, "and he began to drink. He met Travers and cursed the slave-holders. Travers replied with a sneer, which the mountaineer could not understand, except that it hurt. Skelly snatched out his pistol and fired wildly. Travers drew his and would have fired, although not so wildly, but friends seized him. Meanwhile, others overpowered Skelly and Travers is not excited at all, although he watches every movement of his enemy, while seeming to be indifferent."

"You read truly, Harry," said Gardner. "It was a fortunate thing for Skelly that he was overpowered. Somehow, those two men facing each other seem, in a way, to typify conditions in this part of the country at least."

Harry was now watching Travers, who always aroused his interest. A lawyer, twenty-seven or eight years of age, he had little practice, and seemed to wish little. He had a wonderful reputation for dexterity with cards and the pistol. A native of Pendleton, he was the son of parents from one of the Gulf States, and Harry could never quite feel that he was one of their own Kentucky blood and breed.

"You can release me," said Travers quietly to the young men who stood on either side of him holding his arms. "I think the time has come to hunt bigger game than a fool there like Skelly. He is safe from me."

He spoke with a supercilious scorn which impressed

Harry, but which he did not wholly admire. Travers seemed to him to have the quiet deadliness of the cobra. There was something about him that repelled. The men released him. He straightened his long black coat, smoothed the full ruffles of his shirt, and walked away, as if nothing had happened.

Skelly ceased to struggle. The aspect of the crowd, which was largely hostile, sobered him. Steve Allison, the town constable, appeared and, putting his hand heavily upon the mountaineer's shoulder, said:

"You come with me, Skelly."

But old Judge Kendrick intervened.

"Let him go, Steve," he said. "Send him back to the mountains."

"But he tried to kill a man, Judge."

"I know, but extraordinary times demand extraordinary methods. A great and troubled period has come into all our lives. Maybe we're about to face some terrible crisis. Isn't that so?"

"Yes," replied the crowd.

"Then we must not hurry it or make it worse by sudden action. If Skelly is punished, the mountaineers will say it is political. I appeal to you, Dr. Russell, to sustain me."

The white head of the principal showed above the crowd.

"Judge Kendrick is right," he said. "Skelly must be permitted to go. His action, in fact, was due to the strained conditions that have long prevailed among us, and was precipitated by the alarming message that has come today. For the sake of peace, we must let him go."

"All right, then," said Allison, "but he goes without his pistol."

Skelly was put upon his mountain pony, and he rode willingly away amid the snow and the coming dusk, carrying, despite his release, a bitter heart into the mountains, and a tale that would inflame the jealousy with which upland regarded lowland.

The crowd dispersed. Gardner returned to his office, and Harry went home. He lived in the best house in or about Pendleton and his father was its wealthiest citizen. George Kenton, having inherited much land in Kentucky, and two or three plantations further south had added to his property by good management. A strong supporter of slavery, actual contact with the institution on a large scale in the Gulf States had not pleased him, and he had sold his property there, reinvesting the money in his native and, as he believed, more solid state. His title of colonel was real. A graduate of West Point, he had fought bravely with Scott in all the battles in the Valley of Mexico, but now retired and a widower, he lived in Pendleton with Harry, his only child.

Harry approached the house slowly. He knew that his father was a man of strong temper and he wondered how he would take the news from Charleston. All the associations of Colonel Kenton were with the extreme Southern wing, and his influence upon his son was powerful.

But the Pendleton home, standing just beyond the town, gave forth only brightness and welcome. The house itself, large and low, built massively of red brick, stood on the crest of a gentle slope in two acres of ground. The clipped cones of pine trees adorned the slopes, and made parallel rows along the brick walk, leading to the white portico that formed the entrance to the house. Light shone from a half dozen windows.

It seemed fine and glowing to Harry. His father loved his home, and so did he. The twilight had now darkened into night and the snow still drove, but the house stood solid and square to wind and winter, and the flame from its windows made broad bands of red and gold across the snow. Harry went briskly up the walk and then stood for a few moments in the portico, shaking the snow off his overcoat and looking back at the town, which lay in a warm cluster in the hollow below. Many lights twinkled there, and it occurred to Harry that they would twinkle later than usual that night.

He opened the door, hung his hat and overcoat in the hall, and entered the large apartment which his father and he habitually used as a reading and sitting room. It was more than twenty feet square, with a lofty ceiling. A home-made carpet, thick, closely woven, and rich in colors covered the floor. Around the walls were cases containing books, mostly in rich bindings and nearly all English classics. American work was scarcely represented at all. The books read most often by Colonel Kenton were the novels of Walter Scott, whom he preferred greatly to Dickens. Scott always wrote about gentlemen. A great fire of hickory logs blazed on the wide hearth.

Colonel Kenton was alone in the room. He stood at the edge of the hearth, with his back to the fire and his hands crossed behind him. His tanned face was slightly pale, and Harry saw that he had been subjected to great nervous excitement, which had not yet wholly abated.

The colonel was a tall man, broad of chest, but lean and muscular. He regarded his son attentively, and his eyes seemed to ask a question.

"Yes," said Harry, although his father had not spoken a word. "I've heard of it, and I've already seen one of its results."

"What is that?" asked Colonel Kenton quickly.

"As I came through town Bill Skelly, a mountaineer, shot at Arthur Travers. It came out of hot words over the news from Charleston. Nobody was hurt, and they've sent Skelly on his pony toward his mountains."

Colonel Kenton's face clouded.

"I'm sorry," he said. "I fear that Travers will be much too free with stinging remarks. It's a time when men should control their tongues. Do you be careful with yours. You're a youth in years, but you're a man in size, and you should be a man in thought, too. You and I have been close together, and I have trusted you, even when you were a little boy."

"It's so, father," replied Harry, with affection and gratitude.

"And I'm going to trust you yet further. It may be that I shall give you a task requiring great skill and energy."

The colonel looked closely at his son, and he gave silent approval to the tall, well-knit form, and the alert, eager face.

"We'll have supper presently," he said, "and then we will talk with visitors. Some you know and some you don't. One of them, who has come far, is already in the house."

Harry's eyes showed surprise, but he knew better than to

ask questions. The colonel had carried his military training into private life.

"He is a distant relative of ours, very distant, but a relative still," continued Colonel Kenton. "You will meet him at supper. Be ready in a half hour."

The dinner of city life was still called supper in the South, and Harry hastened to his room to prepare. His heart began to throb with excitement. Now they were to have visitors at night and a mysterious stranger was there. He felt dimly the advance of great events.

Harry Kenton was a normal and healthy boy, but the discussions, the debates, and the passions sweeping over the Union throughout the year had sifted into Pendleton also. The news today had merely struck fire to tinder prepared already, and, infused with the spirit of youth, he felt much excitement but no depression. Making a careful toilet he descended to the drawing room a little before the regular time. Although he was early, his father was there before him, standing in his customary attitude with his back to the hearth, and his hands clasped behind him.

"Our guest will be down in a few minutes," said Colonel Kenton. "He comes from Charleston and his name is Raymond Louis Bertrand. I will explain how he is related to us."

He gave a chain of cousins extending on either side from the Kenton family and the Bertrand family until they joined in the middle. It was a slender tie of kinship, but it sufficed in the South. As he finished, Bertrand himself came in, and was introduced formally to his Kentucky cousin. Harry would have taken him for a Frenchman, and he was, in very truth, largely of French blood. His black eyes and hair, his swarthy complexion, gleaming white teeth and quick, volatile manner showed a descendant of France who had come from the ancient soil by way of Haiti, and the great negro rebellion to the coast of South Carolina. He seemed strange and foreign to Harry, and yet he liked him.

"And this is my young cousin, the one who is likely to be so zealous for our cause," he said, smiling at Harry with flashing black eyes. "You are a stalwart lad. They grow bigger and stronger here than on our warm Carolina coast."

"Raymond arrived only three hours ago," said Colonel Kenton in explanation. "He came directly from Charleston, leaving only three hours after the resolution in favor of secession was adopted."

5

"And a rough journey it was," said Bertrand vivaciously. "I was rattled and shaken by the trains, and I made some of the connections by horseback over the wild hills. Then it was a long ride through the snow to your hospitable home here, my good cousin, Colonel Kenton. But I had minute directions, and no one noticed the stranger who came so quietly around the town, and then entered your house."

Harry said nothing but watched him intently. Bertrand spoke with a rapid lightness and grace and an abundance of gesture, to which he was not used in Kentucky. He ate plentifully, and, although his manners were delicate, Harry felt to an increasing degree his foreign aspect and spirit. He did not wonder at it when he learned later that Bertrand, besides being chiefly of French blood, had also been educated in Paris.

"Was there much enthusiasm in South Carolina when the state seceded, Raymond?" asked Colonel Kenton.

"I saw the greatest joy and confidence everywhere," he replied, the color flaming through his olive face. "The whole state is ablaze. Charleston is the heart and soul of our new alliance. Rhett and Yancey of Alabama, and the great orators make the souls of men leap. Ah, sir, if you could only have been in Charleston in the course of recent months! If you could have heard the speakers! If you could have seen how the great and righteous Calhoun's influence lives after him! And then the writers! That able newspaper, the *Mercury*, has thundered daily for our cause. Simms, the novelist, and Timrod and Hayne, the poets have written for it. Let the cities of the North boast of their size and wealth, but they cannot match Charleston in culture and spirit and vivacity!"

Harry saw that Bertrand felt and believed every word he said, and his enthusiasm was communicated to the colonel, whose face flushed, and to Harry, too, whose own heart was beating faster.

"It was a great deed!" exclaimed Colonel Kenton. "South Carolina has always dared to speak her mind, but here in Kentucky some of the cold North's blood flows in our veins and we pause to calculate and consider. We must hasten events. Now, Raymond, we will go into the library. Our friends will be here in a half hour. Harry, you are to stay with us. I told you that you are to be trusted."

They left the table, and went into the great room where the fire had been built anew and was casting a ruddy welcome through the windows. The two men sat down before the blaze and each fell silent, engrossed in his thoughts. Harry felt a pleased excitement. Here was a great and mysterious affair, but he was going to have admittance to the heart of it. He walked to the window, lifted the curtain, and looked out. A slender erect figure was already coming up the walk, and he recognized Travers.

Travers knocked at the door and was received cordially. Colonel Kenton introduced Bertrand, saying:

"The messenger from the South."

Travers shook hands and nodded also to signify that he understood. Then came Culver, the state senator from the district, a man of middle years, bulky, smooth shaven, and oratorical. He was followed soon by Bracken, a tobacco farmer on a great scale, Judge Kendrick, Reid and Wayne, both lawyers, and several others, all of wealth or of influence in that region. Besides Harry, there were ten in the room.

"I believe that we are all here now," said Colonel Kenton. "I keep my son with us because, for reasons that I will explain later, I shall nominate him for the task that is needed."

"We do not question your judgment, colonel," said Senator Culver. "He is a strong and likely lad. But I suggest that we go at once to business. Mr. Bertrand, you will inform us what further steps are to be taken by South Carolina and her neighboring states. South Carolina may set an example, but if the others do not follow, she will merely be a sacrifice."

Bertrand smiled. His smile always lighted up his olive face in a wonderful way. It was a smile, too, of supreme confidence.

"Do not fear," he said. "Alabama, Mississippi, Florida, and Louisiana are ready. We have word from them all. It is only a matter of a few days until every state in the lower south goes out, but we want also and we need greatly those on the border, famous states like your Kentucky and Virginia. Do you not see how you are threatened? With the triumph of the rail-splitter, Lincoln, the seat of power is transferred to the North. It is not alone a question of slavery. The balance of the Union is destroyed. The South loses leadership. Her population is not increasing rapidly, and hereafter she will merely hold the stirrup while the North sits in the saddle."

A murmur arose from the men. More than one clenched his hands, until the nails pressed into the flesh. Harry, still standing by the window, felt the influence of the South Carolinian's words more deeply perhaps than any other. The North appeared to him cold, jealous, and vengeful.

"You are right about Kentucky and Virginia," said Senator Culver. "The secession of two such strong states would strike terror in the North. It would influence the outside world, and we would be in a far better position for war, if it should come. Governor Magoffin will have to call a special session of the legislature, and I think there will be enough of us in both Senate and House to take Kentucky out."

Bertrand's dark face glowed.

"You must do it! You must do it!" he exclaimed. "And if you do our cause is won!"

There was a thoughtful silence, broken at last by Colonel Kenton, who turned an inquiring eye upon Bertrand.

"I wish to ask you about the Knights of the Golden Circle," he said. "I hear that they are making great headway in the Gulf States."

Raymond hesitated a moment. It seemed that he, too, felt for the first time a difference between himself and these men about him who were so much less demonstrative than he. But he recovered his poise quickly.

"I speak to you frankly," he replied. "When our new confederation is formed, it is likely to expand. A hostile union will lie across our northern border, but to the south the way is open. There is our field. Spain grows weak and the great island of Cuba will fall from her grasp. Mexico is torn by one civil war after another. It is a grand country, and it would prosper mightily in strong hands. Beyond lie the unstable states of Central America, also awaiting good rulers."

Colonel Kenton frowned and the lawyers looked doubtful.

"I can't say that I like your prospect," the colonel said. "It seems to me that your knights of the Golden Circle meditate a great slave empire which will eat its way even into South America. Slavery is not wholly popular here. Henry Clay long ago wished it to be abolished, and his is a mighty name among us. It would be best to say little in Kentucky of the Knights of the Golden Circle. Our climate is a little too cold for such a project."

George W. L. Bickley, Knights of the Golden Circle[6]

Bertrand bit his lip. Swift and volatile, he showed disappointment, but, still swift and volatile, he recovered quickly.

"I have no doubt that you are right, Colonel Kenton," he said, in the tone of one who conforms gracefully, "and I shall be careful when I go to Frankfort with Senator Culver to say nothing about it."

But Harry, who watched him all the time, read tenacity and purpose in his eyes. This man would not relinquish his great southern dream, a dream of vast dominion, and he had a powerful society behind him.

"What news, then, will you send to Charleston?" asked Bertrand at length. "Will you tell her that Kentucky, the state of great names, will stand beside her?"

"Such a message shall be carried to her," replied Colonel Kenton, speaking for them all, "and I propose that my son Harry be the messenger. These are troubled times, gentlemen, and full of peril. We dare not trust to the mails, and a lad, carrying letters, would arouse the least suspicion. He is strong and resourceful. I, his father, should know best and I am willing to devote him to the cause."

Harry started when he heard the words of his father, and his heart gave a great leap of mingled surprise and joy. Such a journey, such an enterprise, made an instant appeal to his impulsive and daring spirit. But he did not speak, waiting upon the words of his elders. All of them looked at him, and it seemed to Harry that they were measuring him, both body and mind.

"I have known your boy since his birth," said Senator Culver, "and he is all that you say. There is none stronger and better. The choice is good."

"Good! Aye, good indeed!" said the impetuous Bertrand. "How they will welcome him in Charleston!"

"Then, gentlemen," said Colonel Kenton, very soberly, "you are all agreed that my son shall carry to South Carolina the message that Kentucky will follow her out of the Union?"

"We are," they said, all together.

"I shall be glad and proud to go," said Harry, speaking for the first time.

"I knew it without asking you," said Colonel Kenton. "I suggest to you, friends, that he start before dawn, and that he go to Winton instead of the nearest station. We wish to avoid observation and suspicion. The fewer questions he has to answer, the better it will be for all of us."

They agreed with him again, and, in order that he might be fresh and strong for his journey, Harry was sent to his bedroom. Everything would be made ready for him, and Colonel Kenton would call him at the appointed hour. As he withdrew he bade them in turn good night, and they returned his courtesy gravely.

It was one thing to go to his room, but it was another to sleep. He undressed and sat on the edge of the bed. Only when he was alone did he realize the tremendous change that had come into his life. Nor into his life alone, but into the lives of all he knew, and of millions more.

It had ceased snowing and the wind was still. The earth was clothed in deep and quiet white, and the pines stood up, rows of white cones, silvered by the moonlight. Nothing moved out there. No sound came. He felt awed by the world of night, and the mysterious future which must be full of strange and great events.

He lay down between the covers and, although sleep was long in coming, it came at last and it was without dreams.

Unidentified Confederate Soldier, Mounted Rifles[7]

2. A COURIER TO THE SOUTH

Harry was awakened by his father shaking his shoulder. It was yet dark outside, but a small lamp burned on his table.

"It is time for you to go, Harry," said Colonel Kenton, somewhat unsteadily. "Your horse, bridle and saddle on, is waiting. Your breakfast has been cooked for you, and everything else is ready."

Harry dressed rapidly in his heaviest and warmest clothing. He and his father ate breakfast by lamplight, and when he finished it was not yet dawn. Then the Colonel himself brought him his overcoat, comforter, overshoes, and fur cap.

"The saddlebags are already on your horse," he said, "and they are filled with the things you will need. In this pocket-book you will find five hundred dollars, and here is, also, an order on a bank in Charleston for more. See that you keep both money and order safely. I trust to you to spend the money in the proper manner."

Harry put both in an inside pocket of his waistcoat, and then his father handed him a heavy sealed letter.

"This you must guard with your life," he said. "It is not addressed to anybody, but you can give it to Senator Yancey, who is probably in Charleston, or Governor Pickens, of South Carolina, or General Beauregard, who, I understand, is coming to command the troops there, and whom I knew in former days, or to General Ripley. It contains Kentucky's promise to South Carolina, and it is signed by many of us. And now, Harry, let prudence watch over action. It is no common errand upon which you ride."

The colonel walked with him to the gate where the horse stood. Harry did not know who had brought the animal there, but he believed that his father had done so with his own hand. The boy sprang into the saddle, Colonel Kenton gave him a strong grasp of the hand, undertook to say something but, as he did so, the words choked in his throat, and he walked hastily toward the house.

Harry spoke to his horse, but a hundred yards away, before he came to the first curve in the road, he stopped and looked back. Colonel Kenton was standing in the doorway, his figure made bright in the moonlight. Harry waved his hand and a hand was waved in return. Tears arose to his own eyes, but he was youth in the saddle, with the world before him, and the mist was gone quickly.

The snow was six or eight inches deep, and lay unbroken in the road. But the horse was powerful, shod carefully for snow and ice, and Harry had been almost from infancy an expert rider. His spirits rose. He had no fear of the stillness and the dark. But one could scarcely call it the dark, since brilliant stars rode high in a bright blue heaven, and the forest on either side of him was a vast and intricate tracery of white touched with silver.

He examined his saddle bags, and found in them a silver-mounted pistol and cartridges which he transferred to his belt. The line of the mountains lay near the road, and he remembered Bill Skelly and those like him. The weapon gave him new strength. Skelly and his comrades might come on any pretext they chose.

The road lay straight toward the south, edged on either side by forest. Now and then he passed a silent farm house, set back among the trees, and once a dog barked, but there was no sound, save the tread of the horse's feet in the snow, and his occasional puff when he blew the steam from his nostrils. Harry did not feel the cold. The heavy overcoat protected his body, and the strong action of the heart, pouring the blood in a full tide through his veins, kept him warm.

The east whitened. Dawn came. Thin spires of smoke began to rise from distant houses in the woods or fields. Harry was already many miles from Pendleton, and then something rose in his throat again. He remembered his father standing in the portico, and, strangely enough, the Tacitus lying in his locked desk at the academy. But he crushed it down. His abounding youth made him consider as weak and unworthy, an emotion which a man would merely have reckoned as natural.

8

The station at Winton was a full twenty miles from Pendleton and, with such heavy snow, Harry did not expect to arrive until late in the afternoon. Nor would there be any need for him to get there earlier, as no train for Nashville reached that place until half past six in the evening. His horse showed no signs of weariness, but he checked his speed, and went on at an easy walk.

The road curved nearer to a line of blue hills, which sloped gradually upward for scores of miles, until they became mountains. All were clothed with forest, and every tree was heavy with snow. A line between the trees showed where a path turned off from the main road and entered the hills. As Harry approached it, he heard the crunching of horses' hoofs in the snow. A warning instinct caused him to urge his own horse forward, just as four riders came into view.

He saw that the men in the saddles, who were forty or

fifty yards away, were mountaineers, like Skelly. They wore fur caps; heavy blanket shawls were drooped about their shoulders and every one carried a rifle. As soon as they saw the boy they shouted to him to halt.

Harry's alert senses took alarm. They must have gained some knowledge of his errand and its nature. Perhaps word had been sent from Pendleton by those who were arraying themselves on the other side that he be intercepted. When they cried to him to stop, he struck his horse sharply, shouted to him, and bent far over against his neck. Colonel Kenton had chosen well. The horse responded instantly. He seemed to gather his whole powerful frame compactly together, and shot forward. The nearest mountaineer fired, but the bullet merely whistled where the horse and rider had been, and sent snow flying from the bushes on the other side of the road. A second rifle cracked but it, too, missed the flying target, and the mountaineers, turning into the main road, gave pursuit.

Harry felt a cold shiver along his spine when the leading man pulled trigger. It was the first time in his life that any one had ever fired upon him, and the shiver returned with the second shot. And since they had missed, confidence came. He knew that they could not overtake him, and they would not dare to pursue him long. He glanced back. They were a full hundred yards in the rear, riding all four abreast. He remembered his own pistol, and, drawing it from his belt, he sent a bullet toward the pursuit. It was too long a range for serious work, but he intended it as a warning that he, too, was armed and would fight.

The road still ran through the forest with the hills close on the left. Up went the sun, casting a golden glory over the white earth. Harry beheld afar only a single spire of smoke. The houses were few in that region, and he might go four or five miles without seeing a single human being, save those who pursued. But he was not afraid. His confidence lay chiefly in the powerful animal that he rode, and he saw the distance between him and the four men lengthen from a hundred to two hundred yards. One of them fired another shot at him, but it only shook the snow from a tree fifteen feet away. He could not keep from sending back a taunting cry.

On went the sun up the curve of the heavens, and the brilliant light grew. The forest thinned away. The line of hills retreated, and before him lay fields, extending to both right and left. The eye ranged over a great distance and he counted the smoke of five farm houses. He believed that the men would not pursue him into the open country, but he urged his horse to greater speed, and did not turn in his saddle for a quarter of an hour. When he finally looked back the mountaineers were gone. He could see clearly a half-mile, and he knew now that his surmise had come true. They dared to pursue only in the forest, and having failed, they would withdraw into the hills.

He drew his horse down to a walk, patted his shoulder, and spoke to him words of approval. He was not sorry now that he had passed through the adventure. It would harden him to risks and dangers to come. He made up his mind, also, to say nothing about it. He could send a warning back from Winton, but the men in Pendleton knew how to protect themselves, and the message might fall into wrong hands.

His journey continued in such peace that it was hard to believe men had fired upon him, and in the middle of the afternoon he reached Winton. He left his horse, saddle and bridle at a livery stable, stating that they would be called for by Colonel Kenton, who was known throughout the region, and sought food at the crude little wooden hotel. He was glad that he saw no one whom he knew, because, after the fashion of the country, they would ask him many questions, and he felt relief, too, when the train arrived.

Dark had already come when Harry entered the car. There were no coaches for sleepers, and he must make himself comfortable as best he could on the red plush seat, sprinkled thickly with ashes and cinders from the engine. Fortunately, he had the seat alone, although there were many people in the car.

The train, pouring out a huge volume of black smoke, pulled out of the station with a great clatter that never ceased. Now Harry felt an ebb of the spirits and melancholy. He was leaving behind Pendleton and all that he had known. In the day the excitement, the cold air, and the free world about him had kept him up. Now the swaying and jarring of the train, crude like most others in that early time of railways, gave him a sense of illness.

Railroad bridge[9]

The window at his elbow rattled incessantly, and the ashes and cinders sifted in, blackening his face and hands. Three or four smoking lamps, hung from the ceiling, lighted the car dimly, and disclosed but partly the faces of the people around him. Some were asleep already. Others ate their suppers from baskets. Harry felt of his pockets at intervals to see that his money and letters were safe, and he kept his saddle bags closely on the seat beside him.

The nausea created by the motion of the train passed away soon. He put his face against the dusty window pane and tried to see the country. But he could catch only glimpses of snowy woods and fields, and, once or twice, flashes of water as they crossed rivers. The effort yielded little, and he turned his attention to the people. He noted only one who differed in aspect from the ordinary country passenger.

A man of middle years sat rigidly erect at the far end of the car. He wore a black hat, broad of brim, and all his clothing was black and precise. His face was shaven smoothly, save for a long gray mustache with an upward curve. While the people about him talked in a miscellaneous fashion, he did not join them, and his manner did not invite approach even in those easy times.

Harry was interested greatly. The stranger presently opened a valise, took out some food, and ate delicately. Then he drew a small silver cup from the same valise, filled it at the drinking stand, drank, and returned it to the valise. Without a crumb having fallen on clothing or floor, he resumed his seat and gazed straight before him.

Harry's interest in the stranger increased. He had a fine face, cut clearly, and of a somewhat severe and melancholy cast. Always he gazed straight before him, and his mind seemed to be far from the people in the car. It was obvious that he was not the ordinary traveler, and the boy spent some time in trying to guess his identity. Then he gave it up, because he was growing sleepy.

Excitement and the long physical strain were now telling upon Harry. He leaned his head against the corner of the seat and the wall, drew his overcoat as a blanket about his body and shoulders, and let his eyelids droop. The dim train grew dimmer, and he slept.

The train was due at Nashville between midnight and morning, and Harry was awakened by the conductor a half hour before he reached the city. He shook himself, put on his overcoat that he had used as a blanket, and tried to look through the window. He saw only darkness rushing past, but he knew that he had left Kentucky behind, and it seemed to him that he had come into an alien land, a land of future friends, no doubt, but as yet, the land of the stranger.

All the people in the train were awakening, and were gathering their baggage sleepily about them. But the stranger, who drank from the silver cup, seemed not to have been asleep at all. He still sat rigidly erect, and his melancholy look had not abated. His valise lay on the seat beside him. Harry noticed that it was large and strong, with metal clasps at the corners.

The engine was whistling already for Nashville, and Harry threw his saddle bags over his arm. He was fully awake now, alert and eager. This town of Nashville was full of promise. It had been the home of the great Andrew Jackson, and it was one of the important cities of the South, where cities were measured by influence rather than population, because all, except New Orleans, were small.

As the train slowed down, Harry arose and stood in the aisle. The stranger also stood up, and Harry noticed that his bearing was military. He looked around, his eyes met Harry's—perhaps he had been observing him in the night—and he smiled. It was a rare, illuminating smile that made him wonderfully attractive, and Harry smiled back. He did not know it, but he was growing lonely, with the loneliness of youth, and he wanted a friend.

"You are stopping in Nashville?" said the man with the friendliness of the time.

"For a day only. I am then going further south."

Harry had answered without hesitation. He did not believe it possible that this man could be planning anything against him or his errand. The tall stranger looked upon him with approval.

"I noticed you in the train last night when you slept," he said, speaking in the soft, musical accents of the seaboard South. "Your sleep was very deep, almost like collapse. You showed that you had been through great physical and mental strain, and even before you fell asleep your anxious look indicated that you rode on an errand of importance."

Harry gazed at him in surprise, mingled with a little alarm. The strange man laughed musically and with satisfaction.

"I am neither a detective nor a conspirator," he said. "These are times when men travel upon anxious journeys. I go upon one myself, but since we are in Tennessee, well south of the Mason and Dixon line, I make no secret of it. I am Leonidas Talbot, of South Carolina, until a week ago a colonel in the American army, but now bound for my home in Charleston. You boarded this train at a station in Kentucky, either the nearest or among the nearest to Pendleton. A resemblance, real or fancied, has caused me to notice you closely."

The man was looking at him with frank blue eyes set well apart, and Harry saw no need of concealing his identity.

"My name is Kenton, Henry Kenton—though people generally call me Harry—and I live at Pendleton in

Kentucky," he replied.

Now the smile of Leonidas Talbot, late colonel U. S. A., became rarely sweet.

"I should have guessed it," he said. "The place where you joined us and the strong resemblance should have made me know. You must be the son of Colonel George Kenton."

"Yes," said Harry.

"Then, young sir, let me shake your hand."

His manner seemed so warm and natural that Harry held out his hand, and Colonel Talbot gave it a strong clasp.

"Your father and I have served together," he said. "We were in the same class at West Point, and we fought in the same command against the Indians on the plains. I saw him again at Cerro Gordo, and we were side by side at Contreras, Molino del Rey, and the storming of Chapultepec. He left the service sometime after we came back from Mexico, but I remained in it, until—recent events. It is fitting that I should meet his son here, when we go upon errands which are, perhaps, similar in nature. I infer that your destination is Charleston!"

"Yes," said Harry impulsively, and he was not sorry that he had obeyed the impulse.

"Then we shall go together," said Colonel Talbot. "I take it that many other people are now on their way to this same city of Charleston, which since the secession of South Carolina has become the most famous in the Union."

"I shall be glad if you will take me with you," said Harry. "I know little of Charleston and the lower South, and I need company."

"Then we will go to a hotel," said Colonel Talbot. "On a journey like this two together are better than one alone. I know Nashville fairly well, and while it is of the undoubted South, it will be best for us, while we are here, to keep quiet tongues in our heads. We cannot get a train out of the city until the afternoon."

They were now in the station and everybody was going out. It was not much past midnight, and a cold wind blowing across the hills and the Cumberland River made Harry shiver in his overcoat. Once more he was glad of his new comradeship with a man so much his superior in years and worldly wisdom.

Snow lay on the ground, but not so deep as in Kentucky. Houses, mostly of wood, and low, showed dimly through the dusk. No carriages met the train, and the people were melting away already to their destinations.

"I'll lead the way," said Colonel Talbot. "I know the best hotel, and for travelers who need rest the best is always none too good."

He led briskly through the silent and lonely streets, until they came to a large brick building with several lights shining from the wide and open door. They entered the lobby of the hotel, one carrying his saddle bags, the other his valise, and registered in the book that the sleepy clerk shoved toward them. Several loungers still sat in cane-bottomed chairs along the wall, and they cast curious glances at Harry and the colonel.

The hotel was crowded, the clerk said. People had been crowding into town in the last few days, as there was a great stir in the country owing to the news from Charleston. He could give them only one room, but it had two beds.

"It will do," said the colonel, in his soft but positive voice. "My young friend and I have been traveling hard and we need rest."

Harry would have preferred a room alone, but his trust in Colonel Talbot had already become absolute. This man must be what he claimed to be. There was no trace of deceit about him. His heart had never before warmed so much to a stranger.

Colonel Talbot closed and locked the door of their room. It was a large bare apartment with two windows overlooking the town, and two small beds against opposite walls. The colonel put his valise at the foot of one bed, and walked to the window. The night had lightened somewhat and he saw the roofs of buildings, the dim line of the yellow river, and the dusky haze of hills beyond. He turned his head and looked steadily in the direction in which lay Charleston. A look of ineffable sadness overspread his face.

The light on the table was none too bright, but Harry saw

Colonel Talbot's melancholy eyes, and he could not refrain from asking:

"What's the trouble, colonel?"

The South Carolinian turned from the window, sat down on the edge of the bed and smiled. It was an illuminating smile, almost the smile of youth.

"I'm afraid that everything's the matter, Harry, boy," he said. "South Carolina, the state that I love even more than the Union to which it belongs, or belonged, has gone out, and, Harry, because I'm a son of South Carolina I must go with it—and I don't want to go. But I've been a soldier all my life. I know little of politics. I have grown up with the feeling that I must stay with my people through all things. I must be kin by blood to half the white people in Charleston. How could I desert them?"

"You couldn't," said Harry emphatically.

Colonel Leonidas Talbot smiled. It is possible that, at the moment, he wished for the sanguine decision of youth, which could choose a side and find only wrong in the other.

"In my heart," he continued, "I do not wish to see the Union broken up, although the violence of New England orators and the raid of John Brown has appalled me. But, Harry, pay good heed to me when I say it is not a mere matter of going out of the Union. It may not be possible for South Carolina and the states that follow her to stay out."

"I don't understand you," said the boy.

"It means war! It means war, as surely as the rising of the sun in the morning. Many think that it does not; that the new republic will be formed in peace, but I know better. A great and terrible war is coming. Many of our colored people in Charleston and along the Carolina coast came by the way of the West Indies. They have strange superstitions. They believe that some of their number have the gift of second sight. In my childhood I knew two old women who claimed the power, and they gave apparent proofs that were extraordinary. I feel just now as if I had the gift myself, and I tell you, Harry, although you can see only a dark horizon from the window, I see one that is blood red all the way to the zenith. Alas, our poor country!"

Harry stared at him in amazement. The colonel, although he had called his name, seemed to have forgotten his presence. A vivid and powerful imagination had carried him not only from the room, but far into the future. He recovered himself with an abrupt little shrug of the shoulders.

Camp at night; Edwin Forbes[10]

"I am too old a man to be talking such foolishness to a boy," he said, briskly. "To bed, Harry! To bed! Your sleep on the train was brief and you need more! So do I!"

Harry undressed quickly, and put himself under the covers, and the colonel also retired, although somewhat more leisurely. The boy could not sleep for some time. One vision was present in his mind, that of Charleston, the famous city to which they were going. The effect of Colonel Talbot's ominous words had worn off. He would soon see the city which had been so long a leader in Southern thought and action, and he would see, too, the men who had so boldly taken matters in their own hands. He admired their courage and daring.

It was late when Harry awoke, and the colonel was already up and dressed. But the man waited quietly until the boy was dressed also, and they went down to breakfast together. Despite the lateness of the hour the dining-room was still crowded, and the room buzzed with animated talk. Harry knew very well that Charleston was the absorbing topic, just as it had been the one great thought in his own mind. The people about him seemed to be wholly of Southern sympathies, and he knew very well that Tennessee, although she might take her own time about it, would follow South Carolina out of the Union.

They found two vacant seats at a table, where three men already sat. One was a member of the Legislature, who talked somewhat loudly; the second was a country merchant of middle age, and the third was a young man of twenty-five, who had very little to say. The legislator, whose name was Ramsay, soon learned Colonel Talbot's identity, and he would have proclaimed it to everybody about him, had not the colonel begged him not to do so.

"But you will at least permit me to shake your hand, Colonel Talbot," he said. "One who can give up his commission in the army and come back to us as you have done is the kind of man we need."

Colonel Talbot gave a reluctant hand.

"I am proud to have felt the grasp of one who will win many honors in the coming war," said Ramsay.

"Or more likely fill a grave," said Colonel Talbot, dryly.

The silent young man across the table looked at the South Carolinian with interest, and Harry in his turn examined this stranger. He was built well, shaven smoothly, and did not look like a Tennessean. His thin lips, often pressed closely together, seemed to indicate a capacity for silence, but when he saw Harry looking at him he smiled and said:

"I gather from your conversation that you are going to Charleston. All southern roads seem to lead to that town, and I, too, am going there. My name is Shepard, William J. Shepard, of St. Louis."

Colonel Talbot turned a measuring look upon him. It was so intent and comprehensive that the young man flushed slightly, and moved a little in his seat.

"So you are from St. Louis?" said the colonel. "That is a great city, and you must know something about the feeling there. Can you tell me whether Missouri will go out?"

"I cannot," replied Shepard. "No man can. But many of us are at work."

"What do you think?" persisted Colonel Talbot.

"I am hoping. Missouri is really a Southern state, the daughter of Kentucky, and she ought to join her Southern sisters. As the others go out one by one, I think she will follow. The North will not fight, and we will form a peaceful Southern republic."

Colonel Leonidas Talbot of South Carolina swept him once more with that intent and comprehensive gaze.

"The North will fight," he said. "As I told my young friend here last night, a great and terrible war is coming."

"Do you think so?" asked Shepard, and it seemed to Harry that his tone had become one of overwhelming interest. "Then Charleston, as its center and origin, ought to be ready. How are they prepared there for defense?"

Colonel Talbot's eyes never left Shepard's face and a faint pink tint appeared again in the young man's cheeks.

"There are the forts—Sumter, Moultrie, Johnson and Pinckney," replied the South Carolinian, "and I heard to-day that they are building earthworks, also. All are helping and it is said that Toutant Beauregard is going there to take command."

"A good officer," said Shepard, musingly. "I believe you said you were leaving for Charleston this afternoon?"

"No, I did not say when," replied Colonel Talbot, somewhat sharply. "It is possible that Harry and I may linger a while in Nashville. They do not need us yet in Charleston, although their tempers are pretty warm. There has been so much fiery talk, cumulative for so many years, that they regard northern men with extremely hostile eyes. It would not take much to cause trouble."

Colonel Talbot continued to gaze steadily at Shepard, but the Missourian looked down into his plate. It seemed to Harry that there was some sort of play between them, or rather a thread of suspicion, a fine thread in truth, but strong enough to sustain something. He could see, too, that Colonel Talbot was giving Shepard a warning, a warning, veiled and vague, but nevertheless a warning. But the boy liked Shepard.

His face seemed to him frank and honest, and he would have trusted him.

They rose presently and went into the lobby, where the colonel evaded Shepard, as the place was now crowded. More news had come from Charleston and evidently it was to their liking. There was a great amount of talk. Many of the older men sprinkled their words with expressive oaths. The oaths came so naturally that it seemed to be a habit with them. They chewed tobacco freely, and now and then their white shirt fronts were stained with it. All those who seemed to be of prominence wore long black coats, waistcoats cut low, and trousers of a lighter color.

Nathan Bedford Forrest[11]

Near the wall stood a man of heavy build with a great shaggy head and thick black hair all over his face. He was dressed in a suit of rough gray jeans, with his trousers stuffed into high boots.

He carried in his right hand a short, thick riding whip, with which he occasionally switched the tops of his own boots.

Harry spoke to him civilly, after the custom of the time and place. He took him for a mountaineer, and he judged by the heavy whip he carried, that he was a horse or cattle trader.

"They talk of Charleston," said Harry.

"Yes, they talk an' talk," said the man, biting his words, "an' they do nothin'."

"You think they ought to take Tennessee out right away?"

"No, I'm ag'in it. I don't want to bust up this here Union. But I reckon Tennessee is goin' out, an' most all the other Southern states will go out, too. I 'low the South will get whipped like all tarnation, but if she does I'm a Southerner myself, an' I'll have to git whipped along with her. But talkin' don't do no good fur nobody. If the South goes out, it's hittin' that'll count, an' them that hits fastest, hardest, truest, an' longest will win."

The man was rough in appearance and illiterate in speech, but his manner impressed Harry in an extraordinary manner. It was direct and wonderfully convincing. The boy recognized at once a mind that would steer straight through things toward its goal.

"My name is Harry Kenton," he said politely. "I'm from Kentucky, and my father used to be a colonel in the army."

"Mine," said the mountaineer, "is Nat Forrest, Nathan Bedford Forrest for full and long. I'm a trader in livestock, an' I thought I'd look in here at Nashville an' see what the smart folks was doin'. I'd tell 'em not to let Tennessee go out of the Union, but they wouldn't pay any 'tention to a hoss-tradin' mountaineer, who his neighbors say can't write his name."

"I'm glad to meet you, Mr. Forrest," said Harry, "but I'm afraid we're on different sides of the question."

"Mebbe we are 'til things come to a head," said the mountaineer, laughing, "but, as I said, if Tennessee goes out, I reckon I'll go with her. It's hard to go ag'in your own gang. Leastways, 't ain't in me to do it. Now I've had enough of this gab, an' I'm goin' to skip out. Good-bye, young feller. I wish you well."

Bringing his whip once more, and sharply this time, across the tops of his own boots, he strode out of the hotel. His walk was like his talk, straight and decisive. Harry saw Shepard in the lobby making friends, but, imitating his older comrade, he avoided him, and late that afternoon Colonel Talbot and he left for Charleston.

Unidentified Confederate Soldiers[12]

3. THE HEART OF REBELLION

Harry, with his friend Colonel Leonidas Talbot, approached Charleston on Christmas morning. It was a most momentous day to him. As he came nearer, the place looked greater and greater. He had read much about it in the books in his father's house—old tales of the Revolution and stories of its famous families—and now its name was in the mouths of all men.

Charleston, 1861[13]

He had felt a change in his own Kentucky atmosphere at Nashville, but it had become complete when he drew near to Charleston. It was a different world, different alike in appearance and in thought. The contrast made the thrill all the keener and longer. Colonel Talbot, also, was swayed by emotion, but his was that of one who was coming home.

"I was born here, and I passed my boyhood here," he said. "I could not keep from loving it if I would, and I would not if I could. Look how the cold North melts away. See the great magnolias, the live oaks, and the masses of shrubbery! Harry, I promise you that you shall have a good time in this Charleston of ours."

They had left the railroad some distance back, and had come in by stage. The day was warm and pleasant. Two odors, one of flowers and foliage, and the other of the salt sea, reached Harry. He found both good. He felt for the thousandth time of his pocket-book and papers to see that they were safe, and he was glad that he had come, glad that he had been chosen for such an important errand.

The colonel asked the driver to stop the stage at a cross road, and he pointed out to Harry a low, white house with green blinds, standing on a knoll among magnificent live oaks.

"That is my house, Harry," he said, "and this is Christmas Day. Come and spend it with me there."

Harry felt to the full the kindness of Colonel Leonidas Talbot, for whom he had formed a strong affection. The colonel seemed to him so simple, so honest and, in a way, so unworldly, that he had won his heart almost at once. But he felt that he should decline, as his message must be delivered as soon as he arrived in Charleston.

"I suppose you are right," said the colonel, when the boy had explained why he could not accept. "You take your letters to the gentlemen who are going to make the war, and then you and I and others like us, ranging from your age to mine, will have to fight it."

But Harry was not to be discouraged. He could not see

things in a gray light on that brilliant Christmas morning. Here was Charleston before him and in a few hours he would be in the thick of great events. A thrill of keen anticipation ran through all his veins. The colonel and he stood by the roadside while the obliging driver waited. He offered his hand, saying good-bye.

"It's only for a day," said Colonel Leonidas Talbot, as he gave the hand a strong clasp. "I shall be in Charleston tomorrow, and I shall certainly see you."

Harry sprang back to his place and the stage rolled joyously into Charleston. Harry saw at once that the city was even more crowded than Nashville had been. Its population had increased greatly in a few weeks, and he could feel the quiver of excitement in the air. Citizen soldiers were drilling in open places, and other men were throwing up earthworks.

He left the stage and carried over his arm his baggage, which still consisted only of a pair of saddle bags. He walked to an old-fashioned hotel which Colonel Talbot had selected for him as quiet and good, and as he went he looked at everything with a keen and eager interest. The deep, mellow chiming of bells, from one point and then from another, came to his ears. He knew that they were the bells of St. Philip's and St. Michael's, and he looked up in admiration at their lofty spires. He had often heard, in far Kentucky, of these famous churches and their silver chimes.

It seemed to Harry that the tension and excitement of the people in the streets were of a rather pleasant kind. They had done a great deed, and, keyed to a high pitch by their orators and newspapers, they did not fear the consequences. The crowd seemed foreign to him in many aspects, Gallic rather than American, but very likeable.

He reached his hotel, a brick building behind a high iron fence, kept by a woman of olive complexion, middle years, and pleasant manners, Madame Josephine Delaunay. She looked at him at first with a little doubt, because it was a time in Charleston when one must inspect strangers, but when he mentioned Colonel Leonidas Talbot she broke into a series of smiles.

"Ah, the good colonel!" she exclaimed. "We were children

at school together, but since he became a soldier he has gone far from here. And has he returned to fight for his great mother, South Carolina?"

"He has come back. He has resigned from the army, and he is here to do South Carolina's bidding."

"It is like him," said Madame Delaunay. "Ah, that Leonidas, he has a great soul!"

"I travelled with him from Nashville to Charleston," said Harry, "and I learned to like and admire him."

He had established himself at once in the good graces of Madame Delaunay and she gave him a fine room overlooking a garden, which in season was filled with roses and oranges. Even now, pleasant aromatic odors came to him through the open window. He had been scarcely an hour in Charleston but he liked it already. The old city breathed with an ease and grace to which he was unused. The best name that he knew for it was fragrance.

He had a suit of fresh clothing in his saddle bags, and he arrayed himself with the utmost neatness and care. He felt that he must do so. He could not present himself in rough guise to a people who had every right to be fastidious. He would also obtain further clothing out of the abundant store of money, as his father had wished him to make a good appearance and associate with the best.

Old Post Office and the only remaining palmetto in Charleston, c1860-1865[15]

He descended, and found Madame Delaunay in the garden, where she gave him welcome, with grave courtesy. She seemed to him in manner and bearing a woman of wealth and position, and not the keeper of an inn, doing most of the work with her own hands. He learned later that the two could go together in Charleston, and he learned also, that she was the grand-daughter of a great Haitian sugar planter, who had fled from the island, leaving everything to the followers of

Toussaint l'Ouverture, glad to reach the shores of South Carolina in safety.

Madame Delaunay looked with admiration at the young Kentuckian, so tall and powerful for his age. To her, Kentucky was a part of the cold North.

"Can you tell me where I am likely to find Senator Yancey?" asked Harry. "I have letters which I must deliver to him, and I have heard that he is in Charleston."

"There is to be a meeting of the leaders this afternoon in St. Anthony's Hall in Broad street. You will surely find him there, but you must have your luncheon first. I think you must have travelled far."

"From Kentucky," replied Harry, and then he added impulsively: "I've come to join your people, Madame Delaunay. South Carolina has many and powerful friends in the Upper South."

"She will need them," said Madame Delaunay, but with no tone of apprehension. "This, however, is a city that has withstood much fire and blood and it can withstand much more. Now I'll leave you here in the garden. Come to luncheon at one, and you shall meet my other guests."

Harry sat down on a little wooden bench beneath a magnolia. Here in the garden the odor of grass and foliage was keen, and thrillingly sweet. This was the South, the real South, and its warm passions leaped up in his blood. Much of the talk that he had been hearing recently from those older than he passed through his mind. The Southern states did have a right to go if they chose, and they were being attacked because their prominence aroused jealousy. Slavery was a side issue, a mere pretext. If it were not convenient to hand, some other excuse would be used. Here in Charleston, the first home of secession, among people who were charming in manner and kind, the feeling was very strong upon him.

He left the house after luncheon, and, following Madame Delaunay's instructions, came very quickly to St. Andrew's hall in Broad street, where five days before, the Legislature of South Carolina, after adjourning from Columbia, had passed the ordinance of secession.

Two soldiers in the Palmetto uniform were on guard, but

they quickly let him pass when he showed his letters to Senator Yancey. Inside, a young man, a boy, in fact, not more than a year older than himself, met him. He was slender, dark, and tall, dressed precisely, and his manner had that easy grace which, as Harry had noticed already, seemed to be the characteristic of Charleston.

"My name is Arthur St. Clair," he said, "and I'm a sort of improvised secretary for our leaders who are in council here."

"Mine," said Harry, "is Henry Kenton. I'm a son of Colonel George Kenton, of Kentucky, late a colonel in the United States Army, and I've come with important messages from him, Senator Culver, and other Southern leaders in Kentucky."

"Then you will be truly welcome. Wait a moment and I'll see if they are ready to receive you."

He returned almost instantly, and asked Harry to go in with him. They entered a large room, with a dais at the center of the far wall, and a number of heavy gilt chairs covered with velvet ranged on either side of it. Over the dais hung a large portrait of Queen Victoria as a girl in her coronation robes. A Scotch society had occupied this room, but the people of Charleston had always taken part in their festivities. In those very velvet chairs the chaperons had sat while the dancing had gone on in the hall. Then the leaders of secession had occupied them, when they put through their measure, and now they were sitting there again, deliberating.

William Lowndes Yancey, 1860[10]

A man of middle years and of quick, eager countenance arose when young St. Clair came in with Harry.

"Mr. Yancey," said St. Clair, "this is Henry Kenton, the son of Colonel George Kenton, who has come from Kentucky with important letters."

Yancey gave him his hand and a welcome, and Harry

looked with intense interest at the famous Alabama orator, who, with Slidell, of South Carolina, and Toombs of Georgia, had matched the New England leaders in vehemence and denunciation. Mr. Slidell, an older man, was present and so was Mr. Jamison, of Barnwell, who had presided when secession was carried. There were more present, some prominent, others destined to become so, and Harry was introduced to them one by one.

He gave his letters to Yancey and retired with young St. Clair to the other end of the room, while the leaders read what had been written from Kentucky. Harry was learning to become a good observer, and he watched them closely as they read. He saw a look of pleasure come on the face of every one, and presently Yancey beckoned to him.

"These are fine assurances," said the orator, "and they have been brought by the worthy son of a worthy father. Colonel Kenton, Senator Culver and others, have no doubt that Kentucky will go out with us. Now you are a boy, but boys sometimes see and hear more than men, and you are old enough to think; that is, to think in the real sense. Tell us, what is your own opinion?"

Harry flushed, and paused in embarrassment.

"Go on," said Mr. Yancey, persuasively.

"I do not know much," said Harry slowly, wishing not to speak, but feeling that he was compelled by Mr. Yancey to do so, "but as far as I have seen, Kentucky is sorely divided. The people on the other side are perhaps not as strong and influential as ours, but they are more numerous."

A shade passed over the face of Yancey, but he quickly recovered his good humor.

"You have done right to tell us the truth as you see it," he said, "but we need Kentucky badly. We must have the state and we will get it. Did you hear anything before you left, of one Raymond Bertrand, a South Carolinian?"

"He was at my father's house before I came away. I think it was his intention to go from there to Frankfort with some of our own people, and assist in taking out the state."

Yancey smiled.

"Faithful to his errand," he said. "Raymond Bertrand is a

good lad. He has visions, perhaps, but they are great ones, and he foresees a mighty republic for us extending far south of our present border. But now that you have accomplished your task, what do you mean to do, Mr. Kenton?"

"I want to stay here," replied Harry eagerly. "This is the head and center of all things. I think my father would wish me to do so. I'll enlist with the South Carolina troops and wait for what happens."

"Even if what happens should be war?"

"Most of all if it should be war. Then I shall be one of those who will be needed most."

"A right and proper spirit," said Mr. Jamison, of Barnwell. "When we can command such enthusiasm we are unconquerable. Now, we'll not keep you longer, Mr. Kenton. This is Christmas Day, and one as young as you are is entitled to a share of the hilarity. Look after him, St. Clair."

Harry went out with young St. Clair, whom he was now calling by his first name, Arthur. He, too, was staying with Madame Delaunay, who was a distant relative.

Harry ate Christmas dinner that evening with twenty people, many of types new to him. It made a deep impression upon him then, and one yet greater afterward, because he beheld the spirit of the Old South in its inmost shrine, Charleston. It seemed to him in later days that he had looked upon it as it passed.

They sat in a great dining-room upon a floor level with the ground. The magnolias and live oaks and the shrubs in the garden moved in the gentle wind. Fresh crisp air came through the windows, opened partly, and brought with it, as Harry thought, an aroma of flowers blooming in the farther south. He sat with young St. Clair—the two were already old friends—and Madame Delaunay was at the head of the table, looking more like a great lady who was entertaining her friends than the keeper of an inn.

Madame Delaunay wore a flowing white dress that draped itself in folds, and a lace scarf was thrown about her shoulders. Her heavy hair, intensely black, was bound with a gold fillet, after a fashion that has returned a half century later. A single diamond sparkled upon her finger. She seemed to Harry foreign, handsome, and very distinguished.

About half the people in the room were of French blood, most of whom Harry surmised were descendants of people who had fled from Haiti or Santo Domingo. One, Hector St. Hilaire, almost sixty, but a major in the militia of South Carolina, soon proved that the boy's surmise was right. Lemonade and a mild drink called claret-sanger was served to the boys, but the real claret was served to the major, as to the other elders, and the mellowness of Christmas pervaded his spirit. He drank a toast to Madame Delaunay, and the others drank it with him, standing. Madame Delaunay responded prettily, and, in a few words, she asked protection and good fortune for this South Carolina which they all loved, and which had been a refuge to the ancestors of so many of them. As she sat down she looked up at the wall and Harry's glance followed hers. It was a long dining-room, and he saw there great portraits in massive gilt frames. They were of people French in look, handsome, and dressed with great care and elaboration. The men were in gay coats and knee breeches, silk stockings and buckled shoes. Small swords were at their sides. The women were even more gorgeous in velvet or heavy satin, with their hair drawn high upon their heads and powdered. One had a beauty patch upon her cheek.

Major St. Hilaire saw Harry's look as it sped along the wall. He smiled a little sadly and then, a little cheerfully:

"Those are the ancestors of Madame Delaunay," he said, "and some, I may mention in passing, are my own, also. Our gracious hostess and myself are more or less distantly related—less, I fear—but I boast of it, nevertheless, on every possible occasion. They were great people in a great island, once the richest colony of France, the richest colony in all the world. All those people whom you see upon the walls were educated in Paris or other cities of France, and they returned to a life upon the magnificent plantations of Haiti. What has become of that brightness and glory? Gone like snow under a summer sun. 'Tis nothing but the flower of fancy now. The free black savage has made a wilderness of Haiti, and our enemies in the North would make the same of South Carolina."

A murmur of applause ran around the table. Major St. Hilaire had spoken with rhetorical effect and a certain undoubted pathos. Every face flushed, and Harry saw the tears glistening in the eyes of Madame Delaunay who, despite her fifty years, looked very handsome indeed in her white dress, with the glittering gold fillet about her great masses of hair.

The boy was stirred powerfully. His sensitive spirit responded at once to the fervid atmosphere about him, to the color, the glow, the intensity of a South far warmer than the one he had known. Their passions were his passions, and having seen the black and savage Haiti of which Major St. Hilaire had drawn such a vivid picture, he shuddered lest South Carolina and other states, too, should fall in the same way to destruction.

"It can never happen!" he exclaimed, carried away by impulse. "Kentucky and Virginia and the big states of the Upper South will stand beside her and fight with her!"

"The Secessionist Movement", Charleston hotel entrance,
London Illustrated News 2 Feb 1861[17]

The murmur of applause ran around the table again, and Harry, blushing, made himself as small as he could in his chair.

"Don't regret a good impulse. Mr. Kenton," said a

neighbor, a young man named James McDonald—Harry had noticed that Scotch names seemed to be as numerous as French in South Carolina—"the words that all of us believe to be true leaped from your heart."

Harry did not speak again, unless he was addressed directly, but he listened closely, while the others talked of the great crisis that was so obviously approaching. His interest did not make him neglect the dinner, as he was a strong and hearty youth. There were sweets for which he did not care much, many vegetables, a great turkey, and venison for which he did care, finishing with an ice and coffee that seemed to him very black and bitter.

It was past eight o'clock when they rose and any lingering doubts that Harry may have felt were swept away. He was heart and soul with the South Carolinians. Those people in the far north seemed very cold and hard to him. They could not possibly understand. One must be here among the South Carolinians themselves to see and to know.

Harry went to his room, after a polite good-night to all the others. He was not used to long and heavy dinners, and he felt the wish to rest and take the measure of his situation. He threw back the green blinds and opened the window a little. Once more the easy wind brought him that odor of the far south, whether reality or fancy he could not say. But he turned to another window and looked toward the north. Away from the others and away from a subtle persuasiveness that had been in the air, some of his doubts returned. It would not all be so easy. What were they doing in the far states beyond the Ohio?

He heard footsteps in the hail and a voice that seemed familiar. He had left his door partly open, and, when he turned, he caught a glimpse of a face that he knew. It was young Shepard, whom he and Major Talbot had met in Nashville. Shepard saw Harry also, and saluted him cheerfully.

"I've just arrived," he said, "and through letters from friends in St. Louis, members of one of the old French families there, I've been lucky enough to secure a room at Madame Delaunay's inn."

"Fortune has been with us both," said Harry, somewhat doubtfully, but not knowing what else to say.

"It certainly has," said Shepard, with easy good humor. "I'll see you again in the morning and we'll talk of what we've been through, both of us."

He walked briskly on and Harry heard his firm step ringing on the floor. The boy retired to his own room again and locked the door. He had liked Shepard from the first. He had seemed to him frank and open and no one could deny his right to come to Charleston if he pleased. And yet Colonel Talbot, a man of a delicate and sensitive mind, which quickly registered true impressions, had distrusted him. He had even given Harry a vague warning, which he felt that he could not ignore. He made up his mind that he would not see Shepard in the morning. He would make it a point to rise so early that he could avoid him.

His conclusion formed, he slept soundly until the first sunlight poured in at the window that he had left open. Then, remembering that he intended to avoid Shepard, he jumped out of bed, dressed quickly and went down to breakfast, which he had been told he could get as early as he pleased.

Madame Delaunay was already there, still looking smooth and fresh in the morning air. But St. Clair was the only guest who was as early as Harry. Both greeted him pleasantly and hoped that he had slept well. Their courtesy, although Harry had no doubt of its warmth, was slightly more ornate and formal than that to which he had been used at home. He recognized here an older society, one very ancient for the New World.

The breakfast was also different from the solid one that he always ate at home. It consisted of fruits, eggs, bread, and coffee. There was no meat. But he fared very well, nevertheless. St. Clair, he now learned, was a bank clerk, but after office hours he was drilling steadily in one of the Charleston companies.

"If you enlist, come with me," he said to Harry. "I can get you a place on the staff, and that will suit you."

Harry accepted his offer gladly, although he felt that he could not take up his new duties for a few days. Matters of money and other things were to be arranged.

"All right," said St. Clair. "Take your time. I don't think there's any need to hurry."

Harry left Madame Delaunay's house immediately after breakfast, still firm in his purpose to avoid Shepard, and went to the bank, on which he held drafts properly attested. Not knowing what the future held, and inspired perhaps by some counsel of caution, he drew half of it in gold, intending to keep it about his person, risking the chance of robbery. Then he went toward the bay, anxious to see the sea and those famous forts, Sumter, Moultrie and the others, of which he had heard so much.

It was a fine, crisp morning, one to make the heart of youth leap, and he soon noticed that nearly the whole population of the city was going with him toward the harbor. St. Clair, who had departed for his bank, overtook him, and it was evident to Harry that his friend was not thinking much now of banks.

Confederate Artillery, Charleston, 1861[18]

"What is it, Arthur?" asked Harry.

"They stole a march on us yesterday," replied St. Clair. "See that dark and grim mass rising up sixty feet or more near the center of the harbor, the one with the Stars and Stripes flying so defiantly over it? That's Fort Sumter. Yesterday, while we were enjoying our Christmas dinner and talking of the things that we would do, Major Anderson, who commanded the United States garrison in Fort Moultrie, quietly moved it over to Sumter, which is far stronger. The wives and children of the soldiers and officers have been landed in the city with the request that we send them to their homes in the states, which, of course, we will do. But Major Anderson, who holds the fort in the name of the United States, refuses to give it up to South Carolina, which claims it."

Harry felt an extraordinary thrill, a thrill that was, in many ways, most painful. Talk was one thing, action was another. Here stood South Carolina and the Union face to face, looking at each other through the muzzles of cannon. Sumter had one hundred and forty guns, most of which commanded the city, and the people of Charleston had thrown up great earthworks, mounting many cannon.

Boy as he was, Harry was old enough to see that here were all the elements of a great conflagration. It merely remained for somebody to touch fire to the tow. He was not one to sentimentalize, but the sight of the defiant flag, the most beautiful in all the world, stirred him in every fiber. It was the flag under which both his father and Colonel Talbot had fought.

"It has to be, Harry," said St. Clair, who was watching him closely. "If it comes to a crisis we must fire upon it. If we don't, the South will be enslaved and black ignorance and savagery will be enthroned upon our necks."

"I suppose so," said Harry. "But look how the people gather!"

The Battery and all the harbor were now lined with the men, women, and children of Charleston. Harry saw soldiers moving about Sumter, but no demonstration of any kind occurred there. He had not thought hitherto about the garrison of the forts in Charleston harbor. He recognized for the first time that they might not share the opinions of Charleston, and this name of Anderson was full of significance for him. Major Anderson was a Kentuckian. He had heard his father speak of him; they had served together, but it was now evident to Harry that Anderson would not go with South Carolina.

"You'll see a small boat coming soon from Sumter," said St. Clair. "Some of our people have gone over there to confer with Major Anderson and demand that he give up the fort."

"I don't believe he'll do it," said Harry impulsively. Someone touched him upon the shoulder, and turning quickly he saw Colonel Leonidas Talbot. He shook the colonel's hand with vigor, and introduced him to young St. Clair.

"I have just come into the city," said the colonel, "and I heard only a few minutes ago that Major Anderson had removed his garrison from Moultrie to Sumter."

"It is true," said St. Clair. "He is defiant. He says that he will hold the fort for the Union."

"I had hoped that he would give up," said Colonel Talbot. "It might help the way to a composition."

He pulled his long mustache and looked somberly at the flag. The wind had risen a little, and it whipped about the staff. Its fluttering motions seemed to Harry more significant than ever of defiance. He understood the melancholy ring in Colonel Talbot's voice. He, too, like the boy's father, had fought under that flag, the same flag that had led him up the flame-swept slopes of Cerro Gordo and Chapultepec.

"Here they come," exclaimed St. Clair, "and I know already the answer that they bring!"

The small boat that he had predicted put out from Sumter and quickly landed at the Battery. It contained three commissioners, prominent men of Charleston who had been sent to treat with Major Anderson, and his answer was quickly known to all the crowd. Sumter was the property of the United States, not of South Carolina, and he would hold it for the Union. At that moment the wind strengthened, and the flag stood straight out over the lofty walls of Sumter.

"I knew it would be so," said Colonel Talbot, with a sigh. "Anderson is that kind of a man. Come, boys, we will go back into the city. I am to help in building the fortifications, and as I am about to make a tour of inspection I will take you with me."

Harry found that, although secession was only a few days

old, the work of offense and defense was already far advanced. The planters were pouring into Charleston, bringing their slaves with them, and white and black labored together at the earthworks. Rich men, who had never soiled their hands with toil before now, wielded pick and spade by the side of their black slaves. And it was rumored that Toutant Beauregard, a great engineer officer, now commander at the West Point Military Academy, would speedily resign, and come south to take command of the forces in Charleston.

Strong works were going up along the mainland. The South Carolina forces had also seized Sullivan's Island, Morris Island, and James Island and were mounting guns upon them all. Circling batteries would soon threaten Sumter, and, however defiantly the flag there might snap in the breeze, it must come down.

As they were leaving the last of the batteries Harry noticed the broad, strong back and erect figure of a young man who stood with his hands in his pockets. He knew by his rigid attitude that he was looking intently at the battery and he knew, moreover, that it was Shepard. He wished to avoid him, and he wished also that his companion would not see him. He started to draw Colonel Talbot away, but it was too late. Shepard turned at that moment, and the colonel caught sight of his face.

"That man here among our batteries!" he exclaimed in a menacing tone.

"Come away, colonel!" said Harry hastily. "We don't know anything against him!"

But Shepard himself acted first. He came forward quickly, his hand extended, and his eyes expressing pleasure.

"I missed you this morning, Mr. Kenton," he said. "You were too early for me, but we meet, nevertheless, in a place of the greatest interest. And here is Colonel Talbot, too!"

Harry took the outstretched hand—he could not keep from liking Shepard—but Colonel Talbot, by turning slightly, avoided it without giving the appearance of brusqueness. His courtesy, concerning which the South Carolinians of his type were so particular, would not fail him, and, while he avoided the hand, he promptly introduced Shepard and St. Clair.

"I did not expect to find events so far advanced in Charleston," said Shepard. "With the Federal garrison concentrated in Sumter and the batteries going up everywhere, matters begin to look dangerous."

"I suppose that you have made a careful examination of all the batteries," said Colonel Talbot dryly.

"Casual, not careful," returned Shepard, in his usual cheerful tones. "It is impossible, at such a time, to keep from looking at Sumter, the batteries and all the other preparations. We would not be human if we didn't do it, and I've seen enough to know that the Yankees will have a hot welcome if they undertake to interfere with Charleston."

"You see truly," said Colonel Talbot, with some emphasis.

"A happy chance has put me at the same place as Mr. Kenton," continued Shepard easily. "I have letters which admitted me to the inn of Madame Delaunay, and I met him there last night. We are likely to see much of each other."

Colonel Leonidas Talbot raised his eyebrows. When they walked a little further he excused himself, saying that he was going to meet a committee of defense at St. Andrew's Hall, and Harry and Arthur, after talking a little longer with Shepard, left him near one of the batteries.

"I'm going to my bank," said St. Clair. "I'm already long overdue, but it will be forgiven at such a time as this. And I must say, Harry, that Colonel Talbot does not seem to like your acquaintance, Mr. Shepard."

"It is true, he doesn't, although I don't know just why," said Harry.

He saw Shepard at a distance three more times in the course of the day, but he sedulously avoided a meeting. He noticed that Shepard was always near the batteries and earthworks, but hundreds of others were near them, too. He did not return to Madame Delaunay's until evening, when it was time for dinner, where he found all the guests gathered, with the addition of Shepard.

Madame Delaunay assigned the new man to a seat near the foot of the table and the talk ran on much as it had done at the Christmas dinner, Major St. Hilaire leading, which

Harry surmised was his custom. Shepard, who had been introduced to the others by Madame Delaunay, did not have much to say, nor did the South Carolinians warm to him as they had to Harry. A slight air of constraint appeared and Harry was glad when the dinner was over. Then he and St. Clair slipped away and spent the evening roaming about the city, looking at the old historic places, the fine churches, the homes of the wealthy and again at the earthworks and the harbor forts. The last thing Harry saw as he turned back toward Madame Delaunay's was that defiant flag of the Union, still waving above the dark and looming mass of old Sumter.

He was unlocking the door to his room when Shepard came briskly down the hall, carrying his candle in his hand.

"I want to tell you good-bye, Mr. Kenton," he said, "I thought we were to be together here at the inn for some time, but it is not to be so."

"What has happened?"

"It appears that my room had been engaged already by another man, beginning tomorrow morning. I was not informed of it when I came here, but Madame Delaunay has recalled the fact and I cannot doubt the word of a Charleston lady. It appears also that no other room is vacant, owing to the great number of people who have come into the city in the last week or two. So, I go."

He did not seem at all discouraged, his tone being as cheerful as ever, and he held out his hand. Harry liked this man, although it seemed that others did not, and when he released the hand he said:

"Take good care of yourself, Mr. Shepard. As I see it, the people of Charleston are not taking to you, and we do not know what is going to happen."

"Both statements are true," said Shepard with a laugh as he vanished down the hall. Nothing yet had been able to disturb his poise.

Harry went into his own room, and, throwing open his front window to let in fresh air, he heard the hum of voices. He looked down into a piazza and he saw two figures there, a man and a woman. They were Colonel Talbot and Madame

Delaunay. He closed the blind promptly, feeling that unconsciously he had touched upon something hallowed, the thread of an old romance, a thread which, though slender, was nevertheless yet strong. Nor did he doubt that the suggestion of Colonel Leonidas Talbot had caused the speedy withdrawal of Shepard.

Several more days passed. Harry found that he was taken into the city's heart, and its spell was very strong upon him. He knew that much of his welcome was due to the powerful influence of Colonel Leonidas Talbot and to the warm friendship of Arthur St. Clair, who apparently was related to everybody. A letter came from his father, to whom he had written at once of his purpose, giving his approval, and sending him more money. Colonel Kenton wrote that he would come South himself, but he was needed in Kentucky, where a powerful faction was opposing their plans. He said that Harry's cousin, Dick Mason, had joined the home guards, raised in the interests of the old Union, and was drilling zealously.

News from home[19]

The letter made the boy very thoughtful. The news about his cousin opened his eyes. The line of cleavage between North and South was widening into a gulf. But his spirits rose when he enlisted in the Palmetto Guards, and began to see active service. His quickness and zeal caused him to be used as a messenger, and he was continually passing back and forth among the Confederate leaders in Charleston. He also came into contact with the Union officers in Fort Sumter.

The relations of the town and the garrison were yet on a friendly basis. Men were allowed to come ashore and to buy fresh meat, vegetables, and other provisions. Strict orders kept anyone from offering violence or insult to them. Harry saw Anderson once, but he did not give him his name, deeming it best, because of the stand that he had taken, that no talk should pass between them.

He picked up a copy of the *Mercury* one morning and saw that a steamer, the *Star of the West*, was on its way to Charleston from a northern port with supplies for the garrison in Fort Sumter. He read the brief account, threw down the paper, and rushed out for his friend, St. Clair. He knew that the coming of this vessel would fire the Charleston heart, and he was eager to be upon the scene.

Unidentified Confederate Soldier, South Carolina[20]

4. THE FIRST CAPITAL

Harry and Arthur stood two days later upon the sea wall of Charleston. Sumter rose up black and menacing in the clear wintry air. The muzzles of the cannon seemed to point into the very heart of the city, and over it, as ever, flew the defiant flag, the red and blue burning in vivid colors in the thin January sunshine. The heart of Charleston, that most intense of all Southern cities, had given forth a great throb. The *Star of the West* was coming from the North with provisions for the garrison of beleaguered Sumter. They would see her hull on the horizon in another hour.

Both Harry and Arthur were trembling with excitement. They were not on duty themselves, but they knew that all the South Carolina earthworks and batteries were manned. What would happen? It still seemed almost incredible to Harry that the people of the Union—at least of the Union that was—should fire upon one another, and his pulse beat hard and strong, while he waited with his comrade.

As they stood there gazing out to sea, looking for the black speck that should mark the first smoke of the *Star of the West*, Harry became conscious that another man was standing almost at his elbow. He glanced up and saw Shepard, who nodded to him.

"I did not know that I was standing by you until I had been here some time," said Shepard, as if he sought to indicate that he had not been seeking Harry and his comrade.

"I thought you had left Charleston," said Harry, who had not seen him for a week.

"Not at such a time," said Shepard, quietly. "So much of overwhelming interest is happening here that nobody who is alive can go away."

He put a pair of powerful glasses to his eyes and scanned the sea's rim. He looked a long time, and then his face showed excitement.

"It comes! It comes!" he exclaimed, more to himself than to Harry and Arthur.

Star of the West, c1860-1865[21]

"Is it the steamer? Is it the *Star of the West*?" exclaimed Harry forgetting all doubts of Shepard in the thrill of the moment.

"Yes, the *Star of the West*! It can be no other!" replied Shepard. "It can be no other! Take the glasses and see for yourself!"

When Harry looked he saw, where sea and sky joined, a black dot that gradually lengthened out into a small plume. It was not possible to recognize any ship at that distance, but he felt instinctively that it was the *Star of the West.* He passed the glasses to Arthur, who also took a look, and then drew a deep breath. Harry handed the glasses back to Shepard, saying:

"I see the ship, and I've no doubt that it's the *Star of the West.* Do you know anything about this vessel, Mr. Shepard?"

"I've heard that she's only a small steamer, totally unfitted for offense or defense."

"If the batteries fire upon her she's bound to go back."

"You put it right."

"Then, in effect, this is a test, and it rests with us whether or not to fire the first shot."

"I think you're right again."

Others also saw the growing black plume of smoke rising from the steamer's funnel, and a deep thrilling murmur ran through the crowd gathered on the sea walls. To many the vessel, steaming toward the harbor, was foreign, carrying a foreign flag, but to many others it was not and could never be so.

Shepard passed the glasses to the boy again, and he looked a second time at the ship, which was now taking shape and rising fast upon the water. Then he examined the walls of Sumter and saw men in blue moving there. They, too, were watching the coming steamer with the deepest anxiety.

Arthur took his second look also, and Shepard watched through the glasses a little longer. Then he put them in the case which he hung over his shoulder. Glasses were no longer needed. They could now see with the naked eye what was about to happen—if anything happened at all.

"It will soon be decided," said Shepard, and Harry noticed that his voice trembled. "If the *Star of the West* comes without interference up to the walls of Sumter there will be no war. The minds of men on both sides will cool. But if she is stopped, then—"

He broke off. Something seemed to choke in his throat. Harry and Arthur remained silent.

The ship rose higher and higher. Behind her hung the long black trail of her smoke. Soon, she would be in the range of the batteries. A deep shuddering sigh ran through the crowd, and then came moments of intense, painful silence. The little blue figures lining the walls of Sumter were motionless. The sea moved slowly and sleepily, its waters drenched in wintry sunshine.

On came the *Star of the West*, straight toward the harbor mouth.

"They will not fire! They dare not!" cried Shepard in a tense, strained whisper.

As the last word left his lips there was a heavy crash. A

tongue of fire leaped from one of the batteries, followed by a gush of smoke, and a round shot whistled over the *Star of the West.* A tremendous shout came from the crowd, then it was silent, while that tongue of flame leaped a second time from the mouth of a cannon. Harry saw the water spring up, a spire of white foam, near the steamer, and a moment later a third shot clipped the water close by. He did not know whether the gunners were firing directly at the vessel or merely meant to warn her that she came nearer at her peril, but in any event, the effect was the same. South Carolina with her cannon was warning a foreign ship, the ship of an enemy, to keep away.

The *Star of the West* slowed down and stopped. Then another shout, more tremendous than ever, a shout of triumph, came from the crowd, but Harry felt a chill strike to his heart. Young St. Clair, too, was silent and Harry saw a shadow on his face. He looked for Shepard, but he was gone and the boy had not heard him go.

"It is all over," said St. Clair, with the certainty of prophecy. "The cannon have spoken and it is war. Why, where is Shepard?"

"I don't know. He seems to have slipped away after the first two or three shots."

"I suppose he considered the two or three enough. Look, Harry! The ship is turning! The cannon have driven her off!"

He was right. The *Star of the West*, a small steamer, unable to face heavy guns, had curved about and was making for the open sea. There was another tremendous shout from the crowd, and then silence. Smoke from the cannon drifted lazily over the town, and, caught by a contrary breeze, was blown out over the sea in the track of the retreating steamer, where it met the black trail left by that vessel's own funnel. The crowd, not cheering much now, but talking in rather subdued tones, dispersed.

Harry felt the chill down his spine again. These were great matters. He had looked upon no light event in the harbor of Charleston that day. He and Arthur lingered on the wall, watching that trailing black dot on the horizon, until it died away and was gone forever. The blue figures on the walls of

Sumter had disappeared within, and the fortress stood up, grim and silent. Beyond lay the blue sea, shimmering and peaceful in the wintry sunshine.

"I suppose there is nothing to do but go back to Madame Delaunay's," said Harry.

"Nothing now," replied St. Clair, "but I fancy that later on we'll have all we can do."

"If not more."

"Yes, if not more."

Both boys were very grave and thoughtful as they walked to Madame Delaunay's most excellent inn. They realized that as yet South Carolina stood alone, but in the evening their spirits took a leap. News came that Mississippi also had gone out. Then other planting states followed fast. Florida was but a day behind Mississippi, Alabama went out the next day after Florida, Georgia eight days later, and Louisiana a week after Georgia. Exultation rose high in Charleston.

Price, Birch & Co, dealers in slaves, Alexandria, Virginia[22]

All the Gulf and South Atlantic States were now sure, but the great border states still hung fire. There was a clamor for Virginia, Kentucky, Maryland, and Missouri, and, though the promises from them came thick and fast, they did not go out. But the fiery energy of Charleston and the lower South was moving forward over all obstacles. Already arrangements had been made for a great convention at Montgomery in Alabama, and a new government would be formed differing but little from that of the old Union.

Now Harry began to hear much of a man, of whom he had heard his father speak, but who had slipped entirely from his mind. It was Jefferson Davis, a native of Kentucky like Abraham Lincoln. He had been a brave and gallant soldier at Buena Vista. It was said that he had saved the day against the overwhelming odds of Santa Anna. He had been Secretary of War in the old Union, now dissolved forever, according to the Charleston talk. Other names, too, began to grow familiar in Harry's ears. Much was said about the bluff Bob Toombs of Georgia, who feared no man and who would call the roll of his slaves at the foot of Bunker Hill monument. And there was little wizened Stephens, also of Georgia, a great intellect in a shrunken frame, and Benjamin of the oldest race, who had inherited the wisdom of ages. There would be no lack of numbers and courage and penetration when the great gathering met at Montgomery.

These were busy and on the whole happy days for Harry and St. Clair. Harry drilled with his comrade in the Palmetto Guards now, and, in due time, they were going to Montgomery to assist at the inauguration of the new president, whoever he might be. No vessel had come in place of the *Star of the West*. The North seemed supine, and Sumter, grim and dark though she might be, was alone. The flag of the Stars and Stripes still floated above it. Everywhere else the Palmetto flag waved defiance. But there was still no passage of arms between Sumter and its hostile neighbors. Small boats passed between the fort and the city, carrying provisions to the garrison, and also the news. The Charlestonians told Major Anderson of the states that went out, one by one, and the brave Kentuckian, eating his heart out, looked vainly toward the open sea for the help that never came.

Exultation still rose in Charleston. The ball was rolling finely. It was even gathering more speed and force than the most sanguine had expected. Every day brought the news of some new accession to the cause, some new triumph. The

Alabama militia had seized the forts, Morgan and Gaines; Georgia had occupied Pulaski and Jackson; North Carolina troops had taken possession of the arsenal at Fayetteville, and those of Florida on the same day had taken the one at Chattahoochee. Everywhere the South was accumulating arms, ammunition, and supplies for use—if they should be needed. The leaders had good cause for rejoicing. They were disappointed in nothing, save that northern tier of border states which still hesitated or refused.

Harry in these days wondered that so little seemed to happen in the North. His strong connections and his own good manners had made him a favorite in Charleston. He went everywhere, perhaps most often to the office of the *Mercury*, controlled by the powerful Rhett family, among the most fiery of the Southern leaders. Exchanges still came there from the northern cities, but he read little in them about preparations for war. Many attacked Buchanan, the present President, for weakness, and few expected anything better from the uncouth western figure, Lincoln, who would soon succeed him.

Senate Chamber, Confederacy; Montgomery, AL, Feb 1861[23]

Meanwhile the Confederate convention at Montgomery was acting. In those days apathy and delay seemed to be characteristic of the North, courage and energy of the South.

The new government was being formed with speed and decision. Jefferson Davis, it was said, would be President, and Stephens of Georgia would be Vice-President.

The time for departure to Montgomery drew near. Harry and Arthur were in fine gray uniforms as members of the Palmetto Guards. Arthur, light, volatile, was full of pleased excitement. Harry also felt the thrill of curiosity and anticipation, but he had been in Charleston nearly six weeks now, and while six weeks are short, they had been long enough in such a tense time to make vital changes in his character. He was growing older fast. He was more of a man, and he weighed and measured things more. He recognized that Charleston, while the second city of the South in size and the first in leadership, was only Charleston, after all, far inferior in weight and numbers to the great cities of the North. Often he looked toward the North over the vast, intervening space and tried to reckon what forces lay there.

The evening before their departure they sat on the wide piazza that swept along the entire front of the inn of Madame Delaunay. Colonel Leonidas Talbot and Major Hector St. Hilaire sat with them. They, too, were going to Montgomery. Mid-February had passed, and the day had been one of unusual warmth for that time of the year, like a day in full spring. The wind from the south was keen with the odor of fresh foliage and of roses, and of faint far perfumes, unknown but thrilling. A sky of molten silver clothed city, bay, and forts in enchantment. Nothing seemed further away than war, yet they had to walk but a little distance to see the defiant flag over Sumter, and the hostile Palmetto flags waving not far away.

Madame Delaunay appeared in the doorway. She was dressed as usual in white and her shining black hair was bound with the slender gold fillet.

"We are going away tomorrow, Madame," said Colonel Talbot, "and I know that we cannot find in Montgomery any such pleasant entertainment as my young friends have enjoyed here."

Harry was confirmed in his belief that the thread of an old

romance still formed a firm tie between them.

"But you will come back," said Madame Delaunay. "You will come back very soon. Surely, they will not try to keep us from going our ways in peace."

A sudden thrill of passion and feeling had appeared in her voice.

House near Charleston, 1861[24]

"That no one can tell, Julie," said Colonel Talbot very gravely—it was the first time that Harry had ever heard him call her by her first name—"but it seems to me that I should tell what I think. A Union such as ours has been formed amid so much suffering and hardship, courage and danger, that it is not to be broken in a day. We may come back soon from Montgomery, Julie, but I see war, a great and terrible war, a war, by the side of which those we have had, will dwindle to mere skirmishes. I shut my eyes, but it makes no difference. I see it close at hand, just the same."

Madame Delaunay sighed.

"And you, Major St. Hilaire?" she said.

"There may be a great war, Madame Delaunay," he said, "I fear that Colonel Talbot is right, but we shall win it."

Colonel Talbot said nothing more, nor did Madame Delaunay. Presently she went back into the house. After a long silence the colonel said:

"If I were not sure that our friend Shepard had left Charleston long since, I should say that the figure now passing in the street is his."

African American church, Port Royal, SC, ca 1860-1865[25]

A small lawn filled with shrubbery stretched before the house, but from the piazza they could see into the street. Harry, too, caught a glimpse of a passing figure, and like the colonel he was sure that it was Shepard.

"It is certainly he!" he exclaimed.

"After him!" cried Colonel Talbot, instantly all action. "As sure as we live that man is a spy, drawing maps of our fortifications, and I should have warned the Government before."

The four sprang from the piazza and ran into the street. Harry, although he had originally felt no desire to seize Shepard, was carried along by the impetus. It was the first man-hunt in which he had ever shared, and soon he caught the thrill from the others. The colonel, no doubt, was right. Shepard was a spy and should be taken. He ran as fast as any of them.

Shepard, if Shepard it was, heard the swift footsteps behind him, glanced back and then ran.

"After him!" cried Major St. Hilaire, his volatile blood leaping high. "His flight shows that he's a spy!"

But the fugitive was a man of strength and resource. He

ran swiftly into a cross street, and when they followed him there he leaped over the low fence of a lawn, surrounding a great house, darted into the shrubbery, and the four, although they were joined by others, brought by the alarm, sought for him in vain.

"After all, I'm not sorry he got away," said Colonel Talbot, as they walked back to Madame Delaunay's. "There is no war, and hence, in a military sense, there can be no spies. I doubt whether we should have known what to do with him had we caught him, but I am certain that he has complete maps of all our defenses."

Harry, with Arthur and many others whom he knew, started the next day for Montgomery. Jefferson Davis had already been chosen President, and Alexander H. Stephens Vice-President, and Davis was on his way from his Mississippi home to the same town to be inaugurated. In the excitement over the great event, so near at hand, Harry forgot all about Shepard and his doubts. He bade a regretful farewell to Charleston, which had taken him to its heart, and turned his face to this new place, much smaller, and, as yet, without fame.

Harry, Arthur, and their older friends began the momentous journey across the land of King Cotton, passing through the very heart of the lower South, as they went from Charleston to Montgomery. Davis and Stephens would be inaugurated on the 17th of that month, which was February. But the Palmetto Guards would arrive at Montgomery before Davis himself, who had left his home and who would cross Mississippi, Alabama, and a corner of Georgia before he reached the new capital to receive the chief honor.

Trains were slow and halting, and Harry had ample opportunity to see the land and the people who crowded to the stations to bring news or to hear it. He crossed a low, rolling country with many rivers, great and small. He saw large houses, with white-pillared porticos, sitting back among the trees, and swarms of negro cabins. Much of the region was yet dead and brown from the touch of winter, but in the valleys the green was appearing. Spring was in the air, and the spirits of the Palmetto Guards, nearly all of whom were very young, were rising with it.

The train drew into Montgomery, the little city that stood on the high banks of the Alabama River. Here they were in the very heart of the new Confederacy, and Harry and Arthur were eager to see the many famous Southern men who were gathered there to welcome the new President. Jefferson Davis was expected on the morrow, and would be inaugurated on the day following. They heard that his coming was already a triumphal progress. Vast crowds held his train at many points, merely to see him and listen to a few words. Generally he spoke in the careful, measured manner that was natural to him, but it was said that in Opelika, in Alabama, he had delivered a warning to the North, telling the Northern states that they would interfere with the Southern at their peril.

Harry and Arthur, despite their eagerness to see the town and the great men, were compelled to wait. The Palmetto Guards went into camp on the outskirts, and their commander, Colonel Leonidas Talbot, late of the United States Army, was very strict in discipline. His second in command, Major Hector St. Hilaire, was no whit inferior to him in sternness. Harry had expected that this old descendant of Huguenots, reared in the soft air of Charleston, would be lax, or at least easy of temper, but whatever of military rigor Colonel Talbot forgot, Major St. Hilaire remembered.

The guards were about three hundred in number, and their camp was pitched on a hill, a half mile from the town. The night, after a beautiful day, turned raw and chill, warning that early spring, even in those southern latitudes, was more of a promise than a performance. But the young troops built several great fires and those who were not on guard basked before the glow.

Harry had helped to gather the wood, most of which was furnished by the people living near, and his task was ended. Now he sat on his blanket with his back against a log and, with a great feeling of comfort, saw the flames leap up and grow.

Coffee Call, Winslow Homer[26]

The cooks were at work, and there was an abundance of food. They had brought much themselves, and the enthusiastic neighbors doubled and tripled their supplies. The pleasant aroma of bacon and ham frying over the coals and of boiling coffee arose. He was weary from the long journey and the work that he had done, and he was hungry, too, but he was willing to wait.

All the troops were South Carolinians except Harry and perhaps a dozen others. They were a pleasant lot, quick of temper, perhaps, but he liked them. Their prevailing note was high spirits, and the most cheerful of all was a tall youth named Tom Langdon, whose father owned one of the smaller of the sea islands off the South Carolina coast. He was quite sanguine that everything would go exactly as they wished. The Yankees would not fight, but, if by any chance they did fight, they would get a most terrible thrashing. Tom, with a tin cup full of coffee in one hand and a tin plate containing ham and bread in the other, sat down by the side of Harry and leaned back against the log also. Harry had never seen a picture of more supreme content than his face showed.

"In thirty-six hours we'll have a new President, do you appreciate that fact, Harry Kenton?" asked young Langdon.

"I do," replied Harry, "and it makes me think pretty hard."

"What's the use of worrying? Why, it's just the biggest picnic that I ever took part in, and if the Yankees object to our setting up for ourselves I fancy we'll have to go up there and teach 'em to mind their own business. I wouldn't object, Harry, to a march at somebody else's expense to New York and Philadelphia and Boston. I suppose those cities are worth seeing."

Harry laughed. Langdon's good spirits were contagious even to a nature much more serious.

"I don't look on it as a picnic altogether," he said. "The Yankees will fight very hard, but we live on the land almost wholly, and the grass keeps on growing, whether there's war or not. Besides, we're an outdoor people, good horsemen, hunters, and marksmen. These things ought to help us."

"They will and we'll help ourselves most," said Langdon gaily. "I'm going to be either a general or a great politician, Harry. If it's a long war, I'll come out a general; if it's a short one, I mean to enter public life afterward and be a great orator. Did you ever hear me speak, Harry?"

"No, thank Heaven," replied Harry fervently. "Don't you think that South Carolina has enough orators now? What on earth do all your people find to talk about?"

Langdon laughed with the utmost good nature.

"We fire the human heart," he replied. "'Words, words, empty words,' it is not so. Words in themselves are often deeds, because the deeds start from them or are caused by them. The world has been run with words. All great actions result from them. Now, if we should have a big war, it would be said long afterward that it was caused by words, words spoken at Charleston and Boston, though, of course, the things they say at Boston are wrong, while those said at Charleston are right."

Harry laughed in his turn.

"It's quite certain," he said, "that you'll have no lack of words yourself. I imagine that the sign over your future office will read, 'Thomas Langdon, wholesale dealer in words. Any amount of any quality supplied on demand.'"

"Not a bad idea," said Langdon. "You mean that as satire, but I'll do it. It's no small accomplishment to be a good dictionary. But my thoughts turn back to war. You think I never look beyond today, but I believe the North will come up against us. And you'll have to go into it with all your might, Harry. You are of fighting stock. Your father was in the thick of it in Mexico. Remember the lines:

"We were not many, we who stood
Before the iron sleet that day;
Yet many a gallant spirit would
Give half his years if he but could
Have been with us at Monterey."

"I remember them," said Harry, much stirred. "I have heard my father quote them. He was at Monterey and he says that the Mexicans fought well. I was at Frankfort, the capital of our state, myself with him, when they unveiled the monument to our Kentucky dead and I heard them read O'Hara's poem which he wrote for that day. I tell you, Langdon, it makes my blood jump every time I hear it."

He recited in a sort of low chant:

"The neighing troop, the flashing blade,
The bugle's stirring blast,
The charge, the dreadful cannonade,
The din and shout are past.

"Nor war's wild note, nor glory's peal
Shall fill with fierce delight
Those breasts that never more may feel
The rapture of the fight."

They were very young and, in some respects, it was a sentimental time, much given to poetry. As the darkness closed in and the lights of the little city could be seen no longer, their thoughts took a more solemn turn. Perhaps it would be fairer to call them emotions or feelings rather than thoughts. In the day all had been talk and lightness, but in the night omens and presages came. Langdon was the first to rouse himself. He could not be solemn longer than three minutes.

"It's certain that the President is coming tomorrow, Harry, isn't it?" he asked.

"Beyond a doubt. He is so near now that they fix the exact hour, and the Guards are among those to receive him."

"I wonder what he looks like. They say he is a very great man."

They were interrupted by St. Clair, who threw himself down on a blanket beside them.

"That's the third cup of coffee you're taking, Tom," he said to Langdon. "Here, give it to me. I've had none."

Langdon obeyed and St. Clair drank thirstily. Then he took from the inside pocket of his coat a newspaper which he unfolded deliberately.

"This came from Montgomery," he said. "I heard you two quoting poetry, and I thought I'd come over and read some to you. What do you think of this? It was written by a fellow in Boston named Holmes and published when he heard that South Carolina had seceded. He calls it: 'Brother Jonathan's Lament for Sister Caroline.'"

"Read it!" exclaimed the others.

"Here goes:

"She has gone—she has left us in passion and pride,
Our stormy-browed sister so long at our side!
She has torn her own star from our firmament's glow,

And turned on her brother the face of a foe.

"O Caroline, Caroline, child of the sun,
We can never forget that our hearts have been one,
Our foreheads both sprinkled in Liberty's name
From the fountain of blood with the fingers of flame."

St. Clair read well in a full, round voice, and when he stopped with the second verse Harry said:

"It sounds well. I like particularly that expression, 'the fingers of flame.' After all, there's some grief in parting company, breaking up the family, so to speak."

"But he's wrong when he says we left in passion and pride," exclaimed Langdon. "In pride, yes, but not in passion. We may be children of the sun, too, but I've felt some mighty cold winds sweeping down from the Carolina hills, cold enough to make fur-lined overcoats welcome. But we'll forget about cold winds and everything else unpleasant, before such a jolly fire as this."

They finished an abundant supper, and soon relapsed into silence. The flames threw out such a generous heat that they were content to rest their backs against the log, and gaze sleepily into the coals. Beyond the fire, in the shadow, they saw the sentinels walking up and down. Harry felt for the first time that he was really within the iron bands of military discipline. He might choose to leave the camp and go into Montgomery, but he would choose and nothing more. He could not go. Colonel Leonidas Talbot and Major Hector St. Hilaire were friends, but they were masters also, and he was recognizing sooner than some of the youths around him that it was not merely play and spectacle that awaited them.

Unidentified Confederate soldier, Richmond Howitzers[27]

5. THE NEW PRESIDENT

Their great day came. Clear sunlight shone over the town, the hills, and the brown waters of the Alabama. It was a peculiarly Southern country, different, Harry thought, from his own Kentucky, more enthusiastic, perhaps, and less prone to count the cost. The people had come not only on the railroad, but they were arriving now from far places in wagons and on horseback. Men of distinction, almost universally, wore black clothes, the coats very long, black slouch hats, wide of brim, and white shirts with glistening or heavily ruffled fronts. There were also many black people in a state of pleasurable excitement, although the war—if one should come—would be over them.

Harry and his two young friends were anxious to visit Montgomery and take a good look at the town, but they did not ask for leave, as Colonel Talbot had already sternly refused all such applications. The military law continued to lie heavily upon them, and, soon after they finished a solid breakfast with appetites sharpened by the open air, they were ordered to fall into line. Arrayed in their fine new uniforms, to which the last touch of neatness had been added, they marched away to the town. They might see it as a company, but not as individuals.

They walked with even step along the grassy slopes, their fine appearance drawing attention and shouts of approval from the dense masses of people of all ages and all conditions of life who were gathering. Harry, a cadet with a small sword by his side, felt his heart swell as he trod the young turf, and heard the shouting and applause. The South Carolinians were the finest body of men present, and they were conscious of it. Eyes always to the front, they marched straight on, apparently hearing nothing, but really hearing everything.

They reached the houses presently and Harry saw the dome of the capitol on its high hill rising before them, but a moment or two later the Guards, with the Palmetto flag waving proudly in front, wheeled and marched toward the railroad station. There they halted in close ranks and stood at attention. Although the young soldiers remained immovable, there was not a heart in the company that did not throb with excitement. Colonel Talbot and Major St. Hilaire were a little in advance, erect and commanding figures.

Other troops, volunteer companies, were present and they spread to right and left of the South Carolinians. Behind and everywhere except in the cleared space before them gathered the people, a vast mass through which ran the hum and murmur of expectancy. Overhead, the sun leaped out and shone for a while with great brilliancy. "A good omen," many said. And to Harry it all seemed good, too. The excitement, the enthusiasm were contagious. If any prophet of evil was present he had nothing to say.

A jet of smoke standing black against the golden air appeared above a hill, and then came the rumble of a train. It was that which bore the President elect, coming fast, and a sudden great shout went up from the multitude, followed by silence, broken only by the heavy breathing of so many. Harry's heart leaped again, but his will kept his body immovable.

The rumble became a roar, and the jet of smoke turned to a cloud. Then the train drew into the station and stopped. The people began a continuous shout, bands played fiercely, and a tall, thin man of middle years, dressed in black broadcloth, descended from a coach. All the soldiers saluted, the bands played more fiercely than ever, and the shouting of the crowd swelled in volume.

It was the first time that Harry had ever seen Jefferson

Davis, and the face, so unlike that which he expected, impressed him. He saw a cold, gray, silent man with lips pressed tightly together. He did not behold here the Southern fire and passion of which he was hearing so much talk, but rather the reserve and icy resolve of the far North. Harry at first felt a slight chill, but it soon passed. It was better at such a time to have a leader of restraint and dignity than the homely joker, Lincoln, of whom such strange tales came.

Mr. Davis lifted his black hat to the shouting crowd, and bowed again and again. But he did not smile. His face remained throughout set in the same stern mold. As the troops closed up, he entered the carriage waiting for him, and drove slowly toward the heart of the city, the multitude following and breaking at intervals into shouts and cheers.

Jefferson Davis, ca 1860[28]

The Palmetto Guards marched on the right of the carriage, and Harry was able to watch the President-elect all the time. The face held his attention. Its sternness did not relax. It was the face of a man who had seen the world, and who believed in the rule of strength.

The procession led on to a hotel, a large building with a great portico in front. Here it stopped, the bands ceased to play, Mr. Davis descended from the carriage and entered the portico, where a group of men famous in the South stood, ready to welcome him. The troops drew up close to the portico, and back of them, every open space was black with people.

Harry, in the very front rank, saw and heard it all. Mr. Davis stopped as soon as he reached the portico, and Yancey, the famous orator of Alabama, to whom Harry had delivered his letters in Charleston, stepped forward, and, in behalf of the people of the South, made a speech of welcome in a clear, resonant, and emphatic tone. The applause compelled him to stop at times, but throughout, Mr. Davis stood rigid and unsmiling. His countenance expressed none of his thoughts, whatever they may have been. Harry's eyes never wandered from his face, except to glance now and then at the wizened, shrunken, little man who stood near him, Alexander H. Stephens of Georgia, who would take the oath of office as Vice-President of the new Confederacy. He had been present throughout the convention as a delegate from Georgia, and men talked of the mighty mind imprisoned in the weak and dwarfed body.

Harry thrilled more than once as the new President spoke on in calm, measured tones. He was glad to be present at the occurrence of great events, and he was glad to witness this gathering of the mighty. The tide of youth flowed high in him, and he believed himself fortunate to have been at Charleston when the cannon met the *Star of the West*, and yet more fortunate to be now at Montgomery, when the head of the new nation was taking up his duties.

His gaze wandered for the first time from the men in the portico to the crowd without that rimmed them around. His eyes, without any particular purpose, passed from face to face in the front ranks, and then stopped, arrested by a countenance that he had little expected to see. It was the shadow, Shepard, standing there, and listening, and looking as intently as Harry himself. It was not an evil face, cut clearly and eager, but Harry was sorry that he had come. If Colonel Talbot's beliefs about him were true, this was a bad place for Shepard.

But his eyes went back to the new President and the men on the portico before him. The first scene in the first act of a great drama, a mighty tragedy, had begun, and every detail was of absorbing interest to him. Shepard was forgotten in an instant.

Harry noticed that Mr. Davis never mentioned slavery, a subject which was uppermost in the minds of all, North and South, but he alluded to the possibility of war, and thought the new republic ought to have an army and navy. The concluding paragraph of his speech, delivered in measured but feeling tones, seemed very solemn and serious to Harry.

Slave quarters at Brierfield, Jefferson Davis's Plantation[29]

"It is joyous in the midst of perilous times," he said, "to look around upon a people united in heart, where one purpose of high resolve animates and actuates the whole; where the sacrifices to be made are not weighed in the balance against honor and right and liberty and equality. Obstacles may retard, but they cannot long prevent the progress of a movement sanctified in justice and sustained by a virtuous people. Reverently let us invoke the God of our fathers to guide and protect us in our efforts to perpetuate the principles which by his blessing they were able to vindicate, establish, and transmit to their posterity. With the continuance of his favor ever gratefully acknowledged we may look hopefully forward to success, to peace and to prosperity."

The final words were received with a mighty cheer which rose and swelled thrice, and again. Jefferson Davis stood calmly through it all, his face expressing no emotion. The thin lips were pressed together tightly. The points of his high collar touched his thick, close beard. He wore a heavy black bow tie and his coat had broad braided lapels. His hair was thick and slightly long, and his face, though thin, was full of vitality. It seemed to Harry that the grave, slightly narrowed eyes emitted at this moment a single flash of triumph or at least of fervor.

Mr. Davis was sworn in and Mr. Stephens after him, and when the shouting and applause sank for the last time, the great men withdrew into the hotel, and the troops marched away. The head of the new republic had been duly installed, and the separation from the old Union was complete. The enthusiasm was tremendous, but Harry, like many others, had an underlying and faint but persistent feeling of sadness that came from the breaking of old ties. Nor had any news come telling that Kentucky was about to join her sister states of the South.

Montgomery state house, Confederate Congress, 4 Feb 1861[30]

The Palmetto Guards marched back to their old camp, and Harry, Langdon, and St. Clair obtained leave of absence to visit the town. Youth had reasserted itself and Harry was again all excitement and elation. It seemed to him at the moment that he was a boy no longer. The Tacitus lying peacefully in his desk was forgotten. He was a man in a man's great world, doing a man's great work.

But both he and his comrades had all the curiosity and zest of boys as they walked about the little city in the twilight, looking at everything of interest, visiting the Capitol, and then coming back to the Exchange Hotel, which sheltered for a night so many of their great men.

They stayed a while in the lobby of the hotel, which was packed so densely that Harry could scarcely breathe. Most of the men were of the tall, thin but extremely muscular type, either clean shaven or with short beards trimmed closely, and no mustaches. Black was the predominant color in clothing, and they talked with soft, drawling voices. But their talk was sanguine. Most of them asked what the North would do, but they believed that whatever she did do the South would go on her way. The smoke from the pipes and cigars grew thicker, and Harry, leaving his comrades in the crowd, walked out upon the portico.

The crisp, fresh air of the February night came like a heavenly tonic. He remained there a little while, breathing it in, expanding his lungs, and rejoicing. Then he walked over to the exact spot upon which Jefferson Davis had stood, when he delivered his speech of acceptance. He was so full of the scene that he shut his eyes and beheld it again. He tried to imagine the feelings of a man at such a moment, knowing himself the chosen of millions, and feeling that all eyes were upon him. Truly it would be enough to make the dullest heart leap.

He opened his eyes, and although he stood in darkness on the portico, he saw a dusky figure at the far edge of it, standing between two pillars, and looking in at one of the windows. The man, whoever he was, seemed to be intently watching those inside, and Harry saw at once that it was not a look of mere curiosity. It was the gaze of one who wished to understand as well as to know. He moved a little nearer. The figure dropped lightly to the ground and moved swiftly away. Then he saw that it was Shepard.

The boy's feelings toward Shepard had been friendly, but now he felt a sudden rush of hostility. All that Colonel Talbot had hinted about him was true. He was there, spying upon the Confederacy, seeking its inmost secrets, in order that he might report them to its enemies. Harry was armed. He and all his comrades carried new pistols at their belts, and driven by impulse he, too, dropped from the portico and followed Shepard.

He saw the dusky figure ahead of him still going swiftly, but with his hand on the pistol he followed at greater speed. A minute later Shepard turned into a small side street, and Harry followed him there. It was not much more than an alley, dark, silent, and deserted. Montgomery was a small town, in which people retired early after the custom of the times, and tonight, the collapse after so much excitement seemed to have sent them sooner than usual into their homes. It was evident that the matter would lie without interference between Shepard and himself.

Shepard went swiftly on and came soon to the outskirts of the town. He did not look back and Harry wondered whether he knew that he was pursued. The boy thought once or twice of using his pistol, but could not bring himself to do it. There was really no war, merely a bristling of hostile forces, and he could not fire upon anybody, especially upon one who had done him no harm.

Shepard led on, passed through a group of negro cabins, crossed an old cotton field, and entered a grove, with his pursuer not fifty yards behind. The grove was lighted well by the moon, and Harry dashed forward, pistol in hand, resolved at last to call a halt upon the fugitive. A laugh and the blue barrel of a levelled pistol met him. Shepard was sitting upon a fallen log facing him. The moon poured a mass of molten silver directly upon him, showing a face of unusual strength and power, set now with stern resolution. Harry's hand was upon the butt of his own pistol, but he knew that it was useless to raise it. Shepard held him at his mercy.

"Sit down, Mr. Kenton," said Shepard. "Here's another log, where you can face me. You feel chagrin, but you need not. I knew that you were following me, and hence I was able to take you by surprise. Now, tell me, what do you want?"

Harry took the offered log. He was naturally a lad of great courage and resolution, and now his presence of mind returned. He looked calmly at Shepard, who lowered his own pistol.

"I'm not exactly sure what I want," he replied with a little laugh, "but whatever it is, I know now that I'm not going to get it. I've walked into a trap. I believed that you were a spy, and it seemed to me that I ought to seize you. Am I right?"

Shepard laughed also.

"That's a frank question and you shall have a frank reply," he said. "The suspicions of your friend, Colonel Talbot, were correct. Yes, I am a spy, if one can be a spy when there is no war. I am willing to tell you, however, that Shepard is my right name, and I am willing to tell you also, that you and your Charleston friends little foresee the magnitude of the business upon which you have started. I don't believe there is any enmity between you and me and I can tell the thoughts that I have."

"Since you offered me no harm when you had the chance," said Harry, "I give my word that I will seek to offer none myself. Go ahead, I think you have more to say and I want to listen."

Shepard thrust his pistol in his belt and his face relaxed somewhat. As they faced each other on the logs they were not more than ten feet part and the moon poured a shower of silver rays upon both. Although Shepard was a few years the older, the faces showed a likeness, the same clearness of vision and strength of chin.

"I liked you, Harry Kenton, the first time I met you," said Shepard, "and I like you yet. When I saw that you were following me, I led you here in order to say some things to you. You are seeing me now probably for the last time. My spying is over for a long while, at least. A mile further on, a horse, saddled and bridled, is waiting for me. I shall ride all the remainder of the night, board a train in the morning, and, passing through Memphis and Louisville, I shall be in the North in forty-eight hours."

"And what then?"

"I shall tell to those who ought to know what I have seen in Charleston and Montgomery. I have seen the gathering of forces in the South, and I know the spirit that animates your people, but listen to me, Harry Kenton, do you think that a Union such as ours, formed as ours was, can be broken up in a moment, as you would smash a china plate? The forces on the other side are sluggish, but they are mighty. I foresee war, terrible war, crowded with mighty battles. Now, I'm going to offer you my hand and you are going to take it. Don't think any the less of me because I've been playing the spy. You may be one yourself before the year is out."

His manner was winning, and Harry took the offered hand. What right had he to judge? Each to his own opinion. Despite himself, he liked Shepard again.

"I'm glad I've known you, but at the same time I'm glad you're leaving," he said.

Shepard gave the boy's hand a hearty grasp, which was returned in kind. Then he turned and disappeared in the forest. Harry walked slowly back to Montgomery. Shepard had given him deep cause for thought. He approached the Exchange Hotel, thinking that he would find his friends there and return with them to the camp. But it was later than he had supposed. As he drew near he saw that nearly all the lights were out in the hotel, and the building was silent.

W. LaRus, Montgomery Post[31]

He was sure that St. Clair and Langdon had already gone to the camp, and he was about to turn away when he saw a window in the hotel thrown up and a man appear standing full length in the opening.

It was Jefferson Davis. The same flood of moonlight that had poured upon Shepard illuminated his face also. But it was not the face of a triumphant man. It was stern, sad, even gloomy. The thin lips were pressed together more tightly than ever, and the somber eyes looked out over the city, but evidently saw nothing there. Harry felt instinctively that his thoughts were like those of Shepard. He, too, foresaw a great and terrible war, and, so foreseeing, knew that this was no time to rejoice and glorify.

Harry, held by the strong spell of time and place, watched him a full half hour. It was certain now that Jefferson Davis was thinking, not looking at anything, because his head never moved, and his eyes were always turned in the same direction—Harry noticed at last that the direction was the

North.

The new President stepped back, closed the window and no light came from his room. Harry hurried to the camp, where, as he had surmised, he found St. Clair and Langdon. He gave some excuse for his delay, and telling nothing of Shepard, wrapped himself in his blankets. Exhausted by the stirring events of the day and night he fell asleep at once.

Three days later they were on their way back to Charleston. They heard that the inauguration of the new President had not been well received by the doubtful states. Even the border slave states were afraid the lower South had been a little too hasty. But among the youths of the Palmetto Guards there was neither apprehension nor depression. They had been present at the christening of the new nation, and now they were going back to their own Charleston.

"Everything is for the best," said young Langdon, whose unfailing spirits bubbled to the brim, "we'll have down here the tightest and finest republic the world ever heard of. New Orleans will be the biggest city, but our own Charleston will always be the leader, its center of thought."

"What you need, Tom," said Harry, "is a center of thought yourself. Don't be so terribly sanguine and you may save yourself some smashes."

"I wouldn't gain anything even then," replied Langdon joyously. "I'll have such a happy time before the smash comes that I can afford to pay for it. I'm the kind that enjoys life. It's a pleasure to me just to breathe."

"I believe it is," said Harry, looking at him with admiration. "I think I'll call you Happy Tom."

"I take the name with pleasure," said Langdon. "It's a compliment to be called Happy Tom. Happy I was born and happy I am. I'm so happy I must sing:

"Ol Dan Tucker was a mighty fine man,
He washed his face in the frying pan,
He combed his hair with a wagon wheel
And died with a toothache in his heel."

"That's a great poem," said a long North Carolina youth

named Ransome, "but I've got something that beats it all holler. 'Ole Dan Tucker' is nothing to 'Aunt Dinah's Tribberlations.'"

"How does it go?" asked St. Clair.

"It's powerful pathetic, telling a tale of disaster and pain. The first verse will do, and here it is:

"Ole Aunt Dinah, she got drunk,
Felled in a fire and kicked up a chunk,
Red-hot coal popped in her shoe,
Lord a-mighty! how de water flew!"

"We've had French and Italian opera in Charleston," said St. Clair, "and I've heard both in New Orleans, too, but nothing quite so moving as the troubles of Ole Dan Tucker and Ole Aunt Dinah."

They sang other songs and the Guards, who filled two coaches of a train, joined in a great swinging chorus which thundered above the rattle of the engine and the cars, so noisy in those days. Often they sang negro melodies with a plaintive lilt. The slave had given his music to his master. Harry joined with all the zest of an enthusiastic nature. The effect of Shepard's words and of the still, solemn face of Jefferson Davis, framed in the open window, was wholly gone.

Spring was now advancing. All the land was green. The trees were in fresh leaf, and when they stopped at the little stations in the woods, they could hear the birds singing in the deep forest. And as they sped across the open they heard the negroes singing, too, in their deep mellow voices in the fields. Then came the delicate flavor of flowers and Harry knew that they were approaching Charleston. In another hour they were in the city which was, as yet, the heart and soul of the Confederacy. Charleston, with its steepled churches, its quaint houses, and its masses of foliage, much of it in full flower, seemed more attractive than ever to Harry. The city preserved its gay and light tone. It was crowded with people. All the rich planters were there. Society had never been more brilliant than during those tense weeks on the eve of men knew not what. But the Charlestonians were sure of one fact, the most important of all, that everything was going well. Texas had joined the great group of the South, and while the border states still hung back, they would surely join.

Mr. Daggett, Charleston Courier[32]

Harry found that the batteries and earthworks had increased in size and number, forming a formidable circle about the black mass of Sumter, above which the defiant flag still swung in the wind. The guards were distributed among the batteries, but St. Clair, Langdon, and Harry remained together. Toutant Beauregard, after having resigned the command at West Point, as the Southern leaders had expected, came to Charleston and took supreme command there. Harry saw him as he inspected the batteries, a small, dark man, French in look, as he was French in descent, full of nervous energy and vitality. He spoke approving words of all that had been done, and Harry, St. Clair and Tom, glowed with enthusiasm.

"Didn't I tell you that everything would come just right!" exclaimed Happy Tom. "We're the boys to do things. I heard today that they were preparing a big fleet in the North to relieve Sumter, but no matter how big it is, it won't be able to get into Charleston harbor. Will it, old fellow?"

He addressed his remarks to one of the great guns, and he patted the long, polished barrel. Harry agreed with him that Charleston harbor could be held inviolate. He did not believe that ships would have much chance against heavy cannon in earthworks.

He was back in Charleston several days before he had a chance to go to Madame Delaunay's. She was unfeignedly glad to see him, but Harry saw that she had lost some of her bright spirits.

"Colonel Talbot tells me," she said, "that mighty forces are gathering, and I am afraid, I am afraid for all the thousands of gallant boys like you, Harry."

But Harry had little fear for himself. Why should he, when the Southern cause was moving forward so smoothly? They heard a day or two later that the rail-splitter, Lincoln, had been duly inaugurated President of what remained of the old Union, although he had gone to Washington at an unexpected hour, and partly in disguise. On the same day the Confederacy adopted the famous flag of the Stars and Bars, and Harry and his friends were soon singing in unison and with fiery enthusiasm:

"Hurrah! Hurrah! for Southern rights, hurrah!
Hurrah for the bonnie blue flag that bears a single star!"

The spring deepened and with it the tension and excitement. The warm winds from the South blew over Charleston, eternally keen with the odor of rose and orange blossom. The bay moved gently, a molten mass now blue, now green. The blue figures could be seen now and then on the black walls of Sumter, but the fortress was silent, although the muzzles of its guns always threatened.

Harry received several letters from his father. The latest stated that he might want him to return, but he was not needed yet. The state had proved more stubborn than he and his friends had expected. A powerful Union element had been disclosed, and there would be an obstinate fight at Frankfort over the question of going out. He would let him know when to come.

Harry was perhaps less surprised than his father over the conflict of opinion in Kentucky, but his thoughts soon slipped from it, returning to his absorption in the great and thrilling drama in Charleston, which was passing before his eyes, and of which he was a part. April came, and the glory of the spring deepened. The winds blowing from the soft shores of the Gulf grew heavier with the odors of blossom and flower.

Montgomery, AL, slaves farming in fields, 1861[33]

But Charleston thrilled continually with excitement. Fort after fort was seized by the Southerners, almost without opposition and wholly without the shedding of blood. It seemed that the stars in their courses fought for the South, or at least it seemed so to the youthful Harry and his comrades.

"Didn't I tell you everything would come as we wished it?" said the sanguine Langdon. "Abe Lincoln may be the best rail-splitter that ever was, but I fancy he isn't such a terrible fighter."

"Let's wait and see," said Harry, with the impression of Shepard's warning words still strong upon him.

His caution was not in vain. That day the rulers of Charleston received a message from Abraham Lincoln that Sumter would be revictualled, whether Charleston consented or not. The news was spread instantly through the city and fire sprang up in the South Carolina heart. The population, increased far beyond its normal numbers by the influx from the country, talked of nothing else. Beauregard was everywhere giving quick, nervous orders, and always strengthening the already powerful batteries that threatened Sumter.

Unidentified Confederate soldier, Richmond Artillery[34]

6. SUMTER

Harry saw an increase of energy after the arrival of Beauregard. There were fresh rumors about the great fleet the North was going to send down for the relief of Sumter. Major Anderson, the commander in the fort, steadily refused all demands for surrender. It was said freely that the Northern States did not intend to let their Southern sisters go in peace. The *Mercury*, with all the power and fire of the Rhett family behind it, thundered continually for action. Sumter with its guns menacing the city should not be allowed to remain under the hostile flag.

It seemed to Harry afterward that he was in a sort of fever, not a fever that parched and burned, but a fever that made his pulse leap faster, and his heart long for the thrill of conflict. Often he sat with St. Clair and Langdon on their earthworks, and looked at Sumter.

"I wonder when the word will come for us to turn these big guns loose," Langdon said one day, as he looked at the cannon. "Seems to me we ought to take Sumter before that fleet comes."

"But wouldn't it be better for them to make the first hostile movement, Happy?" asked Harry. "Then we'd put them in the wrong."

"What difference does it make if we should happen to fight them, anyhow? The question who began it we'd settle afterwards on victorious fields. Oh, we're bound to win,

Harry! We can't help it. If there's any war, I expect inside of a year to sleep with my boots on in the President's bed in the White House, and then I'd go on to Philadelphia and New York and Boston and show myself as a fair specimen of the unconquerable Southern soldier."

"Happy," said Harry, in a rebuking tone, "you're the most terrific chatterer I ever heard. Before you've done anything whatever, you talk about having done it all."

"And they call us Charlestonians fiery boasters," said St. Clair. "Why, there's nobody in all Charleston who's half a match for this sea islander, Happy Tom Langdon."

Charleston received Lincoln's threat and gave it back. Many were glad that he had made the issue. The enthusiasm swelled yet further, when they heard that the Confederate envoys at Washington, treating for a peaceful separation, had left the capital at once when Lincoln had sent his message that Sumter would be relieved.

"It looks more like war now," said Langdon, with satisfaction, "and I may make my victorious march into the North after all."

Harry said nothing. As events marched forward on swift foot, he felt more intensely their gravity. For every month that had passed since he put the Tacitus in his desk at Pendleton Academy, the boy had grown a year in mind and thought. So, that rumor about the relieving fleet had come true and they might look for it in Charleston in two or three days.

Harry had his place in one of the batteries nearest Sumter, and he often went with Colonel Talbot on tours of inspection and once or twice he was in General Beauregard's own party. The fact that his father had been a graduate of West Point and for years an officer, was of the greatest service to him. In the little army of the United States before the Civil War, the officers constituted a family. Everybody knew who everybody else was, and those of the same age had been at West Point together. General Beauregard and Colonel Kenton had met often, and the Southern commander became very partial to the Colonel's son.

Harry was present when Beauregard, some of his more important officers and the civil authorities of Charleston, conferred after Lincoln's warning message came.

Pierre Gustave Toutant Beauregard, *Harpers* *27 April 1865*[35]

"If Lincoln's fleet tries to force the harbor," said Rhett, "we must fire upon it. Sumter should be ours, and if Lincoln succeeds in revictualling the fort it will be a great blow to our prestige. It will hurt the whole South. What do you think, General?"

"I think as you do, Mr. Rhett," replied Toutant Beauregard. "But have no fear, gentlemen. No fleet that Lincoln may send can reach Sumter. Our batteries are able to blow out of the water every vessel that flies the Northern flag."

"We must reduce Sumter itself before the fleet comes," said Jamison, of Barnwell.

Beauregard smiled slightly.

"We can do that, too," he said, "and I am glad to see that you gentlemen are for action. The fleet, I am accurately informed, consists of the warship *Baltic*, three sloops of war, and two tenders. The *Baltic*, with Fox, the assistant secretary of the Northern Navy, on board, left New York two days ago. The other vessels started earlier, and we may expect the whole fleet in a day."

"Then," said Rhett, "we must send to Sumter another and a final demand for its surrender."

They were all agreed, and Beauregard chose his messengers, putting Harry among the number. Hoisting a white flag, they entered a large boat and were rowed by powerful oarsmen toward Sumter. Harry, looking back, saw the whole front of the harbor lined with people. Even at the distance it looked like a holiday crowd. He saw hundreds of women and girls in white and pink dresses, and there were roses of the same colors in hats and bonnets. Great parasols of every shade threw back the brilliant sunlight. It was still a holiday spectacle, a pageant, and many of the light hearts along the sea wall could not realize that it might yet be something far more.

Anderson, the commander of Sumter, appeared upon the esplanade to meet the boat coming with the white flag. Harry watched him closely. He saw a face worn, but set hard and firm, and a figure upright and steady. The Southerners tied their boat to the wall and climbed upon the esplanade.

"What do you want, gentlemen?" asked Anderson.

"We have come with our final demand for your surrender," replied the chief Southern officer. "If you do not yield we fire upon you."

Anderson shrugged his shoulders.

"I hear that a fleet from New York is coming to my relief."

"It will never be able to force a passage into the harbor."

"That may or may not be, but in any event, gentlemen, I tell you that the flag will not come down. If you fire, we fire back."

He spoke with no quiver in his voice, although his supply of ammunition was low, and the fort had a food supply for only four days.

"Then it is scarcely worthwhile for us to talk longer."

"No, it would be a waste of time by both of us." The Southerners turned back to their boat. Harry was the last and Anderson said to him in a low tone:

"I am sorry to see your father's son here."

"I am where he would wish me to be," replied the boy stiffly.

"Even so, I hope you will come to no harm," said Anderson in a generous tone.

After such a noble rejoinder Harry's heart softened instantly, and he returned the wish. Then he followed the others into the boat, and they pulled back to the mainland.

The crowd surmised from the quick return of the boat the nature of the answer that it brought. It seemed to feel one gigantic throb of passion, and perhaps of relief also, that the issue was made after so many weeks of waiting. Yet the holiday aspect disappeared, as if a cloud had passed suddenly before the sun.

Harry noted the shadow even before he landed. The people had become silent, and faces that had laughed turned grave. As they set foot upon the mainland, they told their news freely, and then the crowd dispersed almost in silence. It was the first time that Harry had seen Charleston, gay and light of heart, in the shadow, but he was sure that it could not last long. His errand over, he returned to his own battery and told Langdon and St. Clair of everything that had happened.

"It's all for the best," said Langdon cheerfully. "Sumter will be ours in another day."

"Wait and see, Happy," said Harry.

"All right, old Wait-and-See, I will," returned Langdon.

Harry tried to suppress, or at least conceal his intense excitement. The whole city was in the same state. The batteries were filled with men of wealth and position, serving as mere volunteer privates. The wives and daughters of many of them were at the Charleston Hotel or the Mills House, or at such inns as that kept by Madame Delaunay. Governor Pickens and his wife were at the Charleston Hotel, and with them were chief officers of the city and state. Nearly everybody knew that something was going to happen, but few knew when it would happen.

Harry noticed a tightening of discipline at their battery. The orders were sharp and they had to be obeyed. Nothing was wasted in politeness. Visitors were no longer allowed to gratify curiosity. Women and girls in their white or pink dresses were not permitted to come near and smile at their husbands or brothers or sweethearts in the trenches. The ammunition was stacked neatly behind the guns, and every man was compelled to be ready at an instant's notice.

"Looks like business," Langdon whispered joyfully to his comrades. "I'm hoping that fleet will come just as soon as it can."

"Happy, you sanguinary wretch," Harry whispered back, "I'm thinking the fleet will come soon enough for you and all the rest of us."

"Upset his coffee", Winslow Homer[36]

The afternoon faded. The sun sank in the hills behind them, and dusk came over city and harbor. But Harry, from the battery, could still see the black bulk of Sumter, and above it the gleaming red and blue of a flag.

Coffee and food were served to his comrades and himself in the battery, and then they remained by their guns waiting. The night deepened. Harry could yet see the flash of waters and the dim bulk of Sumter, but the flag itself was no longer visible. No sound came from the city. The silence there seemed singular and heavy.

The boy felt the night and the waiting. Even Happy Tom ceased to be light and frivolous. The three had nothing to do and they sat together, always looking toward the sea where the smoke of the relieving fleet might appear. Colonel Leonidas Talbot and Major Hector St. Hilaire passed together on a tour of inspection. They gave approving looks to the three trim youths, with the frank open faces, but said nothing and went on. Harry heard their footsteps for a moment or two, and then the oppressive silence came again.

The same stillness endured for a long time, so long that the three began to believe nothing would happen. Despite himself, Harry began to nod and he was forced to bring himself back to earth with a jerk. Then he stretched a little and peered over the earthwork. It was brighter now. A fine moon rode high, and the sea was dusted with starshine. The bulk of Sumter, black no longer, was coated with silver.

"Looks peaceful enough," whispered Langdon. "The ships have heard that you and St. Clair and I are here waiting for them and have turned back."

Harry made no answer. This waiting in the silence and the night made his blood quiver just a little. He was about to turn back when he saw a sudden flash of fire from another point further up. It was followed by a heavy crash that echoed and re-echoed over the still sea and city. Harry's heart leaped, but his body stiffened to attention. Tom and St. Clair by his side pressed against the earthwork.

"What is it?" they whispered.

"The moonlight is good," replied Harry, "but I don't see any ship. It must be a signal of some kind."

"Hush!" said Langdon, "there it goes again!"

Another cannon thundered, and the echoes, as before, came back from sea and shore, followed, as the echoes died, by that strange, heavy silence. But, straining their eyes to the utmost, the three boys could see nothing on the sea. It swayed gently like a vast mass of molten silver in the starshine, and lapped softly against the shore. The report of a third heavy gun came, and then the reports of several more. After that the silence was complete. It had seemed to Harry, his brain surcharged with excitement, like the tolling of great bells. Langdon and St. Clair whispered together, but he said nothing.

It was permitted to the three to lie down in their blankets in the earthwork and sleep, but they did not think of trying it. They wished to know the meaning of those cannon shots and they waited, tense with excitement. It was nearly midnight when Colonel Leonidas Talbot came.

"We have learned that the Northern vessels will appear before Charleston tomorrow," he said, "and the shots were a signal to all our people to be ready. The attack on Sumter will begin in the morning. Now you three boys must go to sleep. We shall need tomorrow soldiers who are fresh and strong, not those who are worn and weak from loss of sleep."

They tried it and found it easier now because they knew the mystery of the shots. Harry became conscious that the night was crisp and cold, and, wrapped in his blanket, he lay with his back against an inner wall of the earthwork. The blood, the result of his tension and excitement, pounded in his ears for some time, but, at last, his pulses became quiet, and his heavy eyes closed.

He was awakened at the first shoot of dawn by Colonel Leonidas Talbot.

"Up, boys!" he said, "snatch a bite of food and a drink of coffee, and make yourselves as neat as possible. General Beauregard is coming to this very battery."

His voice was quick and sharp, and the boys obeyed with the lightning speed of youth. It was a pale dawn. Gray clouds drifted along the sea's far rim, and a sharp wind came out of the Northwest. Heavy waves rolled into the mouths of the narrow and difficult passes that led into the bay.

"The Lord Himself fights for us," Harry heard Colonel Leonidas Talbot murmur. "No ships on such a sea would dare the passes in the face of our guns."

The pale light widened. Sumter was black and threatening again, and the flag waved there before it.

General Beauregard, his staff and a body of civilians arrived, and almost overflowed the battery. Harry noticed among the civilians an old man, seventy-five at least, with long hair, snow white. Despite his years, his face was as keen and eager as that of any boy.

"Who is he?" Harry whispered to St. Clair, who knew everybody.

"His name's Ruffin, but he's not a South Carolinian. He's a Virginian, but he has come to join us, and he's heart and soul with us. He's ready to fight at the drop of a hat."

Harry—their battery stood on Coming's Point—glanced toward the city and uttered a low cry of surprise.

"Look!" he said to his friends, "all Charleston is here."

"Yes, and a lot more of South Carolina, too," said St. Clair.

The people, learning the meaning of those signal guns in the night, were packed in every open space, and the very roofs were black with them. Forty or fifty thousand, men, women and children, were looking on, but nothing more than a murmur ran through the great mass. Harry knew that every heart in the fifty thousand beat, like his own, with strained expectancy.

A great gun in the battery was trained upon Sumter, and the gunner stood ready at the lanyard, but the old man with the long white hair and the keen, eager face, stepping forward, begged General Beauregard to allow him the honor of firing the first shot. The General consented at once, and the old man pulled the lanyard.

There was a terrific crash that almost deafened Harry, a gush of flame, followed by smoke, and a shell, screaming in a curve, dropped upon Sumter. For a few moments no one spoke, and Harry could hear the blood pounding in his ears. In a sudden flash of insight he saw a long and terrible road that they must tread. But neither he nor any other present realized to the full what had happened. The first real shot in the mightiest war of history had been fired, and the years of promises, kept or broken, of mutual jealousies and mutual abuse had ended at the cannon's mouth.

Confederate bombardment of Fort Sumter 13 April 1861[37]

The silence was broken by a shout like the roar of a storm, that came from the people in the town. A puff of smoke rose from Sumter and the fort sent its answering shot, but it struck no enemy and again the shout came from the town, now a cry of derision.

Then all the batteries in the wide curve about Sumter leaped into fiery life. Cannon after cannon poured shot and shell against the black walls. The fort was ringed with fire. It seemed to Harry that the earth rocked. He tried to speak to his comrades, but he could not hear his own voice. He thought he was about to be deafened for his whole life, but Langdon handed him pieces of cotton which he quickly stuffed in his ears. Langdon and St. Clair had already taken the precaution. Happy Tom had proved himself the most forethoughtful of them all. And yet Langdon, careless and easy, was aflame with the fire of battle. It seemed to Harry that he thought little of consequences.

"Listen to it!" he shouted in excited tones to Harry and St. Clair. "Hark to the thudding of the great guns! It's war, the greatest of all games!"

Harry felt an intense excitement also. These were his people. He was of their bone and sinew, and he was with them, heart and soul. He did his part at the guns, and, although his excitement grew, he said nothing. He saw that the return fire from the fort was far inferior to that of the South Carolinians, and that it was doing no damage.

"Using their light guns only," he heard Colonel Talbot say during a momentary lull. "They must be short of ammunition."

The morning wore slowly on. From every battery along the mainland and on the islands, the storm of projectiles yet beat upon Sumter, and, at intervals, the fort replied, still using the light guns. Once Harry heard the whistle of a shell over his head, and he ducked automatically, while the others laughed. Another time, a solid shot sent the dirt flying in all their faces, stinging like driven sand, but that was the nearest any missile ever came to them.

Beauregard, after a while, gave an order for the firing to cease, and the city and harbor rose again, clear and distinct, in the pale sunlight. The great crowd of people was still there, all watching and waiting, The fort was battered and torn, but above it still hung the defiant flag, and there was no offer of surrender.

"Look! Look!" Langdon cried suddenly, reckless of all discipline, as he pointed a forefinger toward the sea.

Harry saw a column of smoke rising, and defining itself clearly against the pale blue sky.

"The Yankee fleet!" cried one of the officers, as he put his glasses to his eyes.

General Beauregard, General Ripley, and officers in every other battery, also were watching that new column of smoke through glasses. The dark spire in truth rose from the *Baltic*, the chief ship of the Union, having on board the energetic Fox himself, and two hundred soldiers. But chance and the elements seemed to have conspired against the secretary. One of his strongest ships had gone to the relief of another fort further south, others had been scattered by a storm, and the *Baltic* had only two sister vessels as she approached, over a rolling gray sea, the fiery volcano that was once the peaceful harbor of Charleston.

Harry saw the first column of smoke increase to three, and they knew then that the number of the Union vessels was far less than had been expected.

"Will they undertake to force the harbor and reach Sumter?" he asked of Colonel Talbot, who was then in the battery.

"If they do," replied the Colonel, "it will be a case of the most reckless folly. They would be sunk in short order, as they come right into the teeth of our guns. The sea itself, is against them. The waves are rolling worse than ever."

Colonel Talbot knew what he was saying. Vainly the men in Sumter looked for relief by sea. They, too, had seen the three ships off the harbor, and they knew whence they came and for what purpose. But they had reached the end of their journey, and had fallen short with the object of it in sight. They were compelled to swing back and forth, while they watched the circle of batteries pour a continuous fire upon the crumbling fort.

After the Southern officers had taken a long look at the Union ships, and had seen that they could do nothing, the fire on Sumter was renewed with increased volume. It lasted all through the day and the vast crowd of spectators did not diminish in numbers. Many of the wealthier were in carriages. If one went away for food or refreshment another took his place.

When the wind at times lifted the smoke, Harry saw that the wooden buildings standing on the esplanade of the fort were burning fiercely, set on fire by the bursting shells. The iron cisterns, too, although he did not know it until later, were smashed, and columns of smoke from the flaming buildings were pouring into the fort, threatening its defenders with destruction.

Night came on, and most of the people, lining the harbor, were compelled to go to their homes, but the fire of the Southern batteries continued, always converging upon the scarred and blackened walls of Sumter, from which came an occasional shot in return. Harry had now grown used to this incessant, rolling crash. He could hear his comrades speak, their voices coming in an under note, and now and then they discussed the result. They agreed that Sumter was bound to fall. The Union fleet could bring it no relief, and such a continuous rain of balls and shells must eventually pound it to pieces.

They ate and drank after dark. They had food in abundance and delicacies of many kinds from which to choose. Charleston poured forth its plenty for its heroes, and in those days of fresh young enthusiasm there was no lack of anything.

"The Yankees hold out well," said Langdon, "but I'm willing to bet a hundred to one that nobody sleeps in that fort tonight. You can't see the smoke of the ships any more. I suppose that for safety in the night they've had to go further out to sea. I'm glad I'm not on one of them, rolling and tumbling in those high waves. Well, everything is for the best, and if Sumter doesn't fall into our laps tonight she'll fall tomorrow, and if she doesn't fall tomorrow she'll fall the next day. What do you say to that, old Wait-and-See?"

"Wait and see," replied Harry so naturally that the others laughed.

The bombardment went on all through the night. Harry continually breathed smoke and the odor of burned gunpowder, which seemed to keep his nerves keyed to a great pitch, and to maintain the heat of his blood. Yet, after a while, he lay down, when his turn at the guns ceased, and slept through sheer exhaustion. His eyes closed to the thunder of cannon and they awoke at dawn to the same heavy thudding.

The fire had not ceased at any time in the course of the night, and Sumter looked like a ruin, but the flag still floated over it. St. Clair and Langdon were awakened a few minutes later, and they also stood up, rubbed their eyes, stared at the fort, and listened to the firing. Harry laughed at their appearance.

"You fellows are certainly grimy," he said. "You look as if you hadn't seen water for a month."

"We can't see ourselves, old Wait-and-See," retorted Langdon, "but I guess we're beauties alongside of you. If I didn't have the honor of your acquaintance, I wouldn't know whether you came from the Indian Territory, Ashantee, or the Cannibal Islands."

"And the music goes merrily on," said St. Clair. "I went to sleep with the cannon firing, and I wake up with them still at it. I suppose a fellow will get used to it after a while."

"You can get used to anything," said an officer who heard them. "Now, you boys eat your breakfasts. Your turn at the guns will come again soon."

They took breakfast willingly, although they found a strong flavor of smoke, sand, and burned gunpowder in everything they ate and drank. Then they went to their guns, but, when a few more shots were fired, a trumpet blew a signal, and it was echoed from battery to battery. Every cannon ceased, and, in the silence and under the lifting smoke, Harry saw a white flag going up on the fort.

Sumter was about to yield.

Unidentified Confederate soldiers[38]

7. THE HOMECOMING

A great and exultant cheer went up from the massed thousands in Charleston. A smile passed over Beauregard's swarthy face and he showed his white teeth. Colonel Leonidas Talbot regarded the white flag with feelings in which triumph and sadness were mingled strangely. But the emotions of Harry and his comrades were, for the moment, those of victory only.

Boats put out both from the fort and the shore. Discipline was relaxed now, and Harry, St. Clair, and Langdon went outside the battery. A light breeze had sprung up, and it was very grateful to Harry, who for hours had breathed the heavy odors of smoke and burned gunpowder. The smoke itself, which had formed a vast cloud over harbor, forts, and city, was now drifting out to sea, leaving all things etched sharply in the dazzling sunlight of a Southern spring day.

"Well, old Wait-and-See, you have waited, and you have seen," said Langdon to Harry. "That white flag and those boats going out mean that Sumter is ours. Everything is for the best and we win everywhere and all the time."

Harry was silent. He was watching the boats. But the negotiations were soon completed. Sumter, a mass of ruins, was given up, and the Star and Bars, taking the place of the Stars and Stripes, gaily snapped defiance to the whole North. "It begins to look well there," said Beauregard, gazing proudly at the new flag.

Confederate flag raised at Fort Sumter 16 Apr 1861[39]

All the amenities were preserved between the captured garrison and their captors. Anderson was sent to the *Baltic*, which still hovered outside, and the Union vessels disappeared on their way back to the North. Peace, but now the peace of triumph, settled again over Charleston, and throughout the South went the joyous tidings that Sumter had been taken. The great state of Virginia, Mother of Presidents, went out of the Union at last, and North Carolina, Tennessee, and Arkansas followed her, but Maryland, Kentucky, and Missouri still hung in the balance.

Lincoln had called for volunteers to put down a rebellion, but Harry heard everywhere in Charleston that the Confederacy was now secure. The Southerners were rising by the thousands to defend it. The women, too, were full of zeal and enthusiasm and they urged the men to go to the front. With the full consent of the lower South the capital was to be moved from Montgomery to Richmond, the capital of Virginia, on the very border of the Confederacy, to look defiantly, as it were, across at Washington over a space which was to become the vast battlefield of America, although few then dreamed it. The progress of President Davis to the new capital, set in the very face of the foe, was to be one huge triumph of faith and loyalty.

Harry heard nothing in Charleston but joyful news. There was not a single note of gloom. Europe, which must have its cotton, would favor the success of the South. Women who had never worked before, sewed night and day on clothing for the soldiers. Men gave freely and without asking to the new government. An extraordinary wave of emotion swept over the South, carrying everybody with it. Charleston shouted anew as the newspapers announced the news of distinguished officers who had gone out with the Southern States. There were the two Johnstons, the one of Virginia and the other of Kentucky; Lee, Bragg, of Buena Vista fame; Longstreet, and many others, some already celebrated in the Mexican War, and others with a greater fame yet to make.

Confederate pickets near Charleston, 1861[40]

Harry heard it all and it was transfused into his own blood. Now a letter came from his father. That obstinate faction in

Kentucky still held the state to the Union. Since Sumter had fallen and Charleston was safe, he wished his son to rejoin him in Pendleton, whence they would proceed together to Frankfort, and help the Southern party. His personal account of the glowing deed that had been done in Charleston harbor would help. He was sure that his old friend, General Beauregard, would release him for this important duty.

Harry's heart and judgment alike responded to the call. He took the letter to General Beauregard, finding him at the Charleston Hotel with Governor Pickens and officers of his staff, and stood aside while the general read it. Beauregard at once wrote an order.

Charleston Hotel, Abbeville Volunteers, 1861[41]

"This is your discharge from the Palmetto Guards," he said. "Colonel Kenton writes wisely. We need Kentucky and I understand that a very little more may bring the state to us. Go with your father. I understand that you have been a brave young soldier here and may you do as well up there."

Harry, feeling pride but not showing it, saluted and left the room, going at once to Madame Delaunay's, where he had left his baggage. He intended to leave early in the morning, but first he sought his friends and told them good-bye.

"Don't forget that we're going to have a great war," said Colonel Leonidas Talbot, "and the first battle line will be far north of Charleston. I shall look for you there."

"God bless you, my boy," said Major Hector St. Hilaire. "May you come back some day to this beautiful Charleston of ours, and find it more beautiful than ever."

"I'll meet you at Richmond later on," said Arthur St. Clair, "and then we'll serve together again."

"I'll join you at the White House in Washington," said Tom Langdon, "and I'll give you the next best bed to sleep in with your boots on."

Harry gave his farewells with deep and genuine regret. Whether their manner was grave or frivolous, he knew that these were good friends of his, and he sincerely hoped that he would meet them again. Madame Delaunay spoke to him almost as if he had been a son of hers, and there was dew in his eyes, because he could never forget her kindness to the lad who had been a stranger.

He resumed his civilian clothing and put his gray uniform, fine and new, of which he was so proud, in his saddle bags. Kentucky had declared herself neutral ground, warning the armies of both North and South to keep off her sacred soil, and he did not wish to invite undue attention. He intended, moreover, to leave the train when he neared Pendleton, at the same little station at which he had taken it when he started south.

It was a different Harry who started home late in April. Four months had made great changes. He bore himself more like a man. His manner was much more considered and grave. He had seen great things and he had done his share of them. He gazed upon a world full of responsibilities and perils.

But he looked back at Charleston the gay, the volatile and the beautiful, with real affection. It was almost buried now in flowers and foliage. Spring was at the full, every breeze was sharply sweet with grassy flavors. The very triumph and joy of living penetrated his soul. Youth swept aside the terrors of war. He was going home after victory. He soon left Charleston out of sight. A last roof or steeple glittered for a moment in the sun and then was gone. Before him lay the uplands and the ridges, and in another day he would be in another land.

He crossed the low mountains, passed through Nashville again, although he did not stop there, his train making immediate connection, and once more and with a thrill, entered his own state. He learned from casual talk on the trains that affairs in Kentucky were very hot. The special session of the Legislature, called by Governor Magoffin, was to meet at Frankfort early in May. The women of the state had already prepared an appeal to the Legislature to save them from the horrors of civil war.

Harry saw that he had not left active life behind him when he came away from Charleston. The feeling of strife had spread over a vast area. The atmosphere of Kentucky, like that of South Carolina, was surcharged with intensity and passion, but it had a difference. All the winds blew in the same direction in South Carolina and they sang one song of triumph, but in Kentucky they were variable and conflicting, and their voices were many.

He felt the difference as soon as he reached the hills of his native state. People were cooler here and they were more prone to look at the two sides of a question. The air, too, was unlike that of South Carolina. There was a sharper tang to it. It whipped his blood as it blew down from the slopes and crests.

It was afternoon when he reached the little station of Winton and left the train, a tall, sturdy boy, the superior of many a man in size, strength and agility. His saddle bags over his arm, he went at once to the liveryman with whom he had left his horse on his journey to Charleston, and asked for another, his best, for the return ride to Pendleton. The liveryman stared at him a moment or two and then burst into an exclamation of surprise.

"Why, it's Harry Kenton!" he said. "Harry, you've changed a lot in so short a time! You were at the bombardment of Fort Sumter, they tell me! It's made a mighty stir in these parts! There were never before such times in old Kentucky! Yes, Harry, I'll give you the best horse I've got, there ain't one more powerful in the state, but pushin' as hard as you will you can't reach Pendleton before dark, an' you look out."

"Look out for what?"

"Bill Skelly an' his gang. Them mountaineers are up. They say they're goin' to beat the rich men of the lowlands an' keep Kentucky in the Union, but between you an' me, Harry, it's the hate they feel for them that think harder an' work harder an' make more than themselves. Bill Skelly is the worst man in the mountains an' he has gathered about him a big gang of toughs. They're carin' mighty little about the Union or the freedom of the slaves, but they expect to make a lot out of this for themselves. Now I tell you again, Harry, to look out as you go through the dark to Pendleton. The country is mighty troubled."

"I will," replied Harry, with vivid recollection of his ride from Pendleton to Winton. "I am armed, Mr. Collins, and I have seen war. I served in one of the batteries that reduced Fort Sumter."

He did not say the last as a boast, but merely as an assurance to the liveryman, who he saw was anxious on his account.

"If you've got pistols, just you think once before you shoot," said Collins. "Things are shorely mighty troubled in these parts an' they're goin' to be worse."

"Have you heard anything of my father? Is he at Pendleton?"

"He was two days ago. He'd been up to Louisville where the Southern leaders had a meetin', but couldn't make things go as they wanted 'em to go, an' so he come back to Pendleton. People are tellin' that he's goin' to Frankfort soon."

Harry thanked him, threw his saddle bags across the horse, a powerful bay, and, giving a final wave of his hand to the sympathetic liveryman, rode away. He had little fear. He carried a pair of heavy double-barreled pistols in holsters, and a smaller weapon in his pocket. The horse, as he soon saw, was of uncommon power and spirit and he snapped his fingers at Skelly and his gang.

He rode first at a long, easy walk, knowing too well to

push hard at the beginning, and the afternoon passed without anything worthy of his notice save the loneliness of the road. In the two hours before sundown he met less than half a dozen persons. All were men, and with a mere nod they went on quickly, regarding him with suspicion. This was not the fashion of a year ago, when they exchanged a friendly word or two, but Harry knew its cause. Now nobody could trust anybody else.

The setting sun was uncommonly red, tinting all the forest with a fiery glow and Harry looked apprehensively at the line of blue hills now on his right, whence danger had come before. But he saw nothing that moved there. No signal lights twinkled. The intervening space was a mass of heavy green foliage, which the eye, now that the twilight was at hand, could penetrate only a few score yards. A northeast wind off the distant mountain tops was cold and sharp, and Harry, who wore no overcoat, shivered a little.

Young though he was, he remembered the liveryman's caution, and he watched the forest on either side, as well as he could. But he depended more upon his keenness of ear. He did not believe the stirring of any large force in the thickets could pass him unheard, and, having nursed the strength of his great horse, he felt that he could leave almost any pursuit far behind.

The twilight sank into a dark and heavy night. The moon and stars lay behind drifting clouds and, now and then, came a swish of cold rain. Harry was not able to see more than a few yards to right or left, when the road ran through the woods, as it did most of the time, and not much further when fields chanced to lie on either side.

He was within a mile of Pendleton, and his heart began to throb, not with thoughts of Skelly, but because he would soon be in his old home again. Ten or fifteen minutes more, and he would see the solid red brick house rising among the clipped pines. But as he passed the junction of a small road coming down from the hills, his attentive ear gave warning. He heard the sound of hoofs and many of them. He drew in for a moment under the boughs and listened.

Harry's instinct warned him against the troop of men that

he heard. Collins, the liveryman, had told him that the country was full of trouble. This region was neither North nor South. It was debatable land, of which raiding bands would take full advantage, and, despite the risk, he wished to know what was on foot. He was almost invisible under the boughs of a great oak which hung over the road, and the horse, after so many miles of hard riding, was willing enough to stand still. The rain swished in his face and the leaves gave forth a chilly rustle, but he held himself firmly to his task.

Guerilla depredations—seizing horses[42]

The hoofbeats came nearer and then ceased. The horsemen stopped at the point, where the narrower road merged into the larger and, as they were clear of the foliage, Harry caught a view of them. There was no moonlight, but his eyes had grown so well used to the darkness that he was able to recognize Skelly, who was in advance, an old army rifle across his saddle bow. Behind him were at least fifty men, and Harry knew they were all mountaineers. They rode the scrubby mountain horses, more like ponies, and every man carried a rifle.

Harry divined instantly that they had come down from the

hills to make a raid upon the Confederate stronghold, Pendleton. War was on, and here was their chance to take revenge upon the more civilized people of the lowlands. Skelly was giving his final orders and Harry could hear him.

"We'll leave the main road, pull down the fences, an' ride across the fields," he said. "We'll first take the house of that rebel and traitor, Colonel Kenton. It'll be helpin' the cause if we burn it clean down to the ground. If anybody tries to stop you, shoot. Then we'll go on to the others."

A growl of approval came from the men, and some shook their rifles as a sign of what they would do. Harry knew them. Mostly moonshiners and fugitives from justice, they cared far more for revenge and spoil than for the Union. He shuddered as he heard their talk. His own home was to be their first point of attack, and those who resisted were to be shot down.

He waited to hear no more, but, keeping in the shadow of the boughs and riding at first in a walk, he went on toward Pendleton. He was sure that Skelly's men had not heard his hoofbeats, as there was no sound of pursuit, and, three or four hundred yards further, he changed from a walk to a gallop. Careless of the dark and of all risks of the road, he drove the horse faster and faster. He was on familiar ground. He knew every hill and dip, almost every tree, but he did not pause to notice anything.

43

Soon he saw a light, then a dark outline, and his heart throbbed greatly. It was his father's house, standing among the clipped pines, and he was in time! Now his horse's feet thundered on the brief stretch of road that was left, and in another minute he was at the gate opening on the lawn. A man, rifle in hand, stood on the front steps, and demanded to know who had come.

"It is I, Harry, father!" cried Harry. "Skelly and his crowd are only a mile behind me, coming to destroy the place!"

Harry heard his father mutter, "Thank God!" which he knew was for his coming. Then he quickly led the horse inside the gate, turned him loose, and ran forward. Colonel Kenton was already coming to meet him and the hands of father and son met in a strong and affectionate clasp.

"We will have to get out and go into the town," said Harry. "You and I alone can't hold them off. Skelly has at least fifty men. I saw them in the road."

"I'm not afraid since you've got safely through," replied Colonel Kenton. "We had a hint that Skelly was coming. That's why you see me with this rifle. I'd have sent you a telegram to stop at Winton, but couldn't reach you in time. Come into the house. Some friends of ours are here, ready to help us hold it against anybody and everybody that Skelly may bring."

Harry, with his saddle bags and holsters over his arm, entered the front hall with his father, who closed the door behind him. A single lamp burned in the hall, but fifteen men, all armed with rifles, stood there. He saw among them Steve Allison, the constable, Bracken the farmer, Senator Culver, and even old Judge Kendrick. Most of them, besides the rifles, carried pistols, and the party, though small, was resolute and grim. They greeted Harry with warmth, but said few words.

"We've food and hot coffee here," said Colonel Kenton. "After your long ride, Harry, you'd better eat."

"A cup of coffee will do," replied the boy. "But let me have a rifle. Skelly and his men will be here in ten minutes."

Old Judge Kendrick smiled.

"You can't complain, colonel," he said, "that your son has not inherited your temperament."

A rifle, loaded and ready, was handed to Harry, and, at the same time he drank a cup of hot coffee, brought by a trembling black boy. Allison meanwhile had opened the door a little and was listening.

"I don't hear 'em yet," he said.

"They'll approach cautiously," said Colonel Kenton. "I think they're likely to leave their horses at the edge of the wood and enter the lawn on foot. We'll put out the light and go outside."

"Good tactics," said Culver, as he promptly blew out the single light. Then all went upon the great front portico, where they stood for a few moments waiting. They could neither see nor hear anything hostile. Drifting clouds still hid the moon and stars, and a swish of light, cold rain came now and then.

There were piazzas on both sides of the house, and a porch in the rear. Colonel Kenton disposed his men deftly in order to meet the foe at any point. The stone pillars would afford protection for the riflemen. He, his son and old Judge Kendrick, held the portico in front.

Harry crouched behind a pillar, his fingers on the trigger of a rifle, and his holster containing the big double-barreled pistols lying at his feet. Impressionable, and with a horror of injustice, his heart was filled with rage. It was merely a band of outlaws who were coming to plunder and destroy his beautiful home and to kill any who resisted. He had respected those who held Sumter so long, but these fought only for their own hand.

A slight sound came from the road, a little distance to the south. He waited until it was repeated and then he was sure.

"They're out there," he whispered to his father at the next pillar.

"I heard them," replied the colonel. "They'll come upon the lawn, hiding behind the pines, and hoping to surprise the house. I fancy the surprise will be theirs, not ours. When you shoot, Harry, shoot to kill, or they will surely kill us. Keep as much as you can behind the pillar, and don't get excited."

Colonel Kenton was quite calm. The old soldier had returned to his work. Wary and prepared, he was not loath to meet the enemy. Harry, keeping his father's orders well in mind, crouched a little lower and waited. Presently he heard a slight rustling, and he knew that Skelly's men were among the dwarf pines on the lawn. The rustling continued and came nearer. Harry glanced at his father, who was behind a pillar not ten feet away.

"Who are you, and what do you want?" called Colonel Kenton into the darkness.

There was no answer and the rustling ceased. Harry heard nothing but the gentle fall of the rain.

"Speak up!" called the colonel once more. "Who are you?"

The answer came. Forty or fifty rifles cracked among the pines. Harry saw little flashes of fire, and he heard bullets hiss so venomously that a chill ran along his spine. There was a patter of lead on every side of the house, but most of the shots came from the front lawn. It was well that the colonel, Harry and the judge, were sheltered by the big pillars, or two or three shots out of so many would have found a mark.

Harry's rage, which had cooled somewhat while he was waiting, returned. He began to peer around the edge of the pillar, and seek a target, but the colonel whispered to him to hold his fire.

"Getting no reply, they'll creep a little closer presently and fire a second volley," he said.

Harry pressed closer to the pillar, kneeling low, as he had learned already that nine out of ten men fire too high in battle. He heard once more the rustling among the pines, and he knew that Skelly's men were advancing. Doubtless they believed that the defenders had fled within the house at the first volley.

He heard suddenly the clicking of gun locks, and the rifles crashed together again, but now the fire was given at much closer range. Harry saw a dusky figure beside a pine not thirty feet away, and he instantly pulled trigger upon it. His father's own rifle cracked at the same time, and two cries of pain came from the lawn. The boy, hot with the fire of battle, snatched the pistols out of the holsters and sent in four more shots.

Rapid reports from the other side of the house showed that the defenders there were also repelling attacks.

But Skelly's men, finding that they could not rush the house, kept up a siege from the ambush of the pines. Bullets rattled like hailstones against the thick brick walls of the house, and several times the smashing of glass told that windows had been shot in. Harry's blood now grew feverishly hot and his anger mounted with it. It was intolerable that these outlaws should attack people in their own homes. Lying almost flat on the floor of the portico he reloaded his rifle and pistols. As he raised his head to seek a new shot, a bullet tipped his ear, burning it like a streak of fire, and flattened against the wall behind him. He fired instantly at the base of the flash and a cry of pain showed that the bullet had struck a human target.

Harry, in his excitement, raised himself a little for another shot, and a second bullet cut dangerously near. A warning command came from his father, veteran warrior of the plains, to keep down, and he obeyed promptly. Then followed a period of long and intensely anxious waiting. Harry thought that if the night would only lighten they could get a clean sweep of the lawn and drive away the mountaineers, but it grew darker instead and the wind rose. He heard the boughs of the clipped pines rustle as they were whipped together, and the cold drops lashed him in the face. He had become soaking wet, lying on the floor of the portico, but he did not notice it.

Harry saw far to his left a single dim light in the dip beyond the forest, and he knew that it shone through a window in one of the houses of Pendleton.

It seemed amazing that so bitter a combat should be going on here, while the people slept peacefully in the town below. But there was not one chance in a thousand that they would hear of the battle on such a night. Then an idea came to him, and creeping to his father he made his proposition. Colonel Kenton opposed it vigorously, but Harry insisted. He knew every inch of the grounds. Why should he not? He had played over them all his life, and he could be in the fields and away in less than two minutes.

Colonel Kenton finally consulted Judge Kendrick, and the judge agreed with Harry. Besieged by so many, they needed help and the boy was the one to bring it. Then Colonel Kenton consented that Harry should go, but pressed his hand and told him to be very careful.

The boy went back into the house, passing through the dark rooms to the rear. As he went, he heard the sound of sobbing. It was the colored servants crying with terror. He found the constable and Senator Culver on watch on the back porch and whispered to them his errand.

"For God's sake, be careful, Harry," the Senator whispered back. "Bad blood is boiling now. Some of Skelly's men have been hit hard, and if they caught you they'd shoot you without mercy."

"But they won't catch me," replied the boy with confidence. Thinking it would be in the way in his rapid flight, he gave his rifle to the senator, and taking the heavy pistols from the holsters, thrust them in the pockets of his coat. Then he dropped lightly from the porch and lay for a few moments in the darkness and on the wet ground, absolutely still.

A strange thrill ran through Harry Kenton when his body touched the damp earth. The contact seemed to bring to him strength and courage. Doubts fled away. He would succeed in the trial. He could not possibly fail. His great-grandfather, Henry Ware, had been a renowned borderer and Indian fighter, one of the most famous in all the annals of Kentucky, gifted with almost preternatural power, surpassing the Indians themselves in the lore and craft of forest and trail. It was said too, that the girl, Lucy Upton, who became Henry Ware's wife and who was Harry's great-grandmother, had received this same gift of forest divination. His own first name had been given to him in honor of that redoubtable great-grandfather.

Now all the instincts of Harry's famous ancestors became intensely alive in him. The blood of those who had been compelled for so many years to watch and fight poured in a full tide through his veins. His bearing became sharper, his eyes saw through the darkness like those of a cat, and a certain sixth sense, hitherto a dormant instinct which would warn of danger, came suddenly to life.

Two parallel rows of honeysuckle bushes ran back some distance to a vegetable garden. He reckoned that the mountaineers would be hiding behind these, and therefore he turned away to the right, where dwarf pines, clipped into cones, grew as on the front lawn. The grass, helped by a wet spring, had grown already to a height of several inches, and Harry was surprised at the ease with which he drew his body through it. Every inch of garment upon him was soaked with rain, but he took no thought of the fact. He felt a certain fierce joy in the wildness of night and storm, and he was ready to defy any number of mountaineers.

The sixth and new sense suddenly gave warning and he lay flat in the wet grass just under one of the pines. Then he saw three men rise from their shelter behind a honeysuckle bush, walk forward, and stand in a group talking about ten feet behind him. Although they were not visible from the house he saw them clearly enough. One of them was Skelly himself, and all three were of villainous face. Straining his ear he could hear what they said and now he was very glad indeed that he had come.

It was the plan of Skelly to wait in silence and patience a long time. The defenders would conclude that he and his men had gone away, and then the mountaineers could either rush the house or set it on fire. If the final resort was fire, they could easily shoot Colonel Kenton and his friends as they ran out. It was Skelly who spoke of this hideous plan, laughing as he spoke, and Harry's hand went instinctively toward the butt of one of the pistols. But his will made him draw it away again, and, motionless in the grass, lying flat upon his face, he continued to listen.

Skelly's plan was accepted and they moved away to tell the others. Harry rose a little, and crept rapidly through the grass toward the vegetable garden.

Again he was surprised at his own skill. Acute of ear as he had become he could scarcely hear the brushing of the grass as he passed. As he approached the garden he saw two more men, rifles in hand, walking about, but paying little heed to them he kept on until he lay against the fence enclosing the garden.

It was a fence of palings, spiked at the top, and climbing it was a problem. Studying the question for a moment or two he decided that it was too dangerous to be risked, and moving cautiously along he began to feel of the palings. At last he came to one that was loose, and he pulled it entirely free at the bottom. Then he slipped through and into the garden. Here were long rows of grapevines, fastened on sticks, and, for a few moments, he lay flat behind one of the rows. He knew that he was not yet entirely safe, as the mountaineers were keen of eye and ear, and an outer guard of skirmishers might be lying in the garden itself. But he was now even keener of eye and hearing than they, and he could detect nothing living near him. The house also, and all about it, was silent. Evidently Skelly's men had settled down to a long siege, and Harry rejoiced in the amount of time they gave him.

He rose to his feet, but, stooped to only half his height, he ran swiftly behind the row of grapevines to the far end of the garden, leaped over the fence, and continued his rapid flight toward Pendleton, where the single light still burned. He surmised that his father had received the warning too late to gather more than a few friends, and that the rest of the town was yet in deep ignorance.

The first house he reached, the one in which the light burned, was that of Gardner, the editor, and he beat heavily upon the door. Gardner himself opened it, and he started back in astonishment at the wild figure covered with mud, a heavy pistol clutched in the right hand.

"In Heaven's name, who are you?" he cried.

"Don't you know me, Mr. Gardner? I'm Harry Kenton, come back from Charleston! Bill Skelly and fifty of his men have ridden down from the mountains and are besieging us in our house, intending to rob and kill! The constable is there and so are Judge Kendrick, Senator Culver, and a few others, but we need help and I've come for it!"

He spoke in such a rapid, tense manner that every word carried conviction.

"Excuse me for not knowing you, Harry," Gardner said, "but you're calling at a rather unusual time in a rather unusual manner, and you have the most thorough mask of mud I ever saw on anybody. Wait a minute and I'll be with you."

He returned in half the time, and the two of them soon had the town up and stirring. Pendleton was largely Southern in sympathy, and even those who held other views did not wholly relish an attack upon one of its prominent men by a band of unclassified mountaineers. Lights sprang up all over the town. Men poured from the houses and there was no house then that did not contain at least one rifle.

In a half hour sixty or seventy men, well-armed with rifles and pistols, were on their way to Colonel Kenton's house. Only a few drops of rain were falling now, and the thin edge of the moon appeared between clouds. There was a little light. The relieving party advanced swiftly and without noise. They were all accustomed to outdoor life and the use of weapons, and they needed few commands. Gardner came nearer than anyone else to being the leader, although Harry kept by his side.

They went on Harry's own trail, passing through the garden and hurrying toward the house. Three or four dim figures fled before them, running between the rows of vines. The Pendleton men fired at them, and then raised a great shout, as they rushed for the lawn. The mountaineers took to instant flight, making for the woods, where they had left their horses.

Colonel Kenton and his friends came from the house, shaking hands joyfully with their deliverers. Lanterns were produced, and they searched the lawn. Three men lay stiff and cold behind the dwarf pines. Harry shuddered. He was seeing for the first time the terrible fruits of civil war. It was not merely the pitched battles of armies, but often neighbor against neighbor, and sometimes the cloak of North or South would be used as a disguise for the basest of motives.

They also found two sanguinary trails leading to the wood in which the mountaineers had hitched their horses, indicating that the defenders of the Kenton house had shot well. But by the next morning Skelly's men had made good their flight far into the hills where no one could follow them. They sent no request for their own dead who were buried by the Pendleton people.

But the town raised a home guard to defend itself against raiders of any kind, and Colonel Kenton and Harry promptly made ready for their journey to Frankfort, where the choice of the state must soon be made, and whither Raymond Bertrand, the South Carolinian, had gone already. Colonel Kenton feared no charge because of the fight with Skelly's men. He was but defending his own home and here, as in the motherland, a man's house was his castle.

Unidentified Confederate soldier[45]

8. THE FIGHT FOR A STATE

Colonel Kenton and Harry avoided Louisville, which was now in the hands of Northern sympathizers, and, travelling partly by rail and partly by stage, reached Frankfort early in May to attend the special session of the Legislature called by Governor Magoffin. Although the skirmishing had taken place already along the edge of highland and lowland, the state still sought to maintain its position of neutrality. There was war within its borders, and yet no war. In feeling, it was Southern, and yet its judgment was with the Union. Thousands of ardent young men had drifted southward to join the armies forming there, and thousands of others, equally ardent, had turned northward to join forces that would oppose those below. Harry, young as he was, recognized that his own state would be more fiercely divided than any other by the great strife.

But Federal and Confederate alike preserved the semblance of peace as they gathered at Frankfort for the political struggle over the state. Colonel Kenton and his son took the train at a point about forty miles from the capital, and they found it crowded with public men going from Louisville to Frankfort. It was the oldest railroad west of the Alleghenies, and among the first ever built. The coaches swung around curves, and dust and particles flew in at the windows, but the speed was a relief after the crawling of the stage and Harry stretched himself luxuriously on the plush seat.

A tall man in civilian attire, holding himself very stiffly, despite the swinging and swaying of the train, rose from his seat, and came forward to greet Colonel Kenton.

Mr. Greenfield, reporter for the Hapkinsville Press, KY[46]

"George," he said, his voice quivering slightly, "you and I have fought together in many battles in Mexico and the West, but it is likely now that we shall fight other battles on this own soil of ours against each other. But, George, let us be friends always, and let us pledge it here and now."

The words might have seemed a little dramatic elsewhere, but not so under the circumstances of time and place. Colonel Kenton's quick response came from the depths of a generous soul.

"John," he said as their two hands met in the grip of brothers of the camp and field, "you and I may be on opposing sides, but we can never be enemies. John, this is my son, Harry. Harry, this is Major John Warren of Mason County and the regular army of the United States; he does not think as we do, but even at West Point he was a stubborn idiot. He and I were continually arguing, and he would never admit that he was always wrong. I never knew him to be right in anything except mathematics, and then he was never wrong."

Major Warren smiled and sat down by his old comrade.

"You've a fine boy there, George," he said, "and I suppose he probably takes his opinions from his father, which is a great mistake. I think if I were to talk to him I could show him his, or rather your, error."

"Not by your system of mathematical reasoning, John. Your method is well enough for the building of a fortress or calculating the range of a gun. But it won't do for the actions of men. You allow nothing for feeling, sentiment, association, propinquity, heredity, climate and, and—"

"Get a dictionary or a book of synonyms, George."

"Perhaps I should. I understand how we happen to differ. But I can't explain it well. Well, maybe it will all blow over. The worries of today are often the jokes of tomorrow."

Major Warren shook his head.

"It may blow over," he said, "but it will be a mighty wind; it will blow a long time, and many things for which you and I care, George, will be blown away by it. When that great and terrible wind stops blowing, our country will be changed forever."

"Don't be so downcast, John, you are not dead yet," said Colonel Kenton, clapping his friend on the shoulder. "You've often seen big clouds go by without either wind or rain."

"How about that attack upon your house and you and your friends? The clouds had something in them then."

"Merely mountain outlaws taking advantage of unsettled conditions."

Harry had listened closely and he knew that his father was only giving voice to his hopes, not to his beliefs. But as they ceased to talk of the great question, his attention wandered to the country through which they were passing. Spring was now deep and green in Kentucky. They were running through a land of deep, rich soil, with an outcrop of white limestone showing here and there above the heavy green grass. A peaceful country and prosperous. It seemed impossible that it should be torn by war, by war between those who lived upon it.

Then the train left the grass lands, cut through a narrow but rough range of hills, entered a gorge, and stopped in Frankfort, the little capital, beside the deep and blue Kentucky.

Frankfort had only a few thousand inhabitants, but Harry found here much of the feeling that he had seen in Nashville and Charleston, with an important difference. There it was all Southern, or nearly so, but here North struggled with South on terms that certainly were not worse than equal.

Although the place was crowded, he and his father were lucky enough to secure a room at the chief hotel, which was also the only one of any importance. The hotel itself swarmed with the opposing factions. Senator Culver and Judge

Kendrick had a room together across the hall from theirs, and next to them four red hot sympathizers with the Union slept on cots in one apartment. Further down the hall Harvey Whitridge, a state senator, huge of stature, much whiskered, and the proud possessor of a voice that could be heard nearly a mile, occupied a room with Samuel Fowler, a tall, thin, quiet member of the Lower House. The two were staunch Unionists.

Everybody knew everybody else in this dissevered gathering. Nearly everybody was kin by blood to everybody else. In a state affected little by immigration families were more or less related. If there was to be a war it would be, so far as they were concerned, a war of cousins against cousins.

Colonel Kenton and Harry had scarcely bathed their faces and set their clothing to rights, when there was a sharp knock at the door and the Colonel admitted Raymond Bertrand, the South Carolinian, dark of complexion, volatile and wonderfully neat in apparel. He seemed at once to Harry to be a messenger from that Charleston which he had liked, and in the life of which he had had a share. Bertrand shook hands with both with great enthusiasm, but his eyes sparkled when he spoke to Harry.

"And you were there when they fired on Sumter!" he exclaimed. "And you had a part in it! What a glorious day! What a glorious deed! And I had to be here in your cold state, trying to make these descendants of stubborn Scotch and English see the right, and follow gladly in the path of our beautiful star, South Carolina!"

"How goes the cause here, Bertrand?" asked Colonel Kenton, breaking in on his prose epic.

Bertrand shrugged his shoulders and his face expressed discontent.

"Not well," he replied, "not as well as I had hoped. There is still something in the name of the Union that stirs the hearts of the Kentuckians. They hesitate. I have worked, I have talked, I have used all the arguments of our illustrious President, Mr. Davis, and of the other great men who have charge of Southern fortunes, and they still hesitate. Their blood is not hot enough. They do not have the vision. They lack the fire and splendor of the South Carolinians!"

Harry felt a little heat, but Colonel Kenton was not disturbed at all by the criticism.

"Perhaps you are right, Bertrand," he said thoughtfully. "We Kentuckians have the reputation of being very quick on the trigger, but we are conservative in big things. This is going to be a great war, a mighty great war, and I suppose our people feel like taking a good long look, and then another, equally as long, before they leap."

Bertrand, hot-blooded and impatient, bit his lip.

"It will not do! It will not do!" he exclaimed. "We must have this state. Virginia has gone out! Kentucky is her daughter! Then why does not she do the same?"

"You must give us time, Bertrand," said Colonel Kenton, still speaking slowly and thoughtfully. "We are not starting upon any summer holiday, and I can understand how the people here feel. I'm going with my people and I'm going to fire on the old flag, under which I've fought so often, but you needn't think it comes so easy. This thing of choosing between the sections is the hardest task that was ever set for a man."

Harry had never heard his father speak with more solemnity. Bertrand was silent, overawed by the older man, but to the boy the words were extremely impressive. His youthful temperament was sensitive to atmosphere. In Charleston he shared the fire, zeal, and enthusiasm of an impressionable people. They saw only one side and, for a while, he saw only one side, too. Here in Frankfort the atmosphere was changed. They saw two sides and he saw two sides with them.

"But you need have no fear about us, Bertrand," continued Colonel Kenton. "My heart is with the South, and so is my boy's. I thought that Kentucky would go out of the Union without a fight, but since there is to be a struggle we'll go through with it, and win it. Don't be afraid, the state will be with you yet."

They talked a little longer and then Bertrand left. Harry politely held the door open for him, and, as he went down the hall, he saw him pass Whitridge and Fowler. Contrary to the custom which still preserved the amenities they did not speak. Bertrand gave them a look of defiance. It seemed to Harry that he wanted to speak, but he pressed his lips firmly together, and, looking straight ahead of him, walked to the stairway, down which he disappeared. As Harry still stood in the open doorway, Whitridge and Fowler approached.

"Can we come in?" Whitridge asked.

"Yes, Harvey," said Colonel Kenton over the boy's shoulder. "Both of you are welcome here at any time."

The two men entered and Harry gave them chairs. Whitridge's creaked beneath him with his mighty weight.

"George," said the Senator pointedly but without animosity, "you and I have known each other a good many years, and we are eighth or tenth cousins, which counts for something in this state. Now, you have come here to Frankfort to pull Kentucky out of the Union, and I've come to pull so hard against you that you can't. You know it and I know it. All's square and above board, but why do you bring here that South Carolina Frenchman to meddle in the affairs of the good old state of Kentucky? Is it any business of his or of the other people down there? Can't we decide it ourselves? We're a big family here in Kentucky, and we oughtn't to bring strangers into the family council, even if we do have a disagreement. Besides, he represents the Knights of the Golden Circle, and what they are planning is plumb foolishness. Even if you are bound to go out and split up the Union, I'd think you wouldn't have anything to do with the wholesale grabbing of Spanish-speaking territories to the southward."

"There's a lot in what you say, Harvey," replied Colonel Kenton, speaking with the utmost good humor, "but I didn't bring Bertrand here; he came of his own accord. Besides, while I'm strong for the South, I think this Knights of the Golden Circle business is bad, just as you do."

"I'm glad you've got that much sense left, George," said Whitridge. "You army men never do know much about politics. It's easy to pull the wool over your eyes."

"Have you and Fowler come here for that purpose?" asked the colonel, smiling.

It was the preliminary to a long argument carried on without temper. Harry listened attentively, but as soon as it was over and Whitridge and Fowler had gone, he tumbled into his bed and went to sleep.

He rose early the next morning, before his father in fact, as he was eager to see more of Frankfort, ate a solid breakfast almost alone, and went into the streets, where the first person he met was his own cousin and schoolmate, Dick Mason. The two boys started, looked first at each other with hostile glances, which changed the next instant to looks of pleasure and welcome, and then shook hands with power and heartiness. They could not be enemies. They were boys together again.

"Why, Dick," exclaimed Harry, "I thought you had gone east to save the Union."

"So I have," replied Dick Mason, "but not as far east as you thought. We've got a big camp down in Garrard County, where the forces of the Kentuckians who favor the Union are gathering. General Nelson commands us. I suppose you've heard that you rebels are gathering on the other side of Frankfort in Owen County under Humphrey Marshall?"

"Yes, Yank, I've heard it," replied Harry. "Now, what are you doing in Frankfort? What business have you got here?"

"Since you ask me a plain question I'll give you a plain answer," replied Dick. "I'm here to scotch you rebels. You don't think you can run away with a state like this, do you?"

"I don't know yet," replied Harry, "but we're going to try. Say, Dick, let's not talk about such things any more for a while. I want to see this town and we can take a look at it together."

"The plan suits me," said Dick promptly. "Come on. I've been here two days and I guess I can be guide."

"We'll take in the Capitol first," said Harry.

Dick led the way and Harry approached with awe and some curiosity the old building which was famous to him. Erected far back, when the state was in its infancy, it still served well its purpose. He and Dick walked together upon the lawns among the trees, but, as soon as the doors were open, they went inside and entered with respect the room in which the great men of their state, the Clays, the Marshalls, the Breckinridges, the Crittendens, the Hardins, and so many others had begun their careers. They were great men not to Kentucky alone, but to the nation as well, and the hearts of the two boys throbbed with pride. They sat down in two of the desks where the members were to meet the next day and fight over the question whether Kentucky was Northern or Southern.

It was very early. Besides themselves there was nobody about but the caretaker. They were sitting in the House and the room was still warmed in winter by great stoves, but they were not needed now, as the windows were open and the fresh breeze of a grass-scented May morning blew in and tumbled the hair of the two youths of the same blood who sat side by side, close friends of their school days again, but who would soon be facing each other across red fields.

The wind which blew so pleasantly on Harry's forehead reminded him of that other wind which had blown so often upon his face at Charleston. But it was not heavy and languorous here. It did not have the lazy perfumes of the breezes that floated up from the warm shores of the Gulf. It was sharp and penetrating. It whipped the blood like the touch of frost. It stirred to action. His cousin's emotions were evidently much like his own.

"Harry," said Dick, "I never thought that Kentucky would be fighting against Kentucky, that Pendleton would be fighting against Pendleton."

Harry was about to reply when his attention was attracted by a heavy footstep. A third person had entered the chamber of the House, and he stood for a while in the aisle, looking curiously about him. Harry saw the man before the stranger saw him and with an instinctive shudder he recognized Bill Skelly. There he stood, huge, black, hairy, and lowering, two heavy pistols shown openly in his belt.

The boys were sitting low in the desks and it was a little while before Skelly noticed them. His attitude was that of triumph, that of one who expects great spoils, like that of a buccaneer who finds his profit in troubled times, preying upon friend and foe alike. Presently he caught sight of the two boys. But his gaze fastened on Harry, and a savage glint appeared in his eyes. Then he strode down the wide aisle and stood near them. But he looked at Harry alone.

"You are Colonel Kenton's son?" he said.

"I am," replied Harry, meeting his fierce stare boldly, "the same whom you tried to murder on the way to Winton, the same who helped to hold our house against you and your gang of assassins."

Guerilla, c1861-1865[47]

Skelly's dark face grew darker as the black blood leaped to his very eyes. But he choked down his passion. The mountaineer was not lacking in cunning.

"Your father and his friends killed some of my men," he said. "I ain't here now to argy with you about the rights an' wrongs of it, but I want to tell you that all the people of the mountains are up for the Union. With them from the lowlands that are the same way, we'll chase you rebels, Jeff Davis and all, clean into the Gulf of Mexico."

Harry deliberately turned his head away, and stared out of a window at the green of lawns and trees. Skelly filled him with abhorrence. He felt as if he were in the presence of a creeping panther, and he would have nothing more to say to him. Skelly looked at him for a few minutes longer, drew himself together in the manner of a savage wild beast about to spring, but relaxed the next moment, laughed softly, and strode out of the chamber.

"That's one of your men," said Harry. "I hope you're proud of him."

"All the mountain people are for us," replied Dick judicially, "and we can't help it if some of the rascals are on our side. You're likely to have men just as bad on yours. I heard about the attack he made upon Uncle George's house, but it was war, I suppose, and this which we have here in Frankfort is only an armed truce. You can't do anything."

"I suppose not. Do you know how long he has been here?"

"He arrived at Camp Dick Robinson only two or three days ago, and I suppose he has taken the first chance to come in and have a look at the capital."

"With the idea of looting it later on."

Dick laughed.

"Don't be bitter, Harry," he said. "It's going to be a fair fight."

"Well, I hope so, here in this little town as well as on the greater field of the country. Are you staying long in Frankfort, Dick?"

"Only today. I'm going back tomorrow to Camp Dick Robinson."

"Well, don't you make friends with that fellow Skelly, even if he is on the same side you are."

"I won't, Harry, have no fear of that."

The two went together to the hotel, and found Colonel Kenton at breakfast. He welcomed his nephew with great affection, and made him sit by him until he had finished his breakfast. While he was drinking his coffee Harry told him of Skelly's presence. The Colonel frowned, but merely uttered three words about him.

"We'll watch him," he said.

Then the three went out and saw the little town grow into life and seethe with the heat of the spirit. Although actual skirmishing had taken place already in the state there was no violence here, except of speech. All the members of the House and Senate were gathered, and so far as Harry could observe the Southerners were in the majority. Others thought so, too. Bertrand was sanguine. His eyes burned with the fire of enthusiasm, lighting up his olive face.

"We'll win. We'll surely win!" he said. "This state which we need so much will be out of the Union inside of two weeks."

But Senator Culver was more guarded in his opinion, or at least in the expression of it.

"It's going to be a mighty hot fight," he said.

Harry and Dick together watched the convening of the Legislature, having chosen seats in the upper lobby of the House. Harry looked for Skelly, but not seeing him he inferred that the mountaineer's leave of absence was short and that he had gone back to camp.

Dick himself left the next morning for Camp Dick Robinson, and Harry shook his hand over and over again as he departed. The feeling between the cousins was strong and it had been renewed by their meeting under such circumstances.

"I may go east," said Dick, as he mounted his horse. "The big things are going to happen there first."

Harry watched him as he rode away and he wondered when they would meet again. Like Colonel Leonidas Talbot he felt now that this was going to be a great war, wide in its sweep.

Harry returned to his hotel, very thoughtful. The second parting with his cousin, who had been his playmate all his life, was painful, and he realized that while he was wondering when and where they would meet again it might never occur at all. He found his father and his friends holding a close conference in his room at the hotel. Senator Culver, Mr. Bracken, Gardner, the editor, and others yet higher in the councils of the Confederacy, were there. Bertrand sat in a corner, saying little, but watching everything with ardent, burning eyes.

Letters had come from the chief Southern leaders. There was one from Jefferson Davis, himself, another from the astute Benjamin, another from Toombs, bold and brusque as befitted his temperament, and yet more from Stephens and Slidell and Yancey and others. Colonel Kenton read them one by one to the twenty men who were crowded into the room. They were appealing, insistent, urgent. Their tone might vary, but the tenor was the same. They must take Kentucky out of the Union and take her out at once. In the West the line of attack upon the South would lead through Kentucky. But if the state threw in her fortunes with the South, the advance of Lincoln's troops would be blocked. The force of example would be immense, and a hundred thousand valiant Kentuckians could easily turn the scale in favor of the Confederacy.

Harry listened to them a long time, but growing tired at last, went out again into the fresh air. Young though he was, he realized that it was one thing for the Southern leaders to ask, but it was another thing for the Kentuckians to deliver. He saw all about him the signs of a powerful opposition, and he saw, too, that these forces, scattered at first, were consolidating fast, presenting a formidable front.

The struggle began and it was waged for days in the picturesque old Capitol. There was no violence, but feeling deepened. Men put restraint upon their words, but their hearts behind them were full of bitterness, bitterness on one side because the Northern sympathizers were so stubborn, and bitterness on the other, because the Southern sympathizers showed the same stubbornness. Friends of a lifetime used but cold words to each other and saw widening between then, a gulf which none could cross. Supporters of either cause poured into the little capital. Tremendous pressure was brought to bear upon House and Senate. Members were compelled to strive with every kind of emotion or appeal, love of the Union, cool judgment in the midst of alarms, state patriotism, kinship, and all the conflicting ties which pull at those who stand upon the border line on the eve of a great civil war. And yet they could come to no decision. Day after day they fought back and forth over points of order and resolutions and the result was always the same. North and South were locked fast within the two rooms of one little Capitol.

They were rimmed around meanwhile by a fiery horizon that steadily came closer and closer. The guns reducing Sumter had been a sufficient signal. North and South were sharply arrayed against each other. The Southern volunteers, full of ardor and fire, continued to pour to their standards. The North, larger and heavier, moved more slowly, but it moved. The whole land swayed under an intense agitation. The news of skirmishes along the border came, magnified and colored in the telling. Men's minds were inflamed more every day.

When Harry had been in Frankfort about a week he received a letter from St. Clair, written from Richmond, urging him, if he could, to get an assignment to the East, and to come to that city, which was to be the permanent capital of the South.

"We are here," he said, "looking the enemy in the face. Langdon and I are in the same company and I see Colonel Talbot and Major St. Hilaire every day. We are going to the front soon, and before the summer is out there will be a big battle followed by our taking of Washington."

"But you must come, Harry, to Richmond and join us before we march. This is a fine town and all the celebrities are crowding in. You never saw such confidence and enthusiasm. Virginia was slow in joining us, but, since she has joined, she is with us heart and soul. Troops are pouring in all the time. Cannon and wagons loaded with ammunition and supplies are hurrying to the front. The Yankees are not threatening Richmond; we are threatening Washington. Be sure and get yourself transferred to the East, Harry, where the great things are going to happen. Friends are waiting for you here. Colonel Talbot and Major St. Hilaire have a lot of power and they will use it for you."

Harry was walking on the hills that look down on the Capitol, when he read the letter and its warm words made his pulses leap with pleasure. He felt now the pull of opposing magnets. He wanted to remain in Frankfort with his father and see the issue, and he also wanted to join those South Carolina comrades of his in the East, where the battle fronts now lowered so ominously.

He thought long over the letter, and, at last sat down by the monument to the Kentucky volunteers who fell at the battle of Buena Vista. The pull of the East was gradually growing the stronger. He did not see what he could do at Frankfort, and he wanted to be off there on the Virginia fields where the bayonets would soon meet.

Unidentified Union and Confederate soldier; each is from Kentucky[48]

The curious feeling that war could not come here in his own land persisted in Harry. It was late in the afternoon with the lower tip of the sun just hid behind the far hills and the landscape that he looked upon was soft and beautiful. The green of spring was deep and tender. Everything rough or ugly was smoothed away by the first mellow touch of the advancing twilight. The hills were clothed in the same robe of green that lay over the valleys, and through the center of the circle flowed the deep Kentucky, serene and blue.

While Harry's thoughts at that moment were on war, he really had no feeling against anybody. It was all general and impersonal. There is something pure and noble about a boy who comes out of a good home, something lofty to which the man later looks back with pride, not because the boy was wise or powerful, but because his heart was good.

The twilight slowly darkened over green fields and blue river. But the noble stone, with its sculptured lines, by the side of which Harry sat, seemed to grow whiter, despite the veil of dusk that was drooping softly over it. The houses in the town below began to sink out of sight and lights appeared in their place.

Night came and found the boy still at his place. He could see only the tint of the blue river now, and the far hills were lost in the darkness. The chill of evening was coming on, and rising, he shook himself a little. Then he followed a path down the steep hill and along the edge of the river. But he paused, standing by the side of a great oak that grew at the Water's margin, and looked up the Kentucky.

Harry could see from the point where he stood no sign of human life. He heard only the murmur of deep waters as they flowed slowly and peacefully by. The spirit of his great ancestor, the famous Henry Ware, who had been the sword of the border, was strong upon him. The Kentucky was to him the most romantic of all rivers, clustered thick with the facts and legends of the great days, when the first of the pioneers came and built homes along its banks. It flowed out of mountains still mysterious, and, for a few moments, Harry's thoughts floated from the strife of the present to a time far back when the slightest noise in the canebrake might mean to the hunter the coming of his quarry.

A faint musical sound, not more than the sigh of a stray breeze, came from a point far up the stream. He listened and the sound pleased him. The lone, weird note was in full accord with the night and his mood, and presently he knew it. It was some mountaineer on a raft singing a plaintive song of his own distant hills. Huge rafts launched on the headwaters of the stream in the mountains in the eastern part of the state came in great numbers down the river, but oftenest at this time of the year. Some stopped at Frankfort, and others went into the Ohio for the cities down that stream.

Harry waited, while the song grew a little in volume, and, penned now between high banks, gave back soft echoes. But the raft came very slowly, only as fast as the current of the river. He thought he would see a light as the men usually cooked and slept in a rude little hut built in the center of the raft. But all was yet in darkness.

The singer, however rude and unlettered a mountaineer he may have been, had a voice and ear, and Harry still listened with the keenest pleasure to the melodious note that came floating down the river. The spell was upon him. His imagination became so vivid that it was not a mountaineer singing. He had gone back into another century. It was one of the great borderers, perhaps Boone himself, who was paddling his canoe upon the stream, the name of which was danger. And Kenton, and Logan and Harrod and the others were abroad in the woods.

He was engrossed so deeply that he did not hear a heavy step behind him, nor did he see a huge bewhiskered figure in the path, holding a clubbed rifle. Yet he turned. It was perhaps the instinct inherited from his great ancestor, who was said to have had a sixth sense. Whatever it may have been, he faced suddenly about, and saw Bill Skelly aiming at him a blow with the clubbed rifle, which would at once crush his skull and send his body into the deep stream.

The same inherited instinct made him leap within the swing of the rifle and clutch at the mountaineer's throat. The heavy butt swished through the air, and the very force of the blow jerked the weapon from Skelly's hands. The next instant he was struggling for his life. Harry was a powerful youth, much stronger than many men, and, at that instant, the spirit and strength of his great ancestor were pouring into his veins. The treacherous attempt upon his life filled him with rage. He was, in very truth, the forest runner of the earlier century, and he strove with all his great might to slay his enemy.

Skelly, six feet two inches tall and two hundred pounds of muscle and sinew, struck the boy fiercely on the side of the head, but the terrible grasp was still at his throat. He was the larger and the stronger, but the sudden leap upon him gave his younger and smaller antagonist an advantage. He had a pistol in his belt, but with that throttling grip upon his throat he forgot it. The hunter had suddenly become the hunted. Filled with rage and venom he had expected an easy triumph, and, instead, he was now fighting for his life.

Skelly struck again and again at the boy, but Harry, with instinctive wisdom, pressed his head close to the man's chin, and Skelly's blows at such short range lacked force behind them. All the while Harry's youthful but powerful arms were pouring strength into the hands that grasped the man's throat. The mountaineer choked and gasped, and, changing his aim from the head, struck Harry again and again in the chest. Then he remembered to draw his pistol, but Harry, raising his knee, struck him violently on the wrist. The pistol dropped to the ground, and Skelly, in the fierce struggle, was unable to regain it.

Neither had uttered a cry. There was not a single shout for help. Skelly would not want to call attention, and Harry recalled afterward that in the tremendous tension of the moment the thought of it never occurred to him. He continued to press savagely upon Skelly's throat, while the mountaineer rained blows upon his chest, blows that would have killed him had Skelly been able to get full purchase for his arms. He heard the heavy gasping breath of the man, and he saw the dark, hideous face close to his own. It was so hairy that it was like the face of some huge anthropoid, with the lips wrinkled back from strong and cruel white teeth.

It seemed to Harry in very truth that he was fighting a great wild beast. His own breath came in short gasps, and at every expansion of the lungs a fierce pain shot through his whole body. A bloody foam rose to his lips. The savage pounding upon his chest was telling. He still retained his grasp upon Skelly's throat, where his fingers were sunk into the flesh, but it was only the grimmest kind of resolution that enabled him to hold on.

Harry saw the fierce light in Skelly's eye turn to joy. The man foresaw his triumph, and he began to curse low, but fast and with savage unction. Harry felt himself weakening, and he made another mighty effort to retain his hold, but the fingers still slipped, and, as Skelly struck him harder than ever in the chest, they flew loose entirely.

He knew that if Skelly had room for the full play of his arm that he would be knocked senseless at the next blow, and to ward it off he seized the man by his huge chest, tripping at the same time with all his might. The two fell, rolled over in their struggling, and then Harry felt himself dropping from a height. The next moment the deep waters of the Kentucky closed over the two, still locked fast in a deadly combat, and the waves circled away in diminishing height from the spot where they had sunk.

Unidentified Confederate soldier[49]

9. THE RIVER JOURNEY

"Best pour a little of this down his throat. It'll cut an' burn, but if there's a spark o' life left in him it'll set it to blazin'."

Harry became conscious of the "cutting" and "burning," and, struggling weakly, he sat up.

"That's better," continued the deep, masculine voice. "You've been layin' on your face, lettin' the Kentucky River run out of your mouth, while we was poundin' you on the back to increase the speed o' the current. It's all out o' you now, an' you're goin' to keep your young life."

The man who spoke was standing almost over Harry, holding a flask in one hand and a lantern in the other. He was obviously a mountaineer, tall, with powerful chest and shoulders, and a short red beard. Near him stood a stalwart boy about Harry's own age. They were in the middle of a raft which had been pulled to the south side of the Kentucky and then tied to the shore.

Harry started to speak, but the words stopped at his lips. His weakness was still great.

"Wa'al," said the man, whimsically. "What was it? Sooicide? Or did you fall in the river, bein' awkward? Or was you tryin' to swim the stream, believin' it was fun to do it? What do you think, Ike?"

"It wasn't no sooicide," replied the youth whom he had called Ike. "Boys don't kill theirse'ves. An' it wasn't no awkwardness, 'cause he don't look like the awkward kind. An'

I guess he wasn't tryin' to swim the Kentucky, else he would have took off his clothes."

"Which cuts out all three o' my guesses, leavin' me nothin' to go on. Now, I ain't in the habit of pickin' floatin' an' unconscious boys out o' the middle o' the river, an' that leaves me in unpleasant doubt, me bein' of an inquirin' turn o' mind."

"It was murder," said Harry, at last finding strength to speak.

"Murder!" exclaimed the man and boy together.

"Yes, murder, that is, an attempt at it. A man set upon me to kill me, and in the struggle we fell in the river, which, with your help, saved my life. Look here!"

He tore open his coat and shirt, revealing his chest, which looked like pounded beef.

"Somebody has shorely been gettin' in good hard licks on you," said the man sympathetically, "an' I reckon you're tellin' nothin' but the truth, these bein' such times as this country never heard of before. My name's Sam Jarvis, an' I came with this raft from the mountains. This lunkhead here is my nephew, Ike Simmons. We was driftin' along into Frankfort as peaceful as you please, an' a singin' with joy 'cause our work was about over. I hears a splash an' says I to Ike, 'What's that?' Says he to me, 'I dunno.' Says I to Ike ag'in, 'Was it a big fish?' Says he to me ag'in, 'I dunno.' He's gittin' a repytation for bein' real smart 'cause he's always sayin, 'I dunno,' an' he's never wrong. Then I sees somethin' with hair on top of it floatin' on the water. Says I, 'Is that a man's head?' Says he, 'I dunno.' But he reaches away out from the raft, grabs you with one hand by them brown locks o' yours, an' hauls you in. I guess you owe your life all right enough to this lunkhead, Ike, my nephew, the son o' my sister Jane."

Ike grinned sympathetically.

"Ain't it time to offer him some dry clothes, Uncle Sam?" he asked.

"Past time, I reckon," replied Jarvis, "but I forgot it askin' questions, me havin' such an inquirin' turn o' mind."

Harry rose, with the help of a strong and friendly hand that Jarvis lent him. His chest felt dreadfully sore. Every breath pained him, and all the strength seemed to have gone from his body.

"I don't know what became o' the other feller," said Jarvis. "Guess he must have swum out all by hisself."

"He undoubtedly did so," replied Harry. "He wasn't hurt, and I fancy that he's some distance from Frankfort by this time. My name is Kenton, Harry Kenton, and I'm the son of Colonel George Kenton, who is here in Frankfort helping to push the ordinance of secession. You've saved my life and he'd repay you."

"We don't need no money," said Jarvis shortly. "Me an' Ike here will have a lot of money when we sell this raft, and we don't lack for nothin'."

"I didn't mean money," said Harry, understanding their pride and independence. "I meant in some other ways, including gratitude. I've been fished out of a river, and a fisherman is entitled to the value of his catch, isn't he?"

"We'll talk about that later on, but me bein' of an inquirin' turn o' mind, I'm wonderin' what your father will say about you when he sees you. I guess I better doctor you up a little before you leave the raft."

Ike returned from the tiny cabin with an extra suit of clothes of his own, made of the roughest kind of gray jeans, home knit yarn socks and a pair of heavy brogan shoes. A second trip brought underclothing of the same rough quality, but Harry changed into them gladly. Jarvis meanwhile produced a bottle filled with a brown liquid.

"You may think this is hoss liniment," he said, "an' p'r'aps it has been used for them purposes, but it's better fur men than animiles. Ole Aunt Suse, who is 'nigh to a hundred, got it from the Injuns an' it's warranted to kill or cure. It'll sting at first, but just you stan' it, an' afore long it will do you a power o' good."

Harry refused to wince while the mountaineer kneaded his bruised chest with the liquid ointment. The burning presently gave way to a soothing sensation.

Harry noticed that neither Jarvis nor Ike asked him the name of his opponent nor anything at all about the struggle or its cause. They treated it as his own private affair, of which he could speak or not as he chose. He had noticed this quality before in mountaineers. They were among the most inquisitive of people, but an innate delicacy would suppress questions which an ordinary man would not hesitate to ask.

"Button up your shirt an' coat," said Jarvis at last, "an' you'll find your chest well in a day or two. Your bein' so healthy helps you a lot. Feelin' better already, boy? Don't 'pear as if you was tearin' out a lung or two every time you drawed breath?"

"I'm almost well," said Harry gratefully, "and, Mr. Jarvis, I'd like to leave my wet clothes here to dry while I'm gone. I'll be back in the morning with my father."

"All right," said Samuel Jarvis, "but I wish you'd come bright an' early. Me an' this lunkhead, Ike, my nephew, ain't used to great cities, an' me bein' of an inquirin' turn o' mind we'll be anxious to see all that's to be seed in Frankfort."

"Don't you fear," replied Harry, full of gratitude, "I'll be back soon in the morning."

"But don't furgit one thing," continued Jarvis. "I hear there's a mighty howdy-do here about the state goin' out o' the Union or stayin' in it. The mountains are jest hummin' with talk about the question, but don't make me take any part in it. Me an' this lunkhead, Ike, my nephew, are here jest to sell logs, not to decide the fate o' states."

"I'll remember that, too," said Harry, as he shook hands warmly with both of them, left the raft, climbed the bank and entered Frankfort.

The little town had few lights in those days and the boy moved along in the dusk, until he came near the Capitol. There he saw the flame of lamps shining from several windows, and he knew that men were still at work, striving to draw a state into the arms of the North or the South. He paused a few minutes at the corner of the lawn and drew many long, deep breaths. The soreness was almost gone from his chest. The oil with which Samuel Jarvis had kneaded his bruises was certainly wonderful, and he hoped that "Aunt Suse," who got it from the Indians, would fill out her second hundred years.

He reached the hotel without meeting any one whom he

knew, and went up the stairway to his room, where he found his father writing at a small desk. Colonel Kenton glanced at him, and noticed at once his change of costume.

"What does that clothing mean, Harry?" he asked. "It's jeans, and it doesn't fit."

"I know it's jeans, and I know it doesn't fit, but I was mighty glad to get it, as everything else I had on was soaked with water."

Colonel Kenton raised his eyebrows.

"I was hunting the bottom of the Kentucky River," continued Harry.

"Fall in?"

"No, thrown in."

Colonel Kenton raised his eyebrows higher than ever.

Harry sat down and told him the whole story, Colonel Kenton listening intently and rarely interrupting.

"It was great good fortune that the men on the raft came just at the right time," he said, when Harry had finished. "There are bad mountaineers and good mountaineers—Jarvis and his nephew represent one type and Skelly the other. Skelly hates us because we drove back his band when they attacked our house. In peaceful times we could have him hunted out and punished, but we cannot follow him into his mountains now. We shall be compelled to let this pass for the present, but as your life would not be safe here you must leave Frankfort, Harry."

"I can't go back to Pendleton," said the boy, "and stay there, doing nothing."

"I had no such purpose. I know that you are bound to be in active life, and I was already meditating a longer journey for you. Listen clearly to me, Harry. The fight here is about over, and we are going to fail. It is by the narrowest of margins, but still we will fail. We who are for the South know it with certainty. Kentucky will refuse to go out of the Union, and it is a great blow to us. I shall have to go back to Pendleton for a week or two and then I will take a command. But since you are bent upon service in the field, I want you to go to the East."

Harry's face flushed with pleasure. It was his dearest wish.

Colonel Kenton, looking at him out of the corner of his eyes, smiled.

"I fancied that you would be quite willing to go," he said. "I had a letter this morning from a man who likes you well, Colonel Leonidas Talbot. He is at Richmond and he says that President Davis, his cabinet, and all the equipment of a capital will arrive there about the last of the month. The enemy is massing before Washington and also toward the West in the Maryland and Virginia mountains. A great battle is sure to be fought in the summer and he wants you on his staff. General Beauregard, whom you knew at Charleston, is to be in supreme command. Can you leave here in a day or two for Richmond?"

Alabama troops join Beauregard at Richmond,

Harry's eyes were sparkling, and the flush was still in his face.

"I could go in an hour," he replied.

"Such an abrupt departure as that is not needed. Moreover the choice of a route is of great importance and requires thought. If you were to take one of the steamers up the Ohio, say to Wheeling, in West Virginia, you would almost surely fall into the hands of the Northern troops. The North also controls about all the railway connections there are between

Kentucky and Virginia."

"Then I must ride across the mountains."

"These new friends of yours who saved you from the river, are they going to stay long in Frankfort?"

"Not more than a day or two, I think. I gathered from what Jarvis said that they were not willing to remain long where trouble was thick."

"How are their sympathies placed in this great division of our people?"

Harry laughed.

"I inferred," he replied, "from what Jarvis said that they intend to keep the peace. He intimated to me that the silence of the mountains was more welcome to him than the cause of either North or South."

Colonel Kenton smiled again.

"Perhaps he is wiser than the rest of us," he said, "but in any event, I think he is our man. He will sell his logs and pull back up the Kentucky in a small boat. I gather from what you say that he came down the most southerly fork of the Kentucky, which, in a general way, is the route you wish to take. You can go with him and his nephew until they reach their home in the mountains. Then you must take a horse, strike south into the old Wilderness Road, cross the ranges into Virginia and reach Richmond. Are you willing?"

He spoke as father to son, and also as man to man.

"I'm more than willing," replied Harry. "I don't think we could choose a better way. Jarvis and his nephew, I know, will be as true as steel, and I'd like that journey in the boat."

"Then it's settled, provided Jarvis and his nephew are willing. We'll see them before breakfast in the morning, and now I think you'd better go to sleep. A boy who was fished out of the Kentucky only an hour or two ago needs rest."

Harry promptly went to bed, but sleep was long in coming. Their mission to Frankfort had failed, and action awaited his young footsteps. Virginia, the mother state of his own, was a mighty name to him, and men already believed the great war would be decided there. The mountains, too, with their wild forests and streams beckoned to him. The old, inherited blood within him made the great pulses leap. But he slept at last and dreamed of far-off things.

Harry and his father rose at the first silver shoot of dawn, and went quickly through the deserted street to a quiet cove in the Kentucky, where Samuel Jarvis had anchored his raft. It was a crisp morning, with a tang in the air that made life feel good. A thin curl of smoke was rising from the raft, showing that the man and his nephew were already up, and cooking in the little hut on the raft.

Harry stepped upon the logs and his father followed him. Jarvis was just pouring coffee from a tin pot into a tin cup, and Ike was turning over some strips of bacon in an iron skillet on an iron stove. Both of them, watchful like all mountaineers, had heard the visitors coming, but they did not look up until they were on the raft.

"Mornin'," called Jarvis cheerfully. "Look, Ike, it's the big fish that we hooked out of the river last night, an' he's got company."

"I want to thank you for saving my son's life," said the Colonel.

"I reckon, then, that you're Colonel George Kenton," said Jarvis. "Wa'al, you don't owe us no thanks. I'm of an inquirin' turn of mind, an' whenever I see a man or boy floatin' along in the river I always fish him out, just to see who an' what he is. My curiosity is pow'ful strong, colonel, an' it leads me to do a lot o' things that I wouldn't do if it wasn't fur it. Set an' take a bite with us. This air is nippin' an' it makes my teeth tremenjous sharp."

"We're with you," said the colonel, who was adaptable, and who saw at once that Jarvis was a man of high character. "It's cool on the river and that coffee will warm one up mighty well."

"It's fine coffee," said Jarvis proudly. "Aunt Suse taught me how to make it. She learned, when you didn't git coffee often, an' you had to make the most of it when you did git it."

"Who is Aunt Suse?"

"Aunt Susan, or Suse as we call her fur short, is back at home in the hills. She's a good hundred, colonel, an' two or three yars more to boot, I reckon, but as spry as a kitten. Full o' tales o' the early days an' the wild beasts an' the Injuns. She says you couldn't make up any story of them times that ain't beat by the truth. When she come up the Wilderness Road from Virginia in the Revolution she was already a young woman. She's knowed Dan'l Boone and Simon Kenton an' all them gran' old fellers. A tremenjous interestin' old lady is my Aunt Suse, colonel."

"I've no doubt of it, Mr. Jarvis." said Colonel Kenton, "but I don't think I can wait a second longer for a cup of that coffee of yours. It smells so good that if you don't give it to me I'll have to take it from you."

Jarvis grinned cheerfully. Harry saw that his father had already made a skillful appeal to the mountaineer's pride.

"Ike, you lunkhead," he said to his nephew, "I told the colonel to set, but we did'nt give him anythin' to set on. Pull up them blocks o' wood fur him an' his son. Now you'll take breakfast with us, won't you, colonel? The bacon an' the corn cakes are ready, too."

"Of course we will," said the colonel, "and gladly, too. It makes me young again to eat this way in the fresh air of a cool morning."

Samuel Jarvis shone as a host. The breakfast was served on a smooth stump put on board for that purpose. The coffee was admirable, and the bacon and thin corn cakes were cooked beautifully. Good butter was spread over the corn cakes, and Harry and his father were surprised at the number they ate. Ike, addressed by his uncle variously and collectively as "lunkhead," "nephew," and "Ike," served. He rarely spoke, but always grinned. Harry found later that while he had little use for his vocal organs he invariably enjoyed life.

"Colonel," said Jarvis, at about the tenth corn cake, "be you fellers down here a-goin' to fight?"

"I suppose we are, Mr. Jarvis!"

"An' is your son thar goin' right into the middle of it?"

"I can't keep him from it, Mr. Jarvis, but he isn't going to stay here in Kentucky. Other plans have been made for him. When are you going back up the Kentucky, Mr. Jarvis?"

"This raft was bargained fur before it started. All I've got to do is to turn it over to its new owners today, go to the bank, an' get the money. Then me an' this lunkhead, Ike, my nephew, both bein' of an inquirin' mind, want to do some sight-seein', but I reckon we'll start back in about two days in the boat that you see tied to the stern of the raft."

"Would you take a passenger in the boat? It's a large one."

Samuel Jarvis pursed his lips.

"Depends on who it is," he replied. "It takes a lot o' time, goin' up stream, to get back to our start, an' a cantankerous passenger in as narrow a place as a rowboat would make it mighty onpleasant for me an' this lunkhead, Ike, my nephew. Wouldn't it, Ike?"

Ike grinned and nodded.

"The passenger that I'm speaking of wouldn't be a passenger altogether," said Colonel Kenton. "He'd like to be one of the crew also, and I don't think he'd make trouble. Anyway, he's got a claim on you already. Having fished him out of the river, where he was unconscious, it's your duty to take care of him for a while. It's my son Harry, who wants to get across the mountains to Virginia, and we'll be greatly obliged to you if you'll take him."

Colonel Kenton had a most winning manner. He already liked Jarvis, and Jarvis liked him.

"I reckon your son is all right," said Jarvis, "an' if he gits cantankerous we kin just pitch him overboard into the Kentucky. But I can't undertake sich a contract without consultin' my junior partner, this lunkhead, my nephew, Ike Simmons. Ike, are you willin' to take Colonel Kenton's son back with us? Ef you're willin' say 'Yes,' ef you ain't willin' say 'No.'"

Ike said nothing, but grinned and nodded.

"The resolution is passed an' Harry Kenton is accepted," said Jarvis. "We start day after tomorrow mornin', early."

Breakfast was finished and Colonel Kenton rose and thanked them. He still said nothing about pay. But after he and Harry had entered the town, he said:

"You couldn't have better friends, Harry. Both the man and boy are as true as steel, and, as they have no intention of taking part in the war, they will just suit you as traveling companions."

They spent the larger part of that day in buying the boy's equipment, doing it as quietly as possible, as the colonel wished his son to depart without attracting any notice. In such times as those secrecy was much to be desired. A rifle, pistols, plenty of ammunition, an extra suit of clothes, a pair of blankets, and a good supply of money were all that he took. One small package which contained a hundred dollars in gold coins he put in an inside pocket of his waistcoat.

"You are to give that to Jarvis just after you start," said the colonel. "We cannot pay him directly for saving you, because he will not take it, but you can insist that this is for your passage."

They were all at the cove before dawn on the appointed morning. Colonel Kenton was to say Harry's good-bye for him to his friends. The whole departure had been arranged with so much skill that they alone knew of it. The boat was strong, shaped well, and had two pairs of oars. A heavy canvas sheet could be erected as a kind of awning or tent in the rear, in case of rain. They carried plenty of food, and Jarvis said that in addition they were more than likely to pick up a deer or two on the way. Both he and Ike carried long-barreled rifles.

The three stepped into the boat.

"Good-bye, Harry," said the colonel, reaching down a strong hand that trembled.

"Good-bye, father," said Harry, returning the clasp with another strong hand that trembled also.

People in that region were not demonstrative. Family affection was strong, but they were reared on the old, stern Puritan plan, and the handshake and the brief words were all. Then Jarvis and his silent nephew bent to the oars and the boat shot up the deep channel of the Kentucky.

Harry looked back, and in the dusk saw his father still standing at the edge of the cove. He waved a hand and the colonel waved back. Then they disappeared around a curve of the hills, and the first light of dawn began to drift over the Kentucky.

Harry was silent for a long time. He was becoming used to sudden and hard traveling and danger, but the second parting with his father moved him deeply. Since he had been twelve or thirteen years of age, they had been not only father and son, but comrades, and, in the intimate association, he had acquired more of a man's mind than was usual in one of his years. He felt now, since he was going to the east and the colonel was remaining in the west, that the parting was likely to be long—perhaps forever.

It was no morbid feeling. It was the consciousness that a great and terrible war was at hand. Although but a youth, he had been in the forefront of things. He had been at Montgomery and Sumter, and he had seen the fire and zeal of the South. He had been at Frankfort, too, and he had seen how the gathering force of the massive North had refused to be moved. His father and his friends, with all their skill and force, strengthened by the power of kinship and sentiment, had been unable to take Kentucky out of the Union.

Envelope postmarked Lebanon, KY, 4 Apr 1861-1865[50]

Harry was so thoroughly absorbed in these thoughts that he did not realize how very long he remained silent. He was sitting in the stern of the boat, with a face naturally joyous, heavily overcast. Jarvis and Ike were rowing and with innate delicacy they did not disturb him. They, too, said nothing. But they were powerful oarsmen, and they sent the heavy skiff shooting up the stream. The Kentucky, a deep river at any time, was high from the spring floods, and the current offered but little resistance. The man of mighty sinews and the boy of sinews almost as mighty, pulled a long and regular stroke, without any quickening of the breath.

The dawn deepened into the full morning. The silver of the river became blue, with a filmy gold mist spread over it by the rising sun. High banks crested with green enclosed them on either side, and beyond lay higher hills, their slopes and summits all living green. The singing of birds came from the bushes on the banks, and a sudden flash of flame told where a scarlet tanager had crossed.

The last house of Frankfort dropped behind them, and soon the boat was shooting along the deep channel cut by the Kentucky through the Bluegrass, then the richest and most beautiful region of the west, abounding in famous men and in the height of its glory. It had never looked more splendid. The grass was deeply luxuriant and young flowers bloomed at the water's edge. The fields were divided by neat stone fences and far off Harry saw men working on the slopes.

Jarvis and Ike were still silent. The man glanced at Harry and saw that he had not yet come from his absorption, but Samuel Jarvis was a joyous soul. He was forty years old, and he had lived forty happy years. The money for his lumber was in his pocket, he did not know ache or pain, and he was going back to his home in an inmost recess of the mountains, from which high point he could view the civil war passing around him and far below. He could restrain himself no longer, and lifting up his voice he sang.

But the song, like nearly all songs the mountaineers sing, had a melancholy note.

"'Nita, 'Nita, Juanita,
Be my own fair bride."

He sang, and the wailing note, confined between the high walls of the stream, took on a great increase in volume and power. Jarvis had one of those uncommon voices sometimes found among the unlearned, a deep, full tenor without a harsh note. When he sang he put his whole heart into the words, and the effect was often wonderful. Harry roused himself suddenly. He was hearing the same song that he had heard the night he went into the river locked fast in Skelly's arms.

"'Nita, 'Nita, Juanita."

rang the tenor note, rising and falling and dying away in wailing echoes, as the boat sped on. Then Harry resolutely turned his face to the future. The will has a powerful effect over the young, and when he made the effort to throw off sadness it fell easily from him. All at once he was embarked with good comrades upon a journey of tremendous interest. Jarvis noticed the change upon his face, but said nothing. He pulled with a long, slow stroke, suited to the solemn refrain of Juanita, which he continued to pour forth with his soul in every word.

They went on, deeper into the Bluegrass. The blue sky above them was now dappled with golden clouds, and the air grew warmer, but Jarvis and his nephew showed no signs of weariness. When Harry judged that the right time had come he asked to relieve Ike at the oar. Ike looked at Jarvis and Jarvis nodded to Ike. Then Ike nodded to Harry, which indicated consent.

But Harry, before taking the oar, drew a small package from his pocket and handed it to Jarvis.

"My father asked me to give you this," he said, "as a remembrance and also as some small recompense for the trouble that I will cause you on this trip."

Jarvis took it, and heard the heavy coins clink together.

"I know without openin' it that this is money," he said, "but bein' of an inquirin' turn o' mind I reckon I've got to look into it an' count it."

He did so deliberately, coin by coin, and his eyes opened a little at the size of the sum.

"It's too much," he said. "Besides you take your turn at the oars."

"It's partly as a souvenir," said Harry, "and it would hurt my father very much if you did not take it. Besides, I should have to leave the boat the first time it tied up, if you refuse."

Jarvis looked humorously at him.

"I believe you are a stubborn sort of feller," he said, "but somehow I've took a kind o' likin' to you. I s'pose it's because I fished you out o' the river. You always think that the fish you ketch yourself are the best. Do you reckon that's the reason why we like him, Ike?"

Ike nodded.

"Then, bein' as we don't want to lose your company, an' seein' that you mean what you say, we'll keep the gold, though half of it must go to that lunkhead, Ike, my nephew."

"Then it's settled," said Harry, "and we'll never say another word about it. You agree to that?"

"Yes," replied Jarvis, and Ike nodded.

Harry took his place at the oar. Although he was not as skillful as Ike, he did well, and the boat sped on upon the deep bosom of the Kentucky. The work was good for Harry. It made his blood flow once more in a full tide and he felt a distinct elation.

Jarvis began singing again. He changed from Juanita to "Poor Nelly Gray":

"And poor Nelly Gray, she is up in Heaven, they say,
And I shall never see my darling anymore."

Harry found his oar swinging to the tune as Ike's had swung to that of Juanita, and he did not feel fatigue. They met few people upon the river. Once a raft passed them, but Jarvis, looking at it keenly, said that it had come down from one of the northern forks of the Kentucky and not from his part of the country. They saw skiffs two or three times, but did not stop to exchange words with their occupants, continuing steadily into the heart of the Bluegrass.

They relieved one another throughout the day and at night, tired but cheerful, drew up their boat at a point, where there was a narrow stretch of grass between the water and the cliff, with a rope ferry three or four hundred yards farther on.

"We'll tie up the boat here, cook supper, and sleep on dry ground," said Jarvis.

Unidentified Confederate soldier[51]

10. OVER THE MOUNTAINS

The boat was secured firmly among the bushes, and finding an abundance of fallen wood along the beach, they pulled it into a heap and kindled a fire. The night, as usual, was cool, but the pleasant flames dispelled the chill, and the cove was very snug and comfortable after a day of hard and continuous work. Jarvis and Ike did the cooking, at which they were adepts.

"After pullin' a boat ten or twelve hours there's nothin' like somethin' warm inside you to make you feel good," said Jarvis. "Ike, you lunkhead, hurry up with that coffee pot. Me an' Harry can't wait more'n a minute longer."

Ike grinned and hurried. A fine bed of coals had now formed, and in a few minutes a great pot of coffee was boiling and throwing out savory odors. Jarvis took a small flat skillet from the boat and fried the corn cakes. Harry fried bacon and strips of dried beef in another. The homely task in good company was most grateful to him. His face reflected his pleasure.

"Providin' it don't rain on you, campin' out is stimulatin' to the body an' soul," said Jarvis. "You don't know what a genuine appetite is until you live under the blue sky by day, and a starry sky by night. Harry, you'll find three tin plates in the locker in the boat. Fetch 'em."

Harry abandoned his skillet for a moment, and brought the plates. Ike, the coffee now being about ready, produced three tin cups, and with these simple preparations they began their supper. The flames went down and the fire became a great bed of coals, glowing in the darkness, and making a circle of light, the edges of which touched the boat. Harry found that Jarvis was telling the truth. The long work and the cool night air, without a roof above him, gave him a hunger, the like of which he had not known for a long time. He ate cake after cake of the corn bread and piece after piece of the meat. Jarvis and Ike kept him full company.

"Didn't I tell you it was fine?" said Jarvis, stretching his long length and sighing with content. "I feel so good that I'm near bustin' into song."

"Then bust," said Harry.

"Soft, o'er the fountain, lingering falls the southern moon,
Far o'er the mountain breaks the day too soon.
In thy dark eyes' splendor, where the warm light loves to dwell,
Weary looks yet tender, speak their fond farewell.
'Nita, Juanita! Ask thy soul if we should part,
'Nita, Juanita! Lean thou on my heart."

The notes of the old melody swelled, and, as before, the deep channel of the river gave them back again in faint and dying echoes. Time and place and the voice of Jarvis, with its haunting quality, threw a spell over Harry. The present rolled away. He was back in the romantic old past, of which he had read so much, with Boone and Kenton and Harrod and the other great forest rangers.

The darkness sank down, deeper and heavier. The stars came out presently and twinkled in the blue. Yet it was still dim in the gorge, save where the glowing bed of coals cast a circle of light. The Kentucky, showing a faint tinge of blue, flowed with a soft murmur. Harry and Ike were lying on the grass, propped each on one elbow, while Jarvis, sitting with his back against a small tree, was still singing:

"When in thy dreaming, moons like these shall shine again
And daylight beaming prove thy dreams are vain,

Wilt thou not, relenting, for thy absent lover sigh?
In thy heart consenting to a prayer gone by,
'Nita, Juanita, let me linger by thy side;
'Nita, Juanita, be thou my own fair bride."

The song ceased and the murmur of the river came more clearly. Harry was drawn deeper and deeper into the old dim past. Lying there in the gorge, with only the river to be seen, the wilderness came back, and the whole land was clothed with the mighty forests. He brought himself back with an effort, when he saw Jarvis looking at him and smiling.

"'Tain't so bad down here on a spring night, is it, Harry?" he said. "Always purvidin', as I said, that it don't rain."

"Where did you get that song, Sam?" asked Harry—they had already fallen into the easy habit of calling one another by their first names.

"From a travelin' feller that wandered up into our mount'ins. He could play it an' sing it most beautiful, an' I took to it right off. It grips you about the heart some way or other, an' it sounds best when you are out at night on a river like this. Harry, I know that you're goin' through our mountins to git to Richmond an' the war. Me an' that lunkhead Ike, my nephew, hev took a likin' to you. Now, what do you want to git your head shot off fur? S'pose you stop up in the hills with us. The huntin's good thar, an' so's the fishin'."

Harry shook his head, but he was very grateful.

"It's good of you to ask me," he said, "but I'm bound to go on."

"Wa'al, if you're boun' to do it I reckon you jest have to, but we're leavin' the invite open. Ef you change your mind on the trip all you've got to do is to say so, an' we'll take you in, ain't that so, Ike?"

Ike grinned and nodded. His uncle looked at him admiringly.

"Ike's a lunkhead," he said, "but he's great to travel with. You kin jest talk an' talk an' he never puts in, but agrees with all you say. Now, fellers, we'll put out the fire an' roll in our blankets. I guess we don't need to keep any watch here."

Harry was soon in a dreamless sleep, but his momentary reversion to the wilderness awoke him after a while. He sat up in his blankets and looked around. A mere mass of black coals showed where the fire had been, and two long dark objects looking like logs in the dim light were his comrades.

He cast the blankets aside entirely and walked a little distance up the stream. The instinct that had awakened him was right. He heard voices and saw a light. Then he remembered the rope ferry and he had no doubt that someone was crossing, although it was midnight and past. He went back and touched Jarvis lightly on the shoulder. The mountaineer awoke instantly and sat up, all his faculties alert.

"What is it?" he asked in a whisper.

"People crossing the river at the ferry above," Harry whispered back.

"Then we'll go and see who they are. Like as not they're soldiers in this war that people seem bound to fight, when they could have a lot more fun at home. Jest let Ike sleep on. He's my sister's son, but I don't b'lieve anybody would ever think of kidnappin' him."

The two went silently among the bushes toward the ferry which crossed the river at a point where the hills on either side dipped low. As they drew near, they heard many voices and the lights increased to a dozen. Jarvis's belief that it was no party of ordinary travelers seemed correct.

"Let's go a little nearer. The bushes will still hide us," whispered the mountaineer to the boy. "They ain't no enemies o' ours, but I guess we'd better keep out o' their business, though my inquirin' turn o' mind makes me anxious to see just who they are."

They walked to the end of the stretch of bushes, and, while yet in shelter, could see clearly all that was going on, especially as there was no effort at concealment on the part of those who were crossing the stream. They numbered at least two hundred men, and all had arms and horses, although they were dismounted now, and the horses, accompanied by small guards, were being carried over the river first. Evidently the men understood their work, as it was being done rapidly and without much noise.

Harry's attention was soon concentrated on three men who stood near the edge of the bushes, not more than thirty feet away. They wore slouch hats and were wrapped in heavy, dark cloaks. They stood with their backs to him, and although they seemed to be taking no part in the management of the crossing, they watched everything intently. Two of them were very tall, but the third was shorter and slender.

The moon brightened presently, and some movement at the ferry caused the three men to turn. Harry started and checked an exclamation at his lips. But the watchful mountaineer had noted his surprise.

"I guess you know 'em, Harry," he said.

"Yes," replied the boy. "See the one in the center with the drooping mustaches and the splendid figure. People have called him the handsomest man in the United States. He was a guest at my father's house last year when he was running for the presidency. It is the man who received more popular votes than Lincoln, but fewer in the Electoral College."

"Breckinridge?"

"Yes, John C. Breckinridge."

"Why, he's younger than I expected. He don't look more'n forty."

"Just about forty, I should say. The other tall man is named Morgan, John H. Morgan. I saw him in Lexington once. He's a great horseman. The third, the slender man who looks as if he were all fire, is named Duke, Basil Duke. I think that he and Morgan are related. I fancy they are going south, or maybe to Virginia."

"Harry, these are your people."

"Yes, Sam, they are my people."

The mountaineer glanced at the tall youth who had found so warm a place in his heart, and hesitated, but only for a moment. Then he spoke in a decided whisper.

"Since they are your people an' are goin' on the same business that you are, though mebbe not by the same road, now is your time to join 'em, 'stead o' workin' your way 'cross the hills with two ignorant mountaineers like me an' that lunkhead, Ike, my nephew."

"No, Sam. I'll confess to you that it's a temptation, but it's likely that they're not going where I mean to go, and where I should go. I'm going to keep on with you unless you and Ike throw me out of the boat."

"Well spoke, boy," said Jarvis.

He did not tell Harry that Colonel Kenton had asked him to watch over his son until he should leave him in the mountains, and that he had given him his sacred promise. He understood what a powerful pull the sight of Breckinridge, Morgan, and Duke had given to Harry, and he knew that if the boy were resolved to go with them he could not stop him.

All the horses were now across. The three leaders took their places in the boat, reached the farther shore and the whole company rode away in the darkness. Despite his resolution Harry felt a pang when the last figure disappeared.

"Our curiosity bein' gratified, I think we'd better go back to sleep," said Jarvis.

"The anchor's weighed, farewell, farewell!"

"We're seein' 'em goin' south, Harry. I dream ahead sometimes, an' I dream with my eyes open. I've seen the horsemen ridin' in the night, an' I see 'em by the thousands ridin' over a hundred battle fields, their horses' hoofs treadin' on dead men."

"Those are good men, brave and generous."

"Oh, I don't mean them in partickler. Not for a minute. I mean a whole nation, strugglin' an' strugglin' an' swayin' an' swayin'. I see things that people neither North nor South ain't dreamed of yet. But sho! What am I runnin' on this way fur? That lunkhead, Ike, my nephew, ain't such a lunkhead as he looks. Them that say nothin' ain't never got nothin' to take back, an' don't never make fools o' theirselves. It's time we was back in our blankets sleepin' sound, 'cause we've got another long day o' hard rowin' before us."

Ike had not awakened and Jarvis and Harry were soon asleep again. But they were up at dawn, and, after a brief breakfast, resumed their journey on the river, going at a good pace toward the southeast. They were hailed two or three times from the bank by armed men, whether of the North or South Harry could not tell, but when they revealed themselves as mere mountaineers on their way back, having sold a raft, they were permitted to continue. After the last such stop Jarvis remarked rather grimly:

"They don't know that there are three good rifles in this boat, backed by five or six pistols, an' that at least two of us, meanin' me and Ike, are 'bout the best shots that ever come out o' the mountains."

But his good nature soon returned. He was not a man who could retain anger long, and before night he was singing again.

"As I strayed from my cot at the close of the day
To muse on the beauties of June,
'Neath a jessamine shade I espied a fair maid
And she sadly complained to the moon."

"But it's not June, Sam," said Harry, "and there is no moon."

"No, but June's comin' next month, an' the moon's comin' tonight; that is, if them clouds straight ahead don't conclude to j'in an' make a fuss."

The clouds did join, and they made quite a "fuss," pouring out a great quantity of rain, which a rising wind whipped about sharply. But Jarvis first steered the boat under the edge of a high bank, where it was protected partly, and they stretched the strong canvas before the first drops of rain fell.

It was sufficient to keep the three and all their supplies dry, and Harry watched the storm beat.

Sullen thunder rolled up from the southwest, and the skies were cut down the center by burning strokes of lightning. The wind whipped the surface of the river into white foamy waves. But Harry heard and beheld it all with a certain pleasure. It was good to see the storm seek them, and yet not find them—behind their canvas cover. He remained close in his place and stared out at the foaming surface of the water. Back went his thoughts again to the far-off troubled time, when the hunter in the vast wilderness depended for his life on the quickness of eye and ear. He had read so much of Boone and Kenton and Harrod, and his own great ancestor, and the impression was so vivid, that the vision was translated into fact.

"I'm feelin' your feelin's too," said Jarvis, who, glancing at him, had read his mind with almost uncanny intuition. "Times like these, the Injuns an' the wild animals all come back, an' I've felt 'em still stronger way up in the mountains, where nothin' of the old days is gone 'cept the Injuns. Ike, I guess it's cold grub for us tonight. We can't cook anythin' in all this rain. Reach into that locker an' bring out the meat an' bread. This ain't so bad, after all. We're snug an' dry, an' we've got plenty to eat, so let the storm howl:

"They bore him away when the day had fled,
And the storm was rolling high,
And they laid him down in his lonely bed,
By the light of an angry sky,

"The lightning flashed and the wild sea lashed
The shore with its foaming wave,
And the thunder passed on the rushing blast
As it howled o'er the rover's grave."

The full tenor rose and swelled above the sweep of wind and rain, and the man's soul was in the words he sang. A great voice with the accompaniment of storm, the water before them, the lightning blazing at intervals, and the thunder rolling in a sublime refrain, moved Harry to his inmost soul. The song ceased, but its echo was long in dying on the river.

"Did you pick up that, too, from a wandering fiddler?" asked Harry.

"No, I don't know where I got it. I s'pose I found scraps here an' thar, but I like to sing it when the night is behavin' jest as it's doin' now. I ain't ever seen the sea, Harry, but it must be a mighty sight, particklarly when the wind's makin' the high waves run."

"Very likely you'd be seasick if you were on it then. I like it best when the waves are not running."

The thunder and lightning ceased after a while, but the rain came with a steady, driving rush. The night had now settled down thick and dark, and, as the banks on either side of the river were very high, Harry felt as if they were in a black canyon. He could see but dimly the surface of the river. All else was lost in the heavy gloom. But the boat had been built so well and the canvas cover was so taut and tight that not a drop entered. His sense of comfort increased, and the regular, even, musical thresh of the rain promoted sleep.

"We won't be waked up tonight by people crossin' the river, that's shore," said Jarvis, "'cause thar ain't no crossin' fur miles, an' if there was a crossin' people wouldn't use that crossin' nohow on a night like this. So, boys, jest wrap your blankets about yourselves an' go to sleep, an' if you don't hurry I'll beat you to that happy land."

The three were off to the realms of slumber within ten minutes, running a race about equal. The rain poured all through the night, but they did not awake until the young sun sent the first beams of day into the gorge. Then Jarvis sat up. He had the faculty of awakening all at once, and he began to furl the canvas awning that had served them so well. The noise awoke the boys who also sat up.

"Get to work, you sleepy heads!" called Jarvis cheerfully. "Look what a fine world it is! Here's the river all washed clean, an' the land all washed clean, too! Stir yourselves, we're goin' to have hot food an' coffee here on the boat.

"I'm dreaming now of Hallie, sweet Hallie,
For the thought of her is one that never dies.
She's sleeping in the valley
And the mocking bird is singing where she lies.
Listen to the mocking bird, singing o'er her grave.
Listen to the mocking bird, singing where the weeping willows wave."

"You sing melancholy songs for one who is as cheerful as you are, Sam," said Harry.

"That's so. I like the weepy ones best. But they don't really make me feel sad, Harry. They jest fill me with a kind o' longin' to reach out an' grab somethin' that always floats jest before my hands. A sort o' pleasant sadness I'd call it.

"Ah, well I yet remember
When we gathered in the cotton side by side;
'Twas in the mild September
And the mocking bird was singing far and wide.
Oh, listen to the mocking bird
Still singing o'er her grave.
Oh, listen to the mocking bird
Still singing where the weeping willows wave."

"Now that ain't what you'd call a right merry song, but I never felt better in my life than I did when I was singin' it. Here you are, breakfast all ready! We'll eat, drink an' away. I'm anxious to see our mountains ag'in."

The boat soon reached a point where lower banks ran for some time, and, from the center of the stream, they saw the noble country outspread before them, a vast mass of shimmering green. The rain had ceased entirely, but the whole earth was sweet and clean from its great bath. Leaves and grass had taken on a deeper tint, and the crisp air was keen with blooming odors.

Although they soon had a considerable current to fight, they made good headway against it. Harry's practice with the oar was giving his muscles the same quality like steel wire which those of Jarvis and Ike had. So they went on for that day and others and drew near to the hills. The eyes of Jarvis kindled when he saw the first line of dark green slopes massing themselves against the eastern horizon.

"The Bluegrass is mighty fine, an' so is the Pennyroyal," he said, "an' I ain't got nothin' ag'in em. I admit their claims before they make 'em, but my true love, it's the mountains an' my mountain home. Mebbe some night, Harry, when we tie up to the bank, we'll see a deer comin' down to drink. What do you say to that?"

Harry's eyes kindled, too.

"I say that I want the first shot."

Jarvis laughed.

"True sperrit," he said. "Nobody will set up a claim ag'inst you, less it's that lunkhead, Ike, my nephew. Are you willin' to let him have it, Ike?"

Ike grinned and nodded.

The Kentucky narrowed and the current grew yet stronger. But changing oftener at the oars they still made good headway. The ranges, dark green on the lower slopes, but blue on the higher ridges beyond them, slowly came nearer. Late in the afternoon they entered the hills, and when night came they had left the lowlands several miles behind. They tied up to a great beech growing almost at the water's edge, and made their camp on the ground. Harry's deer did not come that night, but it did on the following one. Then Jarvis and he after supper went about a mile up the stream, stalking the best drinking places, and they saw a fine buck come gingerly to the river. Harry was lucky enough to bring him down with the first shot, an achievement that filled him with pride, and Jarvis soon skinned and dressed the animal, adding him to their larder.

"I don't shoot deer, 'cept when I need 'em to eat," said Jarvis, "an' we do need this one. We'll broil strips of him over the coals in the mornin'. Don't your mouth water, Harry?"

"It does."

The strips proved the next day to be all that Jarvis had promised, and they continued their journey with renewed elasticity, fair weather keeping them company. Deeper and deeper they went into the mountains. The region had all the aspects of a complete wilderness. Now and then they saw smoke, which Jarvis said was rising from the chimneys of log cabins, and once or twice they saw cabins themselves in sheltered nooks, but nobody hailed them. The news of the war had spread here, of course, but Harry surmised that it had made the mountaineers cautious, suppressing their natural curiosity. He did not object at all to their reticence, as it made traveling easier for him.

They were now rowing along a southerly fork of the Kentucky. Another deer had been killed, falling this time to the rifle of Jarvis, and one night they shot two wild turkeys. Jarvis and his nephew would arrive home full handed in every respect, and his great tenor boomed out joyously over the stream, speeding away in echoes among the lofty peaks and ridges that had now turned from hills into real mountains. They towered far above the stream, and everywhere there were masses of the deepest and densest green. The primeval forest clothed the whole earth, and the war to which Harry was going seemed a faint and far thing.

Traveling now became slow, because they always had a strong current to fight. Harry, at times when the country was not too rough, left the boat and walked along the bank. He could go thus for miles without feeling any weariness. Naturally very strong, he did not realize how much his work at the oar was increasing his power. The thin vital air of the mountains flowed through his lungs, and when Jarvis sang, as he did so often, he felt that he could lift up his feet and march as if to the beat of a drum.

They left the fork of the Kentucky at last and rowed up one of the deep and narrow mountain creeks. Peaks towered all about them, a half mile over their heads, covered from base to crest with unbroken forest. Sometimes the creek flowed between cliffs, and again it opened out into narrow valleys. In a two days' journey up its course they passed only two cabins.

"In ordinary water we'd have stopped thar," said Jarvis at the second cabin. "I know the man who lives in it an' he's to be trusted. We'd have left the boat an' the things with him, an' we'd have walked the rest of the way, but the creek is so high now that we kin make at least twenty miles more an' tie up at Bill Rudd's place. Thar's no goin' further on the water, 'cause the creek takes a fall of fifteen feet thar, an' this boat is too heavy to be carried around it."

They reached Rudd's place about dark. He was a hospitable mountaineer, with a double-roomed log cabin, a wife and two small children. He volunteered gladly to take care of the boat and its belongings, while Jarvis and the boys went on the next day to Jarvis's home about ten miles away.

Rudd and his wife were full of questions. They were eager to hear of the great world which was represented to them by Frankfort, and of the war in the lowlands concerning which they had heard vaguely. Rudd had been to Frankfort once and felt himself a traveler and man of the world. He and his wife knew Jarvis and Ike well, and they glanced rather curiously at Harry.

"He's goin' across the mountains an' down into Virginia on some business of his own which I ain't inquired into much," said Jarvis.

Harry slept in a house that night for the first time in days, and he did not like it. He awoke once with a feeling as if walls were pressing down upon him, and he could not breathe. He arose, opened the door, and stood by it for a few minutes, while the fresh air poured in. Jarvis awoke and chuckled.

"I know what's the matter with you, Harry," he said. "After you've lived out of doors a long time you feel penned up in houses. If it wasn't for rain an' snow I'd do without roofs 'cept in winter. Leave the door wide open, an' we'll both sleep better. Nothin', of course, would wake that lunkhead, Ike, my nephew. I guess you might fight the whole of Buena Vista right over his head, an' if it was his sleepin' time he'd sleep right on."

They left the next morning, taking with them all of Harry's baggage. Jarvis' boat would remain in the creek at this point, and he and Ike would return in due time for their own possessions. They followed a footpath now, but the walk was nothing to them. It was in truth a relief after so much traveling in the boat.

"My legs are long an' they need straightenin'," said Jarvis. "The ten miles before us will jest about take out the kinks."

Jarvis was a bachelor, his house being kept by his widowed sister, Ike's mother, and old Aunt Suse. Now, as they swung along in Indian file at a swift and easy gait, his joyous spirits bubbled forth anew. Lifting up his voice he sang with such tremendous volume that every peak and ridge gave back an individual echo:

"I live for the good of my nation,
And my suns are all growing low,
But I hope that the next generation
Will resemble old Rosin, the beau.

"I've traveled this country all o'er,
And now to the next I will go,
For I know that good quarters await me
To welcome old Rosin, the beau."

"I suppose you don't know how you got that song, either," said Harry.

"No, it just wandered in an' I've picked it up in parts, here an' thar. See that clump o' laurel 'cross the valley thar, Harry? I killed a black bear in it once, the biggest seen in these parts in our times, an' I kin point you at least five spots in which

I've killed deer. You kin trap lots of small game all through here in the winter, an' the furs bring good prices. Oh, the mountains ain't so bad. Look! See the smoke over that low ridge, the thin black line ag'in the sky. It comes from the house o' Samuel Jarvis, Esquire, an' it ain't no bad place, either, a double log house, with a downstairs an' upstairs, an' a frame kitchen behin'. It's fine to see it ag'in, ain't it, Ike?"

Ike smiled and nodded.

In another half hour they crossed the low ridge and swung down into a beautiful little valley, a mile long and a quarter of a mile broad that opened out before them. The smoke still rose from the house, which they now saw clearly, standing among its trees. A brook glinting with gold in the sunshine flowed down the middle of the valley. A luscious greenness covered the whole valley floor. No snugger nook could be found in the mountains.

"As fine as pie!" exclaimed Jarvis exultantly. "Everythin's straight an' right. Ike, I think I see Jane, your mother, standin' in the porch. I'll just give her a signal."

He lifted up his voice and sang "Home, Sweet Home," with tremendous volume. He was heard, as Harry saw a sunbonnet waved vigorously on the porch. The travelers descended rapidly, crossed the brook, and approached the house. A strong woman of middle years shouted joyously and came forward to meet them, leaving a little wizened figure crouched in a chair on the porch.

Mrs. Simmons embraced her brother and son with enthusiasm, and gave a hearty welcome to Harry, whom Jarvis introduced in the most glowing words. Then the three walked to the porch and the bent little figure in the chair. As they went up the steps together old Aunt Suse suddenly straightened up and stood erect. A pair of extraordinary black eyes were blazing from her ancient, wrinkled face. Her hand rose in a kind of military salute, and looking straight at Harry she exclaimed in a high-pitched but strong voice:

"Welcome, welcome, governor, to our house! It is a long time since I've seen you, but I knew that you would come again!"

"Why, what's the matter, Aunt Suse?" asked Jarvis

anxiously.

"It is he! The governor! Governor Ware!" she exclaimed. "He, who was the great defender of the frontier against the Indians! But he looks like a boy again! Yet I would have known him anywhere!"

The blazing eyes and tense voice of the old woman held Harry. She pointed with a withered forefinger which she held aloft and he felt as if an electric current were passing from it to him. A chill ran down his back and the hair lifted a little on his head. Jarvis and his nephew stood staring.

"Walk in, governor," she said. "This house is honored by your coming."

Then, and all in a flash, Harry understood. The mind of the old woman dreaming in the sun had returned to the far past, and she was seeing again with the eyes of her girlhood.

"I'm not Henry Ware, Aunt Susan," he said, "but I'm proud to say that I'm his great-grandson. My name is Kenton, Harry Kenton."

The wrinkled forefinger sank, but the light in her eyes did not die.

"Henry Ware, Harry Kenton!" she murmured. "The same blood, and the spirit is the same. It does not matter. Come into our house and rest after your long journey."

Still erect, she stood on one side and pointed to the open door. Jarvis laughed, but it was a laugh of relief rather than amusement.

"She shorely took you, Harry, for your great-grandfather, Henry Ware, the mighty woodsman and Injun fighter that later on became governor of the state. I guess you look as he did when he was near your age. I've heard her tell tales about him by the mile. Aunt Suse, you know, is more'n a hundred, an' she's got the double gift o' lookin' forrard an' back'ard. Come on in, Harry, this house will belong to you now, an' ef at times she thinks you're the great governor, or the boy that Governor Ware was before he was governor, jest let her think it."

With the wrinkled forefinger still pointing a welcome toward the open door Harry went into the house. He spent two days in the hospitable home of Samuel Jarvis. He would have limited the time to a single day, because Richmond was calling to him very strongly now, but it was necessary to buy a good horse for the journey by land, and Jarvis would not let him start until he had the pick of the region.

The first evening after their arrival they sat on the porch of the mountain home. Ike's mother was with them, but old Aunt Suse had already gone to bed. Throughout the day she had called Harry sometimes by his own name and sometimes "governor," and she had shown a wonderful pride whenever he ran to help her, as he often did.

The twilight was gone some time. The bright stars had sprung out in groups, and a noble moon was shining. A fine, misty, silver light, like gauze, hung over the valley, tinting the high green heads of the near and friendly mountains, and giving a wonderful look of softness and freshness to this safe nook among the peaks and ridges. Harry did not wonder that Jarvis and Ike loved it.

"Aunt Suse give me a big turn when she took you fur the governor," said Jarvis to Harry, "but it ain't so wonderful after all. Often she sees the things of them early times a heap brighter an' clearer than she sees the things of today. As I told you, she knowed Boone an' Kenton an' Logan an' Henry Ware an' all them gran' hunters an' fighters. She was in Lexin'ton nigh on to eighty years ago, when she saw Dan'l Boone an' the rest that lived through our awful defeat at the Blue Licks come back. It was not long after that her fam'ly came back into the mountains. Her dad 'lowed that people would soon be too thick 'roun' him down in that fine country, but they'd never crowd nobody up here an' they ain't done it neither."

"Did you ever hear her tell of Henry Ware's great friend, Paul Cotter?" asked Harry.

"Shorely; lots of times. She knowed Paul Cotter well. He wuzn't as tall an' strong as Henry Ware, but he was great in his way, too. It was him that started the big university at Lexin'ton, an' that become the greatest scholar this state ever knowed. I've heard that he learned to speak eight languages. Do you reckon it was true, Harry? Do you reckon that any man that ever lived could talk eight different ways?"

"It was certainly true. The great Dr. Cotter—and 'Dr.' in his case didn't mean a physician, it meant an M. A. and a Ph. D. and all sorts of learned things—could not only speak eight languages, but he knew also so many other things that I've heard he could forget more in a day and not miss it than the ordinary man would learn in a lifetime."

Jarvis whistled.

"He wuz shorely a big scholar," he said, "but it agrees exactly with what old Aunt Suse says. Paul Cotter was always huntin' fur books, an' books wuz mighty sca'ce in the Kentucky woods then."

"Henry Ware and Paul Cotter always lived near each other," resumed Harry, "and in two cases their grandchildren intermarried. A boy of my own age named Dick Mason, who is the great-grandson of Paul Cotter, is also my first cousin."

"Now that's interestin' an' me bein' of an inquirin' min', I'd like to ask you where this Dick Mason is."

Harry waved his hand toward the north.

"Up there somewhere," he said.

"You mean that he's gone with the North, took one side while you've took the other?"

"Yes, that's it. We couldn't see alike, but we think as much as ever of each other. I met him in Frankfort, where he had come from the Northern camp in Garrard County, but I think he left for the East before I did. The Northern forces hold the railways leading out of Kentucky and he's probably in Washington now."

Jarvis lighted his pipe and puffed a while in silence. At length he drew the stem from his mouth, blew a ring of smoke upward, and said in a tone of conviction:

"It does beat the Dutch how things come about!"

Harry looked questioningly at him.

"I mean your arrivin' here, bein' who you are, an' your meetin' old Aunt Suse, bein' who she is, an' that cousin of yours, Dick Mason, didn't you say was his name, bein' who he is, goin' off to the North."

They sat on the porch later than the custom of the mountaineers, and the beauty of the place deepened. The moon poured a vast flood of misty, silver light over the little valley, hemmed in by its high mountains, and Harry was so affected by the silence and peace that he had no feeling of anger toward anybody, not even toward Bill Skelly, who had tried to kill him.

Unidentified Confederate soldier[54]

11. IN VIRGINIA

Harry left the valley with the keenest feeling of regret, realizing at the parting how strong a friendship he had formed with this family. But he felt that he could not delay any longer. Affairs must be moving now in the great world in the east, and he wished to be at the heart of them. He had a strong, sure-footed horse, and he had supplies and an extra suit of clothes in his saddle bags. The rifle across his back would attract no attention, as all the men in the mountains carried rifles.

Jarvis had instructed Harry carefully about the road or path, and as the boy was already an experienced traveler with an excellent sense of direction, there was no danger of his getting lost in the wilderness.

Jarvis, Ike, and Mrs. Simmons gave him farewells which were full of feeling. Aunt Suse had come down the brick walk, tap-tapping with her cane, as Harry stood at the gate ready to mount his horse.

"Good-bye, Aunt Susan," he said. "I came a stranger, but this house has been made a home to me."

She peered up at him, and Harry saw that once more her old eyes were flaming with the light he had seen there when he arrived.

"Good-bye, governor," she said, holding out a wrinkled and trembling hand. "I am proud that our house has sheltered you, but it is not for the last time. You will come again, and you will be thin and pale and in rags, and you will fall at the door. I see you coming with these two eyes of mine."

"Hush, Aunt Suse," exclaimed Mrs. Simmons. "It is not Governor Ware, it is his great-grandson, and you mustn't send him away tellin' of terrible things that will happen to him."

"I'm not afraid," said Harry, "and I hope that I'll see Aunt Susan and all of you again."

He lifted her hand and kissed it in the old-fashioned manner.

She smiled and he heard her murmur:

"It is the great governor's way. He kissed my hand like that once before, when I went to Frankfort on the lumber raft."

"Good-bye, Harry," repeated Jarvis. "If you're bound to fight I reckon that's jest what you're bound to do, an' it ain't no good for me to say anythin'. Be shore you follow the trail jest as I laid it out to you an' in two days you'll strike the Wilderness Road. After that it's easy."

When Harry rode away something rose in his throat and choked him for a moment. He knew that he would never again find more kindly people than these simple mountaineers. Then in vivid phrases he heard once more the old woman's prophecy: "You will come again, and you will be thin and pale and in rags, and you will fall at the door." For a moment it shadowed the sunlight. Then he laughed at himself. No one could see into the future.

He was now across the valley and his path led along the base of the mountain. He looked back and saw the four standing on the porch, Jarvis, Ike, Mrs. Simmons, and old Aunt Suse. He waved his hand to them and all four waved back. A singular thrill ran through him. Could it be possible that he would come again, and in the manner that the old woman had predicted?

The path, in another minute, curved around the mountain, and the valley was shut from view. Nor, as he rode on, did he catch another glimpse of it. One might roam the mountains for months and never see the home of Samuel Jarvis.

The two days passed without event. The weather remained fair, and no one interfered with him. He slept the first night at a log cabin that Jarvis had named, having reached it in due time, and the second day he reached, also in due time, the old Wilderness Road.

Thence the boy advanced by easy stages into Virginia until he reached a railroad, where he sold his horse and took a train for Richmond, having come in a few days out of the cool, peaceful atmosphere of the mountains into another, which was surcharged everywhere with the fiery breath of war.

Harry realized as he approached the capital the deep intensity of feeling in everybody. The Virginians were less volatile than the South Carolinians, and they had long refused to go out, but now that they were out they were pouring into the Southern army, and they were animated by an extraordinary zeal. He began to hear new or unfamiliar names, Early, and Ewell, and Jackson, and Lee, and Johnston, and Hill, and Stuart, and Ashby, names that he would never forget, but names that as yet meant little to him.

He had letters from his father and he expected to find his friends of Charleston in Richmond or at the front. General Beauregard, whom he knew, would be in command of the army threatening Washington, and he would not go into a camp of strangers.

It was now early in June, and the country was at its best. On both sides of the railway spread the fair Virginia fields, and the earth, save where the ploughed lands stretched, was in its deepest tints of green. Harry, thrusting his head from the window, looked eagerly ahead at the city rising on its hills. Then a shade smaller than Charleston, it, too, was a famous place in the South, and it was full of great associations. Harry, like all the educated boys of the South, honored and admired its public men. They were mighty names to him. He was about to tread streets that had been trod by the famous Jefferson, by Madison, Monroe, Randolph of Roanoke, and many others. The shades of the great Virginians rose in a host before him.

He arrived about noon, and, as he carried no baggage

except his saddle bags and weapons, he was quickly within the city, his papers being in perfect order. He ate dinner, as the noonday meal was then called, and decided to seek General Beauregard at once, having learned from an officer on the train that he was in the city. It was said that he was at the residence of President Davis, called the White House, after that other and more famous one at Washington, in which the lank, awkward man, Abraham Lincoln, now lived.

But Harry paused frequently on the way, as there was nothing to hurry him, and there was much to be seen. If Charleston had been crowded, Richmond was more so. Like all capitals on the verge of a great war, but as yet untouched by its destructive breath, it throbbed with life. The streets swarmed with people, young officers, and soldiers in their uniforms, civilians of all kinds, and many pretty girls in white or light dresses, often with flowers in their hair or on their breasts. Light-heartedness and gaiety seemed predominant.

Harry stopped a while to look at the ancient and noble state house, now the home also of the Confederate Congress, standing in Capitol Square, and the spire of the Bell Tower, on Shockoe Hill. He saw important looking men coming in or going out of the square, but he did not linger long, intending to see the sights another time.

He was informed at the "White House" that General Beauregard was there, and sending in his card he was admitted promptly. Beauregard was sitting with President Davis and Secretary Benjamin in a room furnished plainly, and the general in his quick, nervous manner rose and greeted him warmly.

"You did good service with us at Charleston," he said, "and we welcome you here. We have already heard from your father, who was a comrade in war of both President Davis and myself."

"He wrote us that you were coming across the mountains from Frankfort," said Mr. Davis.

Harry thought that the President already looked worn and anxious.

"Yes, sir," replied the boy, "I came chiefly by the river and the Wilderness Road."

"Your father writes that they worked hard at Frankfort, but that they failed to take Kentucky out," continued the head of the Confederacy.

"The Southern leaders did their best, but they could not move the state."

"And you wish, then, to serve at the front?" continued the President.

"If I may," returned Harry. "In South Carolina I was with Colonel Leonidas Talbot. I have had a letter from him here, and, if it is your pleasure and that of General Beauregard, I shall be glad to join his command."

General Beauregard laughed a little.

"You do well," he said. "I have known Colonel Talbot a long time, and, although he may be slow in choosing he is bound to be in the very thick of events when he does choose. Colonel Talbot is at the front, and you'll probably find him closer than any other officer to the Yankee army. We need everybody whom we can get, especially lads of spirit and fire like you. You shall be a second lieutenant in his command. A train will leave here in four hours. Be ready. It will take you part of the way and you will march on for the rest."

Mr. Benjamin did not speak throughout the interview, but he watched Harry closely. Neither did he speak when he left, but he offered him a limp hand. The boy's view of Richmond was in truth brief, as before night he saw its spires and roofs fading behind him. The train was wholly military. There were four coaches filled with officers and troops, and two more coaches behind them loaded with ammunition.

Harry heard from some of the officers that the army was gathered at a place called Manassas Junction, where Beauregard had taken command on June 1st, and to which he would quickly return. But Harry did not know any of these officers and he felt a little lonely. He slept after a while in the car seat, awakened at times by the jolting or stopping of the train, and arrived some time the next day in a country of green hills and red clay roads, muddy from heavy rains.

They left the train, marched over the hills along one of the muddy roads, and presently saw a vast array of tents, fires, and earthworks, stretching to the horizon. Harry's heart leaped again. This was the great army of the South. Here were regiments and regiments, thousands and thousands of men and here he would find his friends, Colonel Talbot and Major St. Hilaire, and St. Clair and Langdon.

The whole scene was inspiring in the extreme to the heart of youth. Far to the right he saw cavalry galloping back and forth, and to the left he saw infantry drilling. From somewhere in front came the strains of a regimental band playing:

"The hour was sad, I left the maid,
A lingering farewell taking,
Her sighs and tears my steps delayed,
I thought her heart was breaking.
In hurried words her name I blessed,
I breathed the vows that bind me
And to my heart in anguish pressed
The girl I left behind me."

Winslow Homer, War Songs, Oct 1861[55]
Note: "Dixie" was added when published in Harper's

It was a favorite air of the Southern bands, and, much as it stirred Harry now, he was destined to hear it again in moments far more thrilling. He presented his order from

General Beauregard to a sentinel, who passed him to an officer, who in turn told him to go about a quarter of a mile westward, where he would find the regiment of Colonel Talbot quartered.

"It's a mixed regiment," he said, "made up of Virginians, South Carolinians, North Carolinians, and a few Kentuckians and Tennesseans, but it's already one of the best in the service. Colonel Talbot and his second in command, Lieutenant-Colonel St. Hilaire, have been thrashing it into shape in great fashion. They're mostly boys and already they call themselves 'The Invincibles.' You can see the tents of their commanding officers over there by that little creek."

Harry's eyes followed the pointing finger, and again his heart leaped. His friends were there, the two colonels for whom he had such a strong affection, and the two lads of his own age. Theirs looked like a good camp, too. It was arranged neatly, and by its side flowed the clear, cool waters of Young's Branch, a tributary of the little Manassas River. He walked briskly, crossed the brook, stepping from stone to stone, and entered the grounds of the Invincibles. A tall youth rushed forward, seized his hand and shook it violently, meanwhile uttering cries of welcome in an unbroken stream.

"By all the powers, it's our own Harry!" he exclaimed, "the new Harry of the West, whom we were afraid we should never see again. Everything is for the best, but we hardly hoped for this! How did you get here, Harry? And you didn't bring Kentucky rushing to our side, after all! Well, I knew it wasn't your fault, old horse! Ho, St. Clair, come and see who's here!"

St. Clair, who had been lying in the grass behind a tent, appeared and greeted Harry joyfully. But while Langdon was just the same he had changed in appearance. He was thinner and graver, and his intellectual face bore the stamp of rapid maturity.

"It's like greeting one of our very own, Harry," he said. "You were with us in Charleston at the great beginning. We were afraid you would have to stay in the west."

"The big things will begin here," said Harry.

"There can be no doubt of it. Do you know, Harry, that

we are less than thirty miles from Washington! If there were any hill high enough around here we could see the white dome[1] of the Capitol which we hope to take before the summer is over. But we'll take you to the Colonel and Major Hector St. Hilaire, that was, but Lieutenant-Colonel Hector St. Hilaire that is."

Colonel Talbot was sitting at a small table in a tent, the sides of which had been raised all around, leaving only a canvas roof. Lieutenant-Colonel St. Hilaire sat opposite him across the table, and they were studying intently a small map of a region that was soon to be sown deep with history. They looked up when Harry came with his two friends, and gave him the welcome that he knew he would always receive from them.

"I've had a letter from your father," said Colonel Leonidas Talbot, "and I've been expecting you. You are to be a lieutenant on my staff, and the quartermaster will sell you a new uniform as glossy and fine as those of which St. Clair and Langdon are so proud."

He asked him a few more questions about Kentucky and his journey over the mountains, and then, telling St. Clair and Langdon to take care of him, he and Lieutenant-Colonel St. Hilaire went back to the study of their map. Harry noted that both were tanned deeply and that their faces were very serious.

"Come along, Harry," said Langdon. "Let the colonel and the major bear all the troubles. For us everything is for the best. We've got you on our hands and we're going to treat you right. See that deep pool in the brook, where the big oak throws its shade over the water? It's partly natural and it's partly dammed, but it's our swimming hole. You are covered with dust and dirt. Pull off your clothes and jump in there. We'll protect you from ribald attention. There are other swimming holes along here, but this swimming hole belongs to the Invincibles, and we always make good our rights."

Harry was more than willing. In three minutes he jumped into the deep, cool water, swimming, diving, and shaking himself like a big dog. He had enjoyed no such luxury in

1 Anachronism: the painted cast-iron dome was not completed until 1863.

many days, and he felt as if he were being re-created. Langdon and St. Clair sat on the bank and gave him instructions.

"Now jump out," Langdon said at the end of five minutes. "You needn't think because you've just come and are in a way a guest, that you can keep this swimming hole all to yourself. A lot more of the Invincibles need bathing and here come some for their chance."

Harry came out reluctantly, and in a few minutes they were on the way to the quartermaster, where the needed uniform, one that appealed gloriously to his eye, was bought. St. Clair was quiet, but Langdon talked enough for all three.

"The Yankee vanguard is only a few miles away," he said. "You don't have to go far before you see their tents, though I ought to say that each side has another army westward in the mountains. There's been a lot of fighting already, though not much of it here. The first shots on Virginia soil were fired on our front the day General Beauregard arrived to take command of our forces."

"How about those troops in the hills?" asked Harry.

"They've been up and doing. A young Yankee general named McClellan has shown a lot of activity. He has beat us in some skirmishes and he has organized troops as far west as the Ohio. Then he and his generals met our general, Garnett, at Rich Mountain. It was the biggest affair of the war so far, and Garnett was killed. Then a curious fellow of ours named Jackson, and Stuart, a cavalry officer, lost a little battle at a place called Falling Waters."

"Has the luck been against us all along the line?"

"Not at all! A cock-eyed Massachusetts politician, one Ben Butler, a fellow of energy though, broke into the Yorktown country, but Magruder thrashed him at Big Bethel. All those things, though, Harry, are just whiffs of rain before the big storm. We're threatening Washington here with our main army, and here is where they will have to meet us. Lincoln has put General Scott, a Virginian, too, in command of the Northern armies, but as he's so old, somebody else will be the real commander."

Harry felt himself a genuine soldier in his new uniform,

and he soon learned his new duties, which, for the present, would not be many. The two armies, although practically face to face, refused to move. On either side the officers of the old regular force were seeking to beat the raw recruits into shape, and the rival commanders also waited, each for the other to make the first movement.

Harry and St. Clair were sent that night far toward the front with a small detachment to patrol some hill country. They marched in the moonlight, keeping among the trees, and listening for any sounds that might be hostile.

"It's not likely though that we'll be molested," said St. Clair. "The men on both sides don't yet realize fully that they are here to shoot at one another. This is our place, along a little brook, another tributary of the Manassas."

They stopped in a grove and disposed the men, twenty in number, along a line of several hundred yards, with instructions not to fire unless they knew positively what they were shooting at. Harry and St. Clair remained near the middle of the line, at the edge of the brook, where they sat down on the bank. The country was open in front of them, and Harry saw a distant light.

"What's that?" he asked.

"The campfire of a Yankee outpost. I told you they were very near."

"And that, I suppose, is one of their bugles."

A faint but musical note was brought to them by the light wind blowing in their faces.

"That's what it is. It may be the signal of some movement, but they can't attempt anything serious without showing themselves. Our sentinels are posted along here for miles."

The sound of the bugle continued faint and far away. It had a certain weird effect in the night and the loneliness. Harry wished to know who they were at that far campfire. His own cousin, Dick Mason, might be there.

"Although we're arrayed for war," said St. Clair, "the sentinels are often friendly. They even exchange plugs of tobacco and news. The officers have not been able to stop it wholly. Our sentinels tell theirs that we'll be in Washington in a month, and theirs tell ours that they've already engaged rooms in the Richmond hotels for July."

"When two prophets disagree both can't be right," said Harry. "How far away would you say that light is, Arthur?"

"About a mile and a half. Let's scout a little in that direction. There are no commands against it. Enterprise is encouraged."

Meeting of Union & Confederate pickets[56]

"Just what I'd like," said Harry, who was eager for action.

Leaving their own men under the command of a reliable sergeant named Carrick, the two youths crossed the brook and advanced over a fairly level stretch of country toward the fire. Small clusters of trees were scattered here and there, and beyond them was a field of young corn. The two paused in one of the little groves about a hundred yards from their own outposts and looked back. They saw only the dark line of the trees, and behind them, wavering lights which they knew were the campfires of their own army. But the lights at the distance were very small, mere pin points.

"They look more like lanterns carried by 'coon and 'possum hunters than the campfires of an army," said Harry.

"Yes, you'd hardly think they mark the presence of twenty or thirty thousand men," said St. Clair. "Here we are at the cornfield. The plants are not high, but they throw enough shadow to hide us."

They climbed a rail fence, and advanced down the corn rows. The moon was good and there was a plentiful supply of stars, enabling them to see some distance. To their right on a hill was a white Colonial house, with all its windows dark.

"That house would be in a bad place if a battle comes off here, as seems likely," said St. Clair.

"And those who own it are wise in having gone away," said Harry.

"I'm not so sure that they've gone. People hate to give up their homes even in the face of death. Around here they generally stay and put out the lights at dark."

"Well, here we are at the end of the cornfield, and the light is not more than four or five hundred yards away. I think I can see the shadows of human figures against the flames. Come, let's climb the fence and go down through this skirt of bushes."

The suggestion appealed to the daring and curiosity of both, and in a few minutes they were within two hundred yards of the Northern camp. But they lay very close in the undergrowth. They saw a big fire and Harry judged that four or five hundred men were scattered about. Many were asleep on the grass, but others sat up talking. The appearance of all was so extraordinary that Harry gazed in astonishment.

It was not the faces or forms of the men, but their dress that was so peculiar. They were arrayed in huge blouses and vast baggy trousers of a blazing red, fastened at the knee and revealing stockings of a brilliant hue below. Little tasseled caps were perched on the sides of their heads. Harry remembering his geography and the descriptions of nations would have taken them for a gathering of Turkish women, if their masculine faces had been hidden.

"What under the moon are those?" he whispered. "They do look curious," replied St. Clair. "They call them Zouaves, and I think they're from New York. It's a copy of a French military costume which, unless I'm mistaken, France uses in Algeria."

"They'd certainly make a magnificent target on the

battlefield. A Kentucky or Tennessee rifleman who'd miss such a target would die of shame."

"Maybe. But listen, they're singing! What do you think of that for a military tune?"

Harry heard for the first time in his life an extraordinary, choppy air, a rapid beat that rose and fell abruptly, sending a powerful thrill through his heart as he lay there in the bushes. The words were nothing, almost without meaning, but the tune itself was full of compelling power. It set the feet marching toward triumphant battle.

"In Dixie's land I'll take my stand,
Cinnamon seed and sandy bottom,
Look away! Look away!
Down South in Dixie!"

Three or four hundred voices took up the famous battle song, as thrilling and martial as the Marseillaise, then fresh and unhackneyed, and they sang it with enthusiasm and fire, officers joining with the men. It was a singular fact that Harry should first hear Northern troops singing the song which was destined to become the great battle tune of the South.

"What is it?" whispered Harry.

"It's called Dixie. They say it was written by a man in New York for a negro minstrel show. I suppose they sing it in anticipation, meaning that they will soon be in the heart of Dixie, which is the South, our South."

"I don't think those baggy red legs will ever march far into our South," whispered Harry defiantly.

"It is to be seen. Between you and me, Harry, I'm convinced there is no triumphant progress ahead for either North or South. Ah, another force is coming and it's cavalry! Don't you hear the hoof-beats, Harry?"

Harry heard them distinctly and he and his comrade lay more closely than ever in the bushes, because the horsemen, a numerous body, as the heavy tread indicated, were passing very near. The two lads presently saw them riding four abreast toward the campfire, and Harry surmised that they had been scouting in strong force toward the Southern front.

They were large men, deep with tan and riding easily. Harry judged their number at two hundred, and the tail of the company would pass alarmingly near the bushes in which his comrade and he lay.

"Don't you think we'd better creep back?" he whispered to St. Clair. "Some of them taking a short cut may ride right upon us."

"Yes, it's time to make ourselves scarce."

Union pickets[57]

They turned back, going as rapidly as they dared, but that which Harry had feared came to pass. The rear files of the horsemen, evidently intending to go to the other side of the camp, rode through the low bushes. Four of them passed so near the boys that they caught in the moonlight a glimpse of the two stooping figures.

"Who is there? Halt!" sharply cried one of them, an officer. But St. Clair cried also:

"Run, Harry! Run for your life, and keep to the bushes!"

The two dashed at utmost speed down the strip of bushes and they heard the thunder of horses' hoofs in the open on either flank. A half dozen shots were fired and the bullets cut leaves and twigs about them. They heard the Northern men shouting: "Spies! Spies! After them! Seize them!"

Harry in the moment of extreme danger retained his presence of mind: "To the cornfield, Arthur!" he cried to his comrade. "The fence is staked and ridered, and their horses can't jump it. If they stop to pull it down they will give us time to get away!"

"Good plan!" returned St. Clair. "But we'd better bend down as we run. Those bullets make my flesh creep!"

A fresh volley was sent into the bushes, but owing to the wise precaution of bending low, the bullets went over their heads, although Harry felt his hair rising up to meet them. In two or three minutes they were at the fence, and they went over it almost like birds. Harry heard two bullets hit the rails as they leaped—they were in view then for a moment—but they merely increased his speed, as he and St. Clair darted side by side through the corn, bending low again.

They heard the horsemen talking and swearing at the barrier, and then they heard the beat of hoofs again.

"They'll divide and send a force around the field each way!" said St. Clair.

"And some of them will dismount and pursue us through it on foot!"

"We can distance anybody on foot. Harry, when I heard those bullets whistling about me I felt as if I could outrun a horse, or a giraffe, or an antelope, or anything on earth! And thunder, Harry, I feel the same way now!"

Bullets fired from the fence made the ploughed land fly not far from them, and they lengthened their stride. Harry afterward said that he did not remember stepping on that cornfield more than twice. Fortunately for them the field, while not very wide, extended far to right and left, and the pursuing horsemen were compelled to make a great circuit.

Before the thudding hoofs came near they were over the fence again, and, still with wonderful powers of flight, were scudding across the country toward their own lines. They came to one of the clusters of trees and dashing into it lay close, their hearts pounding. Looking back they dimly saw the horsemen, riding at random, evidently at a loss.

"That was certainly close," gasped St. Clair. "I'm not going on any more scouts unless I'm ordered to do so."

"Nor I," said Harry. "I've got enough for one night at least. I suppose I'll never forget those men with the red bags in place of breeches, and that tune, 'Dixie.' As soon as I get my breath back I'm going to make a bee line for our own army."

"And when you make your bee line another just as fast and straight will run beside it."

They rested five minutes and then fled for the brook and their own little detachment behind it.

Unidentified Confederate soldier, Lynchburg Virginia rifles[58]

12. THE FIGHT FOR THE FORT

Before they reached the brook they hailed Sergeant Carrick lest they should be fired upon as enemies, and when his answer came they dropped into a walk, still panting and wiping the perspiration from damp foreheads. They bathed their faces freely in the brook, and sat down on the bank to rest. The sergeant, a regular and a veteran of many border campaigns against the Indians, regarded them benevolently.

"I heard firing in front," he said, "and I thought you might be concerned in it. If it hadn't been for my orders I'd have come forward with some of the men."

"Sergeant," said St. Clair, "if you were in the west again, and you were all alone in the hills or on the plains and a band of yelling Sioux or Blackfeet were to set after you with fell designs upon your scalp, what would you do?"

"I'd run, sir, with all my might. I'd run faster than I ever ran before. I'd run so fast, sir, that my feet wouldn't touch the ground more than once every forty yards. It would be the wisest thing one could do under the circumstances, the only thing, in fact."

"I'm glad to hear you say so, Sergeant Carrick, because you are a man of experience and magnificent sense. What you say proves that Harry and I are full of wisdom. They weren't Sioux or Blackfeet back there and I don't suppose they'd have scalped us, but they were Yankees and their intentions weren't exactly peaceful. So we took your advice before you gave it. If you'll examine the earth out there tomorrow you'll find our footprints only five times to the mile."

Unidentified Confederate soldier, Sergeant[59]

Far to the right and left other scattering shots had been fired, where skirmishers in the night came in touch with one another. Hence the adventure of Harry and St. Clair attracted but little attention. Shots at long range were fired nearly every night, and sometimes it was difficult to keep the raw recruits from pulling trigger merely for the pleasure of hearing the report.

But when Harry and St. Clair related the incident the next morning to Colonel Talbot, he spoke with gravity.

"There are many young men of birth and family in our army," he said, "and they must learn that war is a serious business. It is more than that; it is a deadly business, the most deadly business of all. If the Yankees had caught you two, it would have served you right."

"They scared us badly enough as it was, sir," said St. Clair.

Colonel Leonidas Talbot smiled slightly.

"That part of it at least will do you good," he said. "You young men don't know what war is, and you are growing fat and saucy in a pleasant country in June. But there is something ahead that will take a little of the starch out of you and teach you sense. No, you needn't look inquiringly at me, because I'm not going to tell you what it is, but go get some sleep, which you will need badly, and be ready at four o'clock this afternoon, because the Invincibles march then and you march with them."

Harry and St. Clair saluted and retired. They knew that it was not worthwhile to ask Colonel Talbot any questions. Since he had met him again in Virginia, Harry had recognized a difference in this South Carolina colonel. The kindliness was still there, but there was a new sternness also. The friend was being merged into the commander.

They chose a tent in order to shut out the noise and make sleep possible, but on their way to it they were waylaid by Langdon, who had heard something of their adventure the night before, and who felt chagrin because he had lacked a part in it.

"Although everything generally happens for the best, there is a slip sometimes," he said, "and I want to be in on the next move, whatever it is. There is a rumor that the Invincibles are to march. You have been before the colonel, and you ought to know. Is it true?"

"It is," replied Harry, "but that's all we do know. He was pretty sharp with us, Tom, and among our three selves, we are not going to get any favors from Colonel Leonidas Talbot and Lieutenant-Colonel Hector St. Hilaire because we're friends of theirs and would be likely to meet in the same drawing-rooms, if there were no war."

Harry and St. Clair slept well, despite the noises of a camp, but they were ready at the appointed time, very precise in their new uniforms. Langdon was with them and the three were eager for the movement, the nature of which officers alone seemed to know.

The Invincibles were an infantry regiment and the three youths, like the men, were on foot. They filed off to the left behind the front line of the Southern army, and marched steadily westward, inclining slightly to the north. Many of the men, or rather boys, not yet fast in the bonds of discipline, began to talk, and guess together about their errand. But Colonel Talbot and Lieutenant-Colonel St. Hilaire rode along the line and sternly commanded silence, once or twice making the menace of the sword. The lads scarcely understood it, but they were awed into silence. Then there was no noise but the rattle of their weapons and the steady tread of eight hundred men.

The young troops had been kept in splendid condition, drilling steadily, and they marched well. They passed to the extreme western end of the Confederate camp, and continued into the hills. The sun had passed its zenith when they started and a pleasant, cool breeze blew from the slopes of the western mountains. The sun set late, but the twilight began to fall at last, and they saw about them many places suitable for a camp and supper. But Colonel Talbot, who was now at the head of the line, rode on and gave no sign.

"If I were riding a bay horse fifteen hands high I could go on, too, forever," whispered Langdon to Harry.

"Remember your belief that everything happens for the best and just keep on marching."

The twilight retreated before the dark, but the regiment continued. Harry saw a dusky colonel on a dusky horse at the head of the line, and nearer by was Lieutenant-Colonel St. Hilaire, also riding, silent and stern. The Invincibles were weary. It was now nine o'clock, and they had marched many hours without a rest, but they did not dare to murmur, at least not loud enough to be heard by Colonel Leonidas Talbot and his lieutenant-colonel, Hector St. Hilaire.

"I wonder if this is going on all night," whispered Langdon.

"Very likely," returned Harry, "but remember that everything is for the best."

Langdon gave him a reproachful look, but trudged sturdily on. They halted about an hour later, but only for fifteen or twenty minutes. They had now come into much rougher country, steep, with high hills and populated thinly. Westward, the mountains seemed very near in the clear moonlight. No explanation was given to the Invincibles, but the officers rode among the groups and made a careful inspection of arms and equipment. Then the word to march once more was given.

They did not stop, except for short rests, until about three o'clock in the morning, when they came to the crest of a high ridge, covered with dense forest, but without undergrowth. Then the officers dismounted, and the word was passed to the men that they would remain there until dawn, but before they lay down on the ground Colonel Talbot told them what was expected of them, which was much.

Union Battery[60]

"A strong Northern force is encamped on the slope beyond," he said. "It is in a position from which the left flank of our main army can be threatened. Our enemies there are fortified with earthworks and they have cannon. If they hold the place they are likely to increase heavily in numbers. It is our business to drive them out."

The colonel told some of the officers within Harry's hearing that they could attack before dawn, but night assaults, unless with veteran troops, generally defeated themselves through confusion and uncertainty. Nevertheless, he hoped to surprise the Northern soldiers over their coffee. For that reason the men were compelled to lie down in their blankets in the dark. Not a single light was permitted, but they were allowed to eat some cold food, which they brought in their knapsacks.

Horses, drinking and resting[61]

Although it was June, the night was chill on the high hills, and Harry and his two friends, after their duties were done, wrapped their blankets closely around themselves as they sat on the ground, with their backs against a big tree. The physical relaxation after such hard marching and the sharp wind of the night made Harry shiver, despite his blanket. St. Clair and Langdon shivered, too. They did not know that part of it was that three-o'clock-in-the-morning feeling.

Harry, sensitive, keenly alive to impressions, was oppressed by a certain heavy and uncanny feeling. They were going into battle in the morning—and with men whom he did not hate. The attacks on the *Star of the West* and Sumter had been bombardments, distant affairs, where he did not see the face of his enemy, but here it would be another matter. The real shock of battle would come, and the eyes of men seeking to kill would look into the eyes of others who also sought to kill.

He and St. Clair were not sleepy, as they had slept through most of the day, but Langdon was already nodding. Most of the soldiers also had fallen asleep through exhaustion, and Harry saw them in the dusk lying in long rows. The faint moon throwing a ghostly light over so many motionless forms made the whole scene weird and unreal to Harry. He shook himself to cast off the spell, and, closing his eyes, sought sleep.

But sleep would not come and the obstinate lids lifted again. It had turned a little darker and the motionless forms at the far end of the line were hidden. But those nearer were so still that they seemed to have been put there to stay forever. St. Clair had yielded at last to weariness and with his back against the tree slept by Harry's side.

He saw four figures moving up and down like ghosts through the shadows. They were Colonel Talbot, Lieutenant-Colonel St. Hilaire, and two captains watching their men, seeing that silence and caution were preserved. Harry knew that sentinels were posted further down the ridge, but he could not see them from where he lay. Although it was a long time, the forest and human figures wavered at last, and he dozed for a while. But he soon awoke and saw a faint tint of gray low down in the east, the first timid herald of dawn.

The young soldiers were awakened. They started to rise with a cheerful exchange of chatter, but were sternly commanded to silence. Nevertheless, they talked in whispers and told one another how they would wipe the Yankees off the face of the earth. Workers from the shops in the big cities of the North could not stand before them, the open air sons of the South. They stretched their long limbs, felt their big muscles, and wondered why they were not led forward at once.

But before they marched they were ordered to take food from their knapsacks and eat. Five minutes at most were allowed, and there was to be no nonsense, no loud talking. Some who had come north with negro servants stared at these officers who dared to talk to them as if they were slaves. But the words of anger stopped at their lips. They would take their revenge instead on the Yankees.

Harry and his two friends had fitted themselves already into military discipline and military ways. They ate, not because they were hungry, but because they knew it was a necessity. Meanwhile, the faint gray band in the east was broadening. The note of a bugle, distant, mellow, and musical, came from a point down the slope.

"The Yankee fort," said Langdon. "They're waking up, too. But I'm looking for the best, boys, and inside of two hours that Yankee fort will be a Confederate fort."

The note of the bugle seemed to decide the Southern officers. The men were ordered to see to their arms and march. The officers dismounted as the way would be rough and left their horses behind. The troops formed into several columns and four light guns went down the slope with them. Scouts who had been out in the night came back and reported that the fort, consisting wholly of earthworks, had a garrison of a thousand men with eight guns. They were New York and New England troops and they did not suspect the presence of an enemy. They were just lighting their breakfast fires.

The Southern columns moved forward in quiet, still hidden by the forest, which also yet hid the Northern fort. Harry's heart began to beat heavily, but he forced himself to preserve the appearance of calmness. Pride stiffened his will and backbone. He was a veteran. He had been at Sumter. He had seen the great bombardment, and he had taken a part in it. He must show these raw men how a soldier bore himself in battle, and, moreover, he was an officer whose business it was to lead.

The deep forest endured as they advanced in a diagonal line down the slope. The great civil war of North America was fought mostly in the forest, and often the men were not aware of the presence of one another until they came face to face.

Pickets[62]

They were almost at the bottom where the valley opened out in grass land, and were turning northward when Harry saw two figures ahead of them among the trees. They were men in blue uniforms with rifles in their hands, and they were staring in surprise at the advancing columns in gray. But their surprise lasted only a moment. Then they lifted their rifles, fired straight at the Invincibles, and with warning shouts darted among the trees toward their own troops.

"Forward, lads!" shouted Colonel Talbot. "We're within four hundred yards of the fort, and we must rush it! Officers, to your places!"

Their own bugle sang stirring music, and the men gathered themselves for the forward rush. Up shot the sun, casting a sharp, vivid light over the slopes and valley. The soldiers, feeling that victory was just ahead, advanced with so much speed that the officers began to check them a little, fearing that the Invincibles would be thrown into confusion.

The forest ended. Before them lay a slope, from which the

bushes had been cut away and beyond were trenches, and walls of fresh earth, from which the mouths of cannon protruded. Soldiers in blue, sentinels and seekers of wood for the fires, were hurrying into the earthworks, on the crests of which stood men, dressed in the uniforms of officers.

"Forward, my lads!" shouted Colonel Leonidas Talbot, who was near the front rank, brandishing his sword until the light glittered along its sharp blade. "Into the fort! Into the fort!"

The sun, rising higher, flooded the slopes, the valley, and the fort with brilliant beams. Everything seemed to Harry's excited mind to stand out gigantic and magnified. Black specks began to dance in myriads before his eyes. He heard beside him the sharp, panting breath of his comrades, and the beat of many feet as they rushed on.

He saw the Northern officers on the earthwork disappear, dropping down behind, and the young Southern soldiers raised a great shout of triumph which, as it sank on its dying note, was merged into a tremendous crash. The whole fort seemed to Harry to blaze with red fire, as the heavy guns were fired straight into the faces of the Invincibles. The roar of the cannon was so near that Harry, for an instant, was deafened by the crash. Then he heard groans and cries and saw men falling around him.

In another moment came the swish of rifle bullets, and the ranks of the Invincibles were cut and torn with lead. The young recruits were receiving their baptism of fire and it was accompanied by many wounds and death.

The earthworks in front were hidden for a little while by drifting smoke, but the Invincibles, mad with pain and rage, rushed through it. They were anxious to get at those who were stinging them so terribly, and fortunately for them the defenders did not have time to pour in another volley. Harry saw Colonel Talbot still in front, waving his sword, and near him Lieutenant-Colonel St. Hilaire, also with an uplifted sword, which he pointed straight toward the earthwork.

"On, lads, on!" shouted the colonel. "It is nothing! Another moment and the fort is ours!"

Harry heard the hissing of heavy missiles above him. The

light guns of the Invincibles had unlimbered on the slope, and fired once over their heads into the fort. But they did not dare to fire again, as the next instant the recruits, dripping red, but still wild with rage, were at the earthworks, and driven on with rage climbed them and fired at the huddled mass they saw below.

Harry stumbled as he went down into the fort, but quickly recovered himself and leaped to his feet again. He saw through the flame and smoke faces much like his own, the faces of youth, startled and aghast, scarcely yet comprehending that this was war and that war meant pain and death. The Invincibles, despite the single close volley that had been poured into them, had the advantage of surprise and their officers were men of skill and experience. They had left a long red trail of the fallen as they entered the fort, but after their own single volley they pressed hard with the bayonet. Little as was their military knowledge, those against them had less, and they also had less experience of the woods and hills.

As the Invincibles hurled themselves upon them the defenders slowly gave way and were driven out of the fort. But they carried two of their cannon with them, and when they reached the wood opened a heavy fire upon the pursuing Southern troops, which made the youngsters shiver and reel back.

"They, too, have some regular officers," said Colonel Talbot to Lieutenant-Colonel St. Hilaire. "It's a safe wager that several of our old comrades of Mexico are there."

Thus did West Pointers speak with respect of their fellow West Pointers.

Exulting in their capture of the fort and still driven by rage, the Invincibles attempted to rush the enemy, but they were met by such a deadly fire that many fell, and their officers drew them back to the shelter of the captured earthworks, where they were joined by their own light guns that had been hurried down the slope. Another volley was fired at them, when they went over the earthen walls, and Harry, as he threw himself upon the ground, heard the ferocious whine of the bullets over his head, a sound to which he would grow used through years terribly long.

Harry rose to his feet and began to feel of himself to see if he were wounded. So great had been the tension and so rapid their movements that he had not been conscious of any physical feeling.

"All right, Harry?" asked a voice by his side.

He saw Langdon with a broad red stripe down his cheek. The stripe was of such even width that it seemed to have been painted there, and Harry stared at it in a sort of fascination.

"I know I'm not beautiful, Harry," said Langdon, "neither am I killed or mortally wounded. But my feelings are hurt. That bullet, fired by some mill hand who probably never pulled a trigger before, just grazed the top of my head, but it has pumped enough out of my veins to irrigate my face with a beautiful scarlet flow."

"The mill hands may never have pulled trigger before," said Harry, "but it looks as if they were learning how fast enough. Down, Tom!"

Again the smoke and fire burst from the forest, and the bullets whined in hundreds over their heads. Two heavier crashes showed that the cannon were also coming into play, and one shell striking within the fort, exploded, wounding a half dozen men.

"I suppose that everything happens for the best," said Langdon, "but having got into the fort, it looks as if we couldn't get out again. With the help of the earthwork I can hide from the bullets, but how are you to dodge a shell which can come in a curve over the highest kind of a wall, drop right in the middle of the crowd, burst, and send pieces in a hundred directions?"

"You can't," said St. Clair, who appeared suddenly.

He was covered with dirt and his fine new uniform was torn.

"What has happened to you?" asked Harry.

"I've just had practical proof that it's hard to dodge a bursting shell," replied St. Clair calmly. "I'm in luck that no part of the shell itself hit me, but it sent the dirt flying against me so hard that it stung, and I think that some pieces of gravel have played havoc with my coat and trousers."

"Hark! there go our cannon!" exclaimed Harry. "We'll drive them out of those woods."

"None too soon for me," said St. Clair, looking ruefully at his torn uniform. "I'd take it as a politeness on their part if they used bullets only and not shells."

Twenty-minute halt; Edwin Forbes[63]

They had not yet come down to the stern discipline of war, but their talk was stopped speedily by the senior officers, who put them to work arranging the young recruits along the earthworks, whence they could reply with comparative safety to the fire from the wood. But Harry noted that the raking fire of their own cannon had been effective. The Northern troops had retreated to a more distant point in the forest, where they were beyond the range of rifles, but it seemed that they had no intention of going any further, as from time to time a shell from their cannon still curved and fell in the fort or near it. The Southern guns, including those that had been captured, replied, but, of necessity, shot and shell were sent at random into the forest which now hid the whole Northern force.

"It seems to me," said St. Clair to Harry, "that while we have taken the fort we have merely made an exchange. Instead of being besiegers we have turned ourselves into the besieged."

"And while I'm expecting everything to turn out for the best," said Langdon, "I don't know that we've made anything at all by the exchange. We're in the fort, but the mechanics and mill hands are on the slope in a good position to pepper us."

"Or to wait for reinforcements," said Harry.

"I hadn't thought of that," said St. Clair. "They may send up into the mountains and bring four or five times our numbers. Patterson's army must be somewhere near."

"But we'll hope that they won't," said Langdon.

The Northern troops ceased their fire presently, but the officers, examining the woods with their glasses, said they were still there. Then came the grim task of burying the dead, which was done inside the earthworks. Nearly two score of the Invincibles had fallen to rise no more, and about a hundred were wounded. It was no small loss even for a veteran force, and Colonel Talbot and Lieutenant-Colonel St. Hilaire looked grave. Many of the recruits had turned white, and they had strange, sinking sensations.

There was little laughter or display of triumph inside the earthworks, nor was there any increase of cheer when the recruits saw the senior officers draw aside and engage in anxious talk.

"I'm thinking that idea of yours, Harry, about Yankee reinforcements, must have occurred to Colonel Talbot also," said Langdon. "It seems that we have nothing else to fear. The Yankees that we drove out are not strong enough to come back and drive us out. So they must be looking for a heavy force from Patterson's army."

The conference of the officers was quickly over, and then the men were put to work building higher the walls of earth and deepening the ditches. Many picks and spades had been captured in the fort, and others used bayonets. All, besides the guard, toiled hard two or three hours without interruption.

It was now noon, and food was served. An abundance of water in barrels had been found in the fort and the men drank it eagerly as the sun was warm and the work with spade and shovel made them very thirsty. The three boys, despite their rank, had been taking turns with the men and they leaned wearily against the earthwork.

The clatter of tools had ceased. The men ate and drank in silence. No sound came from the Northern troops in the wood. A heavy, ominous silence brooded over the little valley which had seen so much battle and passion. Harry felt relaxed and for the moment nerveless. His eyes wandered to the new earth, beneath which the dead lay, and he shivered. The wounded were lying patiently on their blankets and those of their comrades and they did not complain. The surgeons had done their best for them and the more skillful among the soldiers had helped.

Soldiers in tents, army camp[64]

The silence was very heavy upon Harry's nerves. Overhead great birds hovered on black wings, and when he saw them he shuddered. St. Clair saw them, too.

"No pleasant sight," he said. "I feel stronger since I've had food and water, Harry, but I'm thinking that we're going to be besieged in this fort, and we're not overburdened with supplies. I wonder what the colonel will do."

"He'll try to hold it," said Langdon. "He was sent here for that purpose, and we all know what the colonel is."

"He will certainly stay," said Harry.

After a good rest they resumed work with pick, shovel, and bayonet, throwing the earthworks higher and ever higher. It was clear to the three lads that Colonel Talbot expected a heavy attack.

"Perhaps we have underrated our mill hands and mechanics," said St. Clair, in his precise, dandyish way. "They may not ride as well or shoot as well as we do, but they seem to be in no hurry about going back to their factories."

Harry glanced at him. St. Clair was always extremely particular about his dress. It was a matter to which he gave time and thought freely. Now, despite all his digging, he was again trim, immaculate, and showed no signs of perspiration. He would have died rather than betray nervousness or excitement.

"I've no doubt that we've underrated them," said Harry. "Just as the people up North have underrated us. Colonel Talbot told me long ago that this was going to be a terribly big war, and now I know he was right."

A long time passed without any demonstration on the part of the enemy. The sun reached the zenith and blazed redly upon the men in the fort. Harry looked longingly at the dark green woods. He remembered cool brooks, swelling into deep pools here and there in just such woods as these, in which he used to bathe when he was a little boy. An intense wish to swim again in the cool waters seized him. He believed it was so intense because those beautiful woods there on the slope, where the running water must be, were filled with the Northern riflemen.

Three scouts, sent out by Colonel Talbot, returned with reports that justified his suspicions. A heavy force, evidently from Patterson's army operating in the hills and mountains, was marching down the valley to join those who had been driven from the fort. The junction would be formed within an hour. Harry was present when the report was made and he understood its significance. He rejoiced that the walls of earth had been thrown so much higher and that the trenches had been dug so much deeper.

In the middle of the afternoon, when the cool shade was beginning to fall on the eastern forest, they noticed a movement in the woods. They saw the swaying of bushes and the officers, who had glasses, caught glimpses of the men moving in the undergrowth. Then came a mighty crash and the shells from a battery of great guns sang in the air and burst about them. It was well for the Invincibles that they had dug their trenches deep, as two of the shells burst inside the fort. Harry was with Colonel Talbot, now acting as an aide, and he heard the leader's quiet comment:

"The reinforcements have brought more big guns. They will deliver a heavy cannonade and then under cover of the smoke they will charge. Lieutenant Kenton, tell our gunners that it is my positive orders that they are not to fire a single shot until I give the word. The Yankees can see us, but we cannot see them, and we'll save our ammunition for their charge. Keep well down in the trench, Lieutenant Kenton!"

The Invincibles hugged their shelter gladly enough while the fire from the great guns continued. A second battery opened from a point further down the slope, and the fort was swept by a cross-fire of ball and shell. Yet the loss of life was small. The trenches were so deep and so well constructed that only chance pieces of shell struck human targets.

Harry remained with Colonel Talbot, ready to carry any order that he might give. The colonel peered over the earthwork at intervals and searched the woods closely with a powerful pair of glasses. His face was very grave, but Harry presently saw him smile a little. He wondered, but he had learned enough of discipline now not to ask questions of his commanding officer. At length he heard the colonel mutter:

Horses pulling cannon on wagon uphill during battle[65]

"It is Carrington! It surely must be Carrington!" A third battery now opened at a point almost midway between the other two, and the smile of the colonel came again, but now it lingered longer.

"It is bound to be Carrington!" he said. "It cannot possibly be any other! That way of opening with a battery on one flank, then on the other, and then with a third midway between was always his, and the accuracy of aim is his, too! Heavens, what an artillery officer! I doubt whether there is such another in either army, or in the world! And he is better, too, than ever!"

He caught Harry looking at him in wonder, and he smiled once more.

"A friend of mine commands the Northern artillery," he said. "I have not seen him, of course, but he is making all the signs and using all the passwords. We are exactly the same age, and we were chums at West Point. We were together in the Indian wars, and together in all the battles from Vera Cruz to the City of Mexico. It's John Carrington, and he's from New York! He's perfectly wonderful with the guns! Lord, lad, look how he lives up to his reputation! Not a shot misses! He must have been training those gunners for months! Thunder, but that was magnificent!"

A huge shell struck squarely in the center of the earthwork, burst with a terrible crash, and sent steel splinters and fragments flying in every direction. A rain of dirt followed the rain of steel, and, when the colonel wiped the last mote from his eye, he said triumphantly and joyously:

"It's Carrington! Not a shadow of doubt can be left! Only such gunners as those he trains can plump shells squarely among us at that range! Oh, I tell you, Harry, he's a marvel. Has the wonderful mathematical and engineering eye!"

The eyes of Colonel Leonidas Talbot beamed with admiration of his old comrade, mingled with a strong affection. Nevertheless, he did not relax his vigilance and caution for an instant. He made the circuit of the fort and saw that everything was ready. The Southern riflemen lined every earthwork, and the guns had been wheeled into the best positions, with the gunners ready. Then he returned to his old place.

"The charge will come soon, Lieutenant Kenton," he said to Harry. "Their cannonade serves a double purpose. It keeps us busy dodging ball and shell, and it creates a bank of smoke through which their infantry can advance almost to the fort and yet remain hidden. See how the smoke covers the whole side of the mountain. Oh, Carrington is doing splendidly! I have never known him to do better!"

Harry wished that Carrington would not do quite so well. He was tired of crouching in a ditch. He was growing somewhat used to the hideous howling of the shells, but it was still unsafe anywhere except in the trenches. It seemed to him, too, that the cannon fire was increasing in volume. The slopes and the valley gave back a continuous crash of rolling thunder. Heavier and heavier grew the bank of smoke over and against the forest. It was impossible to see what was going on there, but Harry had no doubt that the Northern regiments were massing themselves for the attack.

The youth remained with Colonel Talbot, being held by the latter to carry orders when needed to other points in the fort. St. Clair and Langdon were kept near for a similar use and they were crouching in the same trench.

"If everything happens for the best it's time it was happening," said Langdon in an impatient whisper. "These shells and cannon balls flying over me make my head ache and scare me to death besides. If the Yankees don't hurry up and charge, they'll find me dead, killed by the collapse of worn-out nerves."

"I intend to be ready when they come," said St. Clair. "I've made every preparation that I can call to mind."

"Which means that your coat must be setting just right and that your collar isn't ruffled," rejoined Langdon. "Yes, Arthur, you are ready now. You are certainly the neatest and best dressed man in the regiment. If the Yankees take us they can't say that they captured a slovenly prisoner."

"Then," said St. Clair, smiling, "let them come on."

"Their cannon fire is sinking!" exclaimed Colonel Talbot. "In a minute it will cease and then will come the charge! 'Tis Carrington's way, and a good way! Hark! Listen to it! The signal! Ready, men! Ready! Here they come!"

The great cannonade ceased so abruptly that for a few moments the stillness was more awful than the thunder of the guns had been. The recruits could hear the great pulses in their temples throbbing. Then the silence was pierced by the shrill notes of a brazen bugle, steadily rising higher and always calling insistently to the men to come. Then they heard the heavy thud of many men advancing with swiftness and regularity.

The Southern troops were at the earthworks in double rows, and the gunners were at the guns, all eager, all watching intently for what might come out of the smoke. But the rising breeze suddenly caught the great bank of mists and vapors and whirled the whole aside. Then Harry saw. He saw a long line of men, their front bristling with the blue steel of bayonets, and behind them other lines and yet other lines.

It seemed to Harry that the points of the bayonets were almost in his face, and then, at the shouted command, the whole earthwork burst into a blaze. The cannon and hundreds of rifles sent their deadly volleys into the blue masses at short range. The fort had turned into a volcano, pouring forth a rain of fire and deadly missiles. The front line of the Northern force was shot away, but the next line took its place and rushed at the fort with those behind pressing close after them. The defenders loaded and fired as fast as they could and the high walls of earth helped them. The loose dirt gave away as the Northern men attempted to climb them, and dirt and men fell together back to the bottom. The Northern gunners in the rear of the attack could not fire for fear of hitting their own troops, but the Southern cannon at the embrasures had a clear target. Shot and shell crashed into the Northern ranks, and the deadly hail of bullets beat upon them without ceasing. But still they came.

"The mechanics and mill hands are as good as anybody, it appears!" shouted St. Clair in Harry's ear, and Harry nodded.

But the defenses of the fort were too strong. The charge, driven home with reckless courage, beat in vain upon those high earthen walls, behind which the defenders, standing upon narrow platforms, sent showers of bullets into ranks so close that few could miss. The assailants broke at last and once more the shrill notes of the brazen bugle pierced the air. But instead of saying come, it said: "Fall back! Fall back!" and the great clouds of smoke that had protected the Northern advance now covered the Northern retreat.

The firing had been so rapid and so heavy that the whole field in front of the fort was covered with smoke, through which they caught only the gleam of bayonets and glimpses of battle flags. But they knew that the Northern troops were retiring, carrying with them their wounded, but leaving the dead behind. Harry, excited and eager, was about to leap upon the crest of the earthwork, but Colonel Talbot sharply ordered him down.

Artillery going into action; Edwin Forbes[66]

"You'd be killed inside of a minute!" he cried. "Carrington is out there with the guns! As soon as their troops are far enough back he'll open on us with the cannon, and he'll rake this fort like a hurricane beating upon a forest. Only the earthworks will protect us from certain destruction."

He sent the order, fierce and sharp, along the line, for everyone to keep under cover, and there was ample proof soon that he knew his man. The Northern infantry had retired and the smoke in front was beginning to lift, when the figure of a tall man in blue appeared on a hillock at the edge of the forest. Harry, who had snatched up a rifle, levelled it instantly and took aim. But before his finger could pull the trigger Colonel Talbot knocked it down again.

"My God!" he exclaimed. "I was barely in time to save him! It was Carrington himself!"

"But he is our enemy! Our powerful enemy!"

"Our enemy! Our official enemy, yes! But my friend! My life-long friend! We were boys together at West Point! We slept under the same blanket on the icy plateaux of Mexico. No, Harry, I could not let you or any other slay him!"

The figure disappeared from the hillock and the next moment the great guns opened again from the forest. The orders of Colonel Talbot had not been given a moment too soon. Huge shells and balls raked the fort once more and the defenders crouched lower than ever in the trenches. Harry surmised that the new cannonade was intended mainly to prevent a possible return attack by the Southern troops, but they were too cautious to venture from their earthworks. The Invincibles had grown many years older in a few hours.

When it became evident that no sally would be made from the fort, the fire of the cannon in front ceased, and the smoke lifted, disclosing a field black with the slain. Harry looked, shuddered, and refused to look again. But Colonel Talbot examined field and forest long and anxiously through his glasses.

"They are there yet, and they will remain," he announced at last. "We have beaten back the assault. They may hold us here until a great army comes, and with heavy loss to them, but we are yet besieged. Carrington will not let us rest. He will send a shell to some part of this fort every three or four minutes. You will see."

They heard a roar and hiss a minute later, and a shell burst inside the walls. Through all the afternoon Carrington played upon the shaken nerves of the Invincibles. It seemed that he could make his shells hit wherever he wished. If a recruit left a trench it was only to make a rush for another. If their nerves settled down for a moment, that solemn boom from the forest and the shriek of the shell made them jump again.

"Wonderful! Wonderful!" murmured Colonel Talbot, "but terribly trying to new men! Carrington certainly grows better with the years."

Harry tried to compose himself and rest, as he lay in the trench with St. Clair and Langdon. They had had their battle face to face and all three of them were terribly shaken, but they recovered themselves at last, despite the shells which burst at short but irregular intervals inside the fort. Thus the last hours of the afternoon waned, and as the twilight came, they went more freely about the fort.

Colonel Talbot called a conference of the senior officers in a corner of the enclosure well under the shelter of the earthen walls, and after some minutes of anxious talking they sent for the three youths. Harry, St. Clair, and Langdon responded with alacrity, sure that something of the utmost importance was afoot.

Unidentified Confederate soldier, Artillery[67]

13. THE SEEKER FOR HELP

Colonel Talbot, Lieutenant-Colonel St. Hilaire, and four other officers were in a deep alcove that had been dug just under the highest earthwork, where they were not likely to be interrupted in their deliberations by any fragment of an exploding shell. The only light was that of the stars and the early moon which had now come out, but it was sufficient to show faces oppressed by the utmost anxiety. Three other men also had been summoned to the council.

"We have chosen you six for an important errand," said Colonel Talbot, "but you are to go upon it singly, and not collectively. As you see, we are besieged here by a greatly superior force. Its assault has been repulsed, but it will not go away. It will bombard us incessantly, and, since we are not strong enough to break through their lines and have limited supplies of food and water, we must fall in a day or two, unless we get help. We want you to make your way over the hills tonight to General Beauregard's army and bring aid. Even should five be captured or slain the sixth may get through. Lieutenant Kenton, you will go first. You will recall that the horses of the officers were left on the crest of the mountain with a small guard. They may be there yet, and if you can secure a mount, so much the better. But the moment you leave this fort you must rely absolutely upon your own skill and judgment."

Harry bowed. It was a great trust and he felt elation because he had been chosen first. He was again a courier, and he would do his best.

"I should advise you not to take either a rifle or a sword," said Colonel Talbot, "as they will be in the way of speed. But you'd better have two pistols. Now, go! I send you upon a dangerous errand, but I hope that the son of George Kenton, my old friend, will succeed. Hark! There is Carrington again! How strangely this war arrays comrades against one another!"

A shell burst almost at the center of the fort, and, for a few moments, the air was full of earth and flying fragments of steel. But in another minute Harry made his preparations, dropped over the rear earthwork and crouched for a little while against it. Before him stretched an open space of several hundred yards and here he felt was his greatest danger. The Northern sharpshooters might be lurking at the edge of the forest, and he ran great danger of being picked off as he fled. He looked up hopefully at the skies and saw a few clouds, but they did not promise much. Starshine and moonshine together gave enough light for a good sharpshooter.

Bending until he was half stooped, he took his chance and ran across the clearing. His flesh quivered, fearing the sudden impact of a bullet upon it, but no crack of a rifle came and he darted into the protecting shades of the forest. He lay a few minutes among the trees, until his lungs filled with fresh air. Then he rose and advanced cautiously up the slope, which lay to the south of the fort. The besieging force was massed on the northern side of the fort, but it was probable that they had outposts here also, to guard against such errands as the one upon which Harry himself was bent.

Yet he felt sure of getting through. One youth in a forest was hard to find. The clouds at which he had looked so hopefully were really growing a little heavier now. It would take good eyes to find him and swift feet to catch him. He paused again halfway up the slope, and saw a flash of flame from the Northern forest. Then came the thunderous roar of one of Carrington's guns, all the louder in the still night, and he saw the shell burst just over the fort.

He knew that these guns would play all night on the Southern recruits, allowing them but little rest and sleep and shaking their nerves still further.

But he must not pause for the guns. A hundred yards further and he sank quietly into a clump of bushes. Voices had warned him and he lay quite still while a Northern officer and twenty soldiers passed. They were so near that he heard them talking and they spoke of the recapture of the fort within two days at least. When they were lost among the trees he rose and advanced more rapidly than before.

He met no interruption until he reached the crest of the mountain, when he ran almost into the arms of a sentinel. The man in the darkness did not see the color of his uniform and hailed him for news.

Union pickets' hut[68]

"Nothing," replied Harry hastily, as he darted away. "I carry a message from our commander to a detachment stationed further on!"

But the sentinel, catching sight of his uniform, and exclaiming: "A Johnny Reb!" threw up his rifle and fired. Luckily for Harry it was such a hurried shot that the bullet only made his flesh creep, and passed on, cutting the twigs. Then Harry lifted himself up and ran. Lifting himself up describes it truly. He had all the motives which can make a boy run, pressing danger, love of life, devotion to his cause, and a burning desire to do his errand. Hence he lifted his feet, spurned the earth behind him, and fled down the slope at amazing speed. Several more shots were fired, but the bullets flew at random and did not come near him.

Harry did not stop until he was two or three miles from the fort, when he knew that he was safe from anything but a chance meeting with the Northern troops. Then he lay down under a big tree and panted. But his breathing soon became easy, and, rising, he examined the region. He always had a good idea of locality, and soon he found the road by which the Invincibles had come. No one could mistake the tracks made by the cannon wheels. He would retrace his steps on that road as fast as he could. He saw that it was useless now to look for the men with the horses. Fear of capture had compelled them to move long since, and a search would merely waste time.

He tightened his belt, squared his shoulders, and bending a little forward, ran at a long, easy gait along the trail. He was a strong and enduring youth, trained to the woods and hills, and, with occasional stops for rest, he knew that he could continue until he reached the camp at Manassas. He wondered if the others had got through. He hoped they had, but he was still anxious to be the first who should reach Beauregard, an ambition not unworthy on the part of youth.

He stopped after midnight for a longer rest than usual. Colonel Talbot, at the last moment, had made him take a small knapsack with some food in it, and now he was grateful for his commander's foresight. He ate, drank from a tiny brook that he heard trickling among the trees, and felt as if he had been made anew. He wisely protracted this stop to half an hour and then he went forward at an increased gait.

His flight, save for short rests, continued without interruption until morning. Always he looked about for a horse, intending in such an emergency to take a horse by force and gallop to Beauregard. But the country was populated very thinly and he saw none. He must continue to rely upon his own good lungs, strong muscles, and dauntless spirit.

Dawn came, bathing the hills in gray light and unveiling the green of the valleys below. Then the sun showed an edge of red fire in the east, and the full day was at hand. Harry saw below him many horsemen in smooth array. They seemed to have just started, as a huge campfire a little further up the valley was still burning.

To the weary and anxious boy it seemed a most gallant command, fresh as the dawn, splendid horses, splendid men, overflowing with life and strength and spirits. His eyes traveled to one who was a little in advance of all the others, and rested there. The figure that held his gaze was scarcely modern, it was more like that of a knight of old romance.

He saw a young man, tall, and built very powerfully, riding upon an immense black horse. His hair and beard were long and thick, of a golden brown that looked like pure flowing gold in the brilliant rays of the young sun. His coat had two rows of shining brass buttons down the front, and was sewn thickly with gold braid. Heavy gold braid covered the seams of his trousers and a great sash of yellow silk was tied around his waist. Spurs of gold gleamed in the sun. Long yellow gloves covered his hands. His hat was of the finest felt, the brim pinned back with a golden star, while a black ostrich plume waved over the crown.

Harry gazed at this singular and striking figure with wonder. He had seen in the pictures knights of old France wearing such a garb as this, and yet it did not seem so strange here. These were strange times. Everything was out of the normal, and the brilliant colors which would have seemed so dandyish to him at other times appealed to him now.

He suddenly recalled that these men were in gray uniforms, and he, too, wore a gray uniform. They were his own people, cavalry of the Southern army. Recovering his presence of mind, he ran forward, shouting and waving his hands. The leader was the first to notice him and gave the order to halt. The whole command stopped with beautiful precision, the ranks remaining even. Then the leader, looking more than ever like a mediaeval knight, rode slowly forward on his great black horse to meet the youth who was running to meet him.

James Ewell Brown Stuart[69]

When Harry came near he saw that the man was young, under thirty. He gazed steadily at the boy out of deep blue eyes, and his hair and beard rippled like molten gold under the light breeze.

"Who are you?" he asked.

"My name is Kenton, Henry Kenton, and I am a lieutenant in the regiment of the Invincibles, commanded by Colonel Leonidas Talbot! We were sent to take a fort on the other side of the mountain and took it, but the regiment is besieged there by a much larger Northern force, and I came through in the night for help."

The man stroked his golden beard and a light leaped up in his eye. Any dandyish or foppish quality that he might have seemed to have disappeared at once, and Harry saw only the soldier.

"Ah, I have heard of this expedition," he said, "and so the Invincibles are in a trap. We had started on another errand, but we will go to the relief of Colonel Talbot. My name is Stuart, lad, J. E. B. Stuart, and this is my command."

It was Harry's first meeting with the famous Jeb Stuart, the most picturesque of all the Southern cavalry leaders, although not superior to the illiterate man of genius, Forrest. Stuart inspired supreme confidence in him. His manner, the very brilliancy of his clothes, seemed to say that here was one who would dare anything.

"We have some extra horses," said Stuart, "you shall mount one and guide us."

"The country is very difficult for cavalry," said Harry. "The slopes are steep and are wooded heavily."

"For ordinary cavalry, yes," replied Stuart, proudly, "but these horsemen of mine can go anywhere. But we will not rely upon cavalry alone. I will send two men at full speed to the main army for infantry reinforcements. Meanwhile, we will hurry forward."

Mounted on a good horse, Harry felt like a new being, and his spirits rose rapidly as the whole troop set off at a swift pace. He rode by the side of Stuart, who asked him many questions. Harry saw that he was not only brilliant and dashing, but thorough. He was planning to relieve Colonel Talbot, but he had no intention of dashing into a trap.

Soon they were deep in the hills and here they picked up a weary youth, dodging about among the trees. It was St. Clair. He had run the gauntlet, but he had been pursued so hotly that he had been forced to lie hidden in the forest a long time. He had made his uniform look as spruce as possible and he held himself with dignity when the horsemen approached, but he could not conceal the fact that he was exhausted.

"I congratulate you, Harry," he said, when he also was astride a horse. "It is likely that you are the only one who has got through so far. I'm quite sure that Langdon was driven back, and I don't know what has become of the others. But it was great luck to find such a command as this."

He looked somewhat enviously at Jeb Stuart's magnificent raiment, and again pulled and brushed at his own.

"You cannot expect to equal it," said Harry, smiling.

"Not unless my opportunities improve greatly. I must say, also, that the colors are a little too bright for me, although they suit him. Everything must be in harmony, Harry, and it is certainly true of Stuart and his uniform that they are in perfect accord. Good clothes, Harry, give one courage and backbone."

Confederate Cavalry, 1st Virginia[70]

Stuart and his men continued to advance rapidly, although they were now deep in the hills, and Harry realized to the full that it was a splendid command, splendid men, and splendid horses, led by a cavalryman of genius. Stuart neglected no precaution. He sent scouts ahead and threw out flankers. When they reached the forest the ranks opened out, and, without losing touch, a thousand men rode among the trees as easily as they had ridden in the open fields.

They reached the crest of the last slope and Stuart, sitting his horse with Harry and St. Clair on either side, looked through his glasses at the valley below.

"Our people still hold it," he said. "I can see their gray uniforms and I have no doubt the besiegers are still in the forest. Yes, there's their signal!"

The heavy report of a cannon shot rolled up the valley and Harry saw a shell burst over the fort. Carrington was still at work, playing upon the nerves of the defenders.

"While we have ridden through the forest," said Stuart, "a cavalry charge here is not possible. We must dismount, leaving one man in every ten to hold the horses, signal to Colonel Talbot that help has come, and then attack on foot."

A bugler advanced on horseback at Stuart's command, blew a long and thrilling call, and then another man beside him broke out an immense Confederate flag.

"They see us in the fort and recognize us," said Stuart. "Hark to the cheer!"

The faint sound of many voices in unison came up from the valley, and Harry knew it to be the Invincibles expressing joy that help had come. The fort then opened with its own guns, and Stuart's dismounted horsemen, who were armed with carbines, advanced through the forest, using the trees for shelter, and attacking the Northern force on the flank. They and the Invincibles together were not strong enough to drive off the enemy, but the heavy skirmishing lasted until the middle of the afternoon, when a whole brigade of infantry came up from the main army. Then the Northern troops retreated slowly and defiantly, carrying with them all their wounded and every gun.

"I've got to take my hat off to the mill hands and mechanics," said St. Clair. "I think, Harry, that if it hadn't been for your skill and luck in getting through we would soon have been living our lives according to their will."

Colonel Talbot congratulated Harry, but his words were few.

"Lad," he said, "you have done well."

Then he and Stuart consulted. Harry, meanwhile, found Langdon, who had been driven back, as St Clair had suspected. He had also sustained a slight wound in the arm, but he was rejoicing over their final success.

"Everything happens for the best," he said. "You might have been driven back, Harry, as I was. You might not have met Stuart. This little wound in my arm might have been a big one in my heart. But none of those things happened. Here I am almost unhurt, and here we are victorious."

"Victorious, perhaps, but without spoils," said St. Clair. "We've got this fort, but we know it will take a big force to keep it. I don't like the way these mill hands and mechanics fight. They hang on too long. After we drove them out of the fort they ought to have retreated up the valley and left us in peace. If they act this way when they're raw, what'll they do when they are seasoned?"

After the conference with Colonel Talbot, Stuart and his cavalry pursued the Northern force up the valley, not for attack, but for observation. Stuart came back at nightfall and reported that their retreat was covered by the heavy guns, and, if they were attacked with much success, it must be done by at least five thousand men.

"Carrington again," said Colonel Talbot, smiling and rubbing his hands. "You and your horsemen, Stuart, could never get a chance at the Northern recruits, unless you rode first over Carrington's guns. From whatever point you approached their muzzles would be sure to face you."

"The colonel is undoubtedly right about his friend Carrington," said St. Clair to Harry and Langdon. "I guess those guns scared us more than anything else."

Stuart and his command left them about midnight. A brilliant moon and a myriad of stars made the night so bright that Harry saw for a long time the splendid man on the splendid horse, leading his men to some new task. Then he lay down and slept heavily until dawn. They remained in the fort two days longer, and then came an order from Beauregard for them to abandon it, and rejoin the main army. The shifting of forces had now made the place useless to either side, and the Invincibles and their new comrades gladly marched back over the mountain and into the lowlands.

Harry found a letter from his father awaiting him. Colonel Kenton was now in Tennessee, where he had been joined by a large number of recruits from Kentucky. He would have preferred to have his son with him, but he was far from sure of his own movements. The regiment might yet be sent to the east. There was great uncertainty about the western commanders, and the Confederate resistance there had not solidified as it had in the east.

Coffee Boilers; Edwin Forbes[71]

Harry expected prompt action on the Virginia field, but it did not come. The two armies lay facing each other for many days. June deepened and the days grew hot. Off in the mountains to the west there were many skirmishes, with success divided about equally. So far as Harry could tell, these encounters meant nothing. Their own battle at the fort meant nothing, either. The fort was now useless, and the two sides faced each other as before. Some of the Invincibles, however, were gone forever. Harry missed young comrades whom he had learned to like. But in the great stir of war, when one day in its effects counted as ten, their memories faded fast. It was impossible, when a boy was a member of a great army facing another great army, to remember the fallen long. Although the long summer days passed without more fighting, there was something to do every hour. New troops were arriving almost daily and they must be broken in. Entrenchments were dug and abandoned for new entrenchments elsewhere, which were abandoned in their turn for entrenchments yet newer. They moved to successive camps, but meanwhile they became physically tougher and more enduring.

The life in the open air agreed with Harry wonderfully. He had already learned from Colonel Talbot and Lieutenant-Colonel St. Hilaire how to take care of himself, and he and St. Clair and Langdon suffered from none of the diseases to which young soldiers are so susceptible. But the long delays and uncertainties preyed upon them, although they made no complaint except among themselves, and then they showed irony rather than irritation.

"Sleeping out here under the trees is good," said Langdon, "but it isn't like sleeping in the White House at Washington, which, as I told you before, I've chosen as my boarding house for the coming autumn."

"There may be a delay in your plans, Tom," said Harry. "I'd make them flexible if I were you."

"I intend to carry 'em out sooner or later. What's that you're reading, Arthur?"

"A New York newspaper. I won't let you see it, Tom, but I'll read portions of it to you. I'll have to expurgate it or you'd have a rush of blood to the head, you're so excitable. It makes a lot of fun of us. Tells that old joke, 'hay foot, straw foot,' when we drill. Says the Yankees now have three hundred thousand men under the best of commanders, and that the Yankee fleet will soon close up all our ports. Says a belt of steel will be stretched about us."

"Then," said Langdon, "just as soon as they get that belt of steel stretched we'll break it in two in a half dozen places. But go on with those feats of fancy that you're reading from that paper."

"Makes fun of our government. Says McDowell will be in Richmond in a month."

"Just the time that Tom gives himself to get into Washington," interrupted Harry. "But go on."

"Makes fun of our army, too, especially of us South Carolinians. Says we've brought servants along to spread tents for us, load our guns for us, and take care of us generally. Says that even in war we won't work."

"They're right, so far as Tom is concerned," said Harry. "We're going to give him a watch as the laziest man among the Invincibles."

"It's not laziness, it's wisdom," said Langdon. "What's the use of working when you don't have to, especially in a June as hot as this one is? I conserve my energy. Besides, I'm going to take care of myself in ways that you fellows don't know anything about. Watch me."

He took his clasp-knife and dug a little hole in the ground. Then he repeated over it solemnly and slowly:

"God made man and man made money;
God made the bee and the bee made honey;
God made Satan and Satan made sin;
God made a little hole to put the devil in."

"What do you mean by that, Tom?" asked Harry. "I learned it from some fellows over in a Maryland company. It's a charm that the children in that state have to ward off evil. I've a great belief in the instincts of children, and I'm protecting myself against cannon and rifles in the battle that's bound to come. Say, you fellows do it, too. I'm not superstitious, I wouldn't dream of depending on such things, but anyway, a charm don't hurt. Now go ahead; just to oblige me."

Harry and St. Clair dug their holes and repeated the lines. Langdon sighed with relief.

"It won't do any harm and it may do some good," he said.

They were interrupted by an orderly who summoned Harry to Colonel Talbot's tent. The colonel had complimented the boy on his energy and courage in bringing Stuart to his relief, when he was besieged in the fort, and he had also received the official thanks of General Beauregard. Proud of his success, he was anxious for some new duty of an active nature, and he hoped that it was at hand. Langdon and St. Clair looked at him enviously.

"He ought to have sent for us, too," said Langdon. "Colonel Talbot has too high an opinion of you, Harry."

"I've been lucky," said Harry, as he walked lightly away. He found that Colonel Talbot was not alone in his tent. General Beauregard was there also. "You have proved yourself, Lieutenant Kenton," said General Beauregard in flattering and persuasive tones. "You did well in the far south and you performed a great service when you took relief to Colonel Talbot. For that reason we have chosen you for a duty yet more arduous."

Beauregard paused as if he were weighing the effect of his words upon Harry. He had a singular charm of manner when he willed and now he used it all. Colonel Talbot looked keenly at the boy.

"You have shown coolness and judgment," continued Beauregard, "and they are invaluable qualities for such a task as the one we wish you to perform."

"I shall do my best, whatever it is," said Harry, proudly.

"You know that we have spent the month of June here, waiting," continued General Beauregard in those soft, persuasive tones, "and that the fighting, what there is of it, has been going on in the mountains to the west. But this state of affairs cannot endure much longer. We have reason to believe that the Northern advance in great force will soon be made, but we wish to know, meanwhile, what is going on behind their lines, what forces are coming down from Washington, what is the state of their defenses, and any other information that you may obtain. If you can get through their lines you can bring us news which may have vital results."

He paused and looked thoughtfully at the boy. His manner was that of one conferring a great honor, and the impression upon Harry was strong. But he remembered. This was the duty of a spy, or something like it. He recalled Shepard and the risk he ran. Spies die ingloriously. Yet he might do a great service. Beauregard read his mind.

"We ask you to be a scout, not a spy," he said. "You may ride in your own uniform, and, if you are taken, you will merely be a prisoner of war."

Harry's last doubt disappeared.

"I will do my best, sir," he said.

"No one can do more," said Beauregard.

"When do you wish me to start?"

"As soon as you can get ready. How long will that be? Your horse will be provided for you."

"In a half hour."

"Good," said Beauregard. "Now, I will leave you with Colonel Talbot, who will give you a few parting instructions."

He left the tent, but, as he went, gave Harry a strong clasp of the hand.

"Now, my boy," said Colonel Leonidas Talbot, when they were alone in the tent, "I've but little more to say to you. It is an arduous task that you've undertaken, and one full of danger. You must temper courage with caution. You will be of no use to our cause unless you come back. And, Harry, you are your father's son; I want to see you come back for your own sake, too. Good-bye, your horse will be waiting."

Harry quickly made ready. St. Clair and Langdon, burning with curiosity, besieged him with questions, but he merely replied that he was riding on an errand for Colonel Talbot. He did not know when he would come back, but if it should be a long time they must not forget him.

"A long time?" said St. Clair. "A long time, Harry, means that you've got a dangerous mission. We'll wish you safely through it, old fellow."

"And don't forget the charm!" exclaimed Langdon. "Of course I don't believe in such foolishness, I wouldn't think of it for a minute, but, anyway, they don't do any harm. Good-bye and God bless you, Harry."

"The same from me, Harry," said St. Clair.

The strong grip of their hands still thrilled his blood as he rode away. His pass carried him through the Southern lines, and then he went toward the northwest, intending to pass through the hills, and reach the rear of the Northern force. He carried no rifle, and his gray uniform, somewhat faded now, would not attract distant attention. Still, he did not care to be observed even by non-combatants, and he turned his horse into the first stretch of forest that he could reach.

Harry, being young, felt the full importance of his errand, but it was vague in its nature. He was to follow his own judgment and discover what was going on between the

Northern army and Washington, no very great distance. When he was well hidden within the forest he stopped and considered. He might meet Federal scouts on errands like his own, but the horse they had given him was a powerful animal, and he had good weapons in his belt. It was Virginia soil, too, and the people, generally, were in sympathy with the South. He relied upon this fact more than upon any other.

The belt of forest into which he had ridden, ran along the crest of a hill, where the soil evidently had been considered too thin for profitable cultivation. Yet the growth of trees and bushes was heavy, and Harry decided to keep in the middle of it, as long as it continued northward in the direction in which he was going. He found a narrow path among the trees, and with his hand on a pistol butt he rode along it.

He expected to meet someone, but evidently the war had driven away all who used the path, and he continued in a welcome silence and desolation. Coming from an army where he always heard many sounds, this silence impressed him at last. Here in the woods there was a singular peace. The June sun had been hot that year in Virginia, but in the sheltered places the leaves were not burned. A moist, fresh greenness enclosed him and presently he heard the trickle of running water.

He came to a little brook, not more than a foot wide and only two or three inches deep, but running joyfully over its pebbly bottom. Both Harry and his horse drank of the water, which was cold, and then they went with the stream, which followed the slow downward slope of the hill toward the north. After a mile, he turned to the edge of the forest and looked over the valley. He caught his breath at the great panorama of green hills and of armies upon them that was spread out before him. Down there under the southern horizon were the long lines of his own people, and toward Washington, but much nearer to him, were the lines of a detachment of the Northern army. Between, he caught the flash of water from Bull Run, Young's Branch and the lesser streams. Behind the Northern force the sun glinted on a long line of bayonets and he knew that it was made by a regiment marching to join the others. The spectacle, with all the somber aspects of war, softened by the distance, was inspiring. Harry drew a long breath and then another. It was in truth more like a spectacle than war's actuality. He counted five colonial houses, white and pillared, standing among green trees and shrubbery. Smoke was rising from their chimneys, as if the people who lived in them were going about their peaceful occupations.

He turned back into the forest, and rode until he came to its end, two or three miles further on. Here the brook darted down through pasture land to merge its waters finally into those of Bull Run. Harry left it regretfully. It had been a good comrade with its pleasant chatter over the pebbles.

Two miles of open country lay before him, and beyond was another cloak of trees. He decided to ride for the forest, and remain there until dark. He would not then be more than fifteen miles from Washington, and he could make the remaining distance under the cover of darkness. He followed a narrow road between two fields, in one of which he saw a farmer ploughing, an old man, gnarled and knotty, whose mind seemed bent wholly upon his work. He was ploughing young corn, and although he could not keep from seeing Harry, he took no apparent notice of him.

The boy rode on, but the picture of the grim old man ploughing between the two armies lingered with him. The fence enclosing the two fields was high, staked, and ridered, and presently he was glad of it. He beheld on a hill to his right, about a half mile away, four horsemen, and the color of their uniforms was blue. He bent low over his horse that they might not see him, and rode on, the pulses in his temples beating heavily. He was glad that gray was not an assertive color, and he was glad that his own gray had been faded by the hot June sun.

Half way to the protecting wood he saw one of the men on the hill, undoubtedly an officer, put glasses to his eyes. Harry was sure at first that he had been discovered, but the man turned the glasses on Beauregard's camp, and the boy rode on unnoticed, praying that the same luck would attend him in the other half of the distance.

Unidentified Confederate soldier[72]

14. IN WASHINGTON

A quarter of a mile from the forest, the wood ascended considerably, throwing him into relief. He felt some shivers here, as he did not know who might be watching him. Field glasses were ugly things when a man was trying to hide. He glanced at the little group that he had seen on the hill, and he noticed now that the officer with the glasses was looking at him. But Harry was a long distance away, and he had the courage and prudence of mind to keep from falling into a panic. He did not believe that they could tell the color of his uniform at that range, but if he whipped his horse into a gallop, pursuit would certainly come from somewhere.

He rode slowly on, letting his figure sway negligently, and he did not look back again at the group on the hill, where the officer was watching him. But he looked from side to side, fearing that horsemen in blue might appear galloping across the fields. It was a supreme test of nerve and will. More than once he felt an almost irresistible temptation to lash his horse and gallop for the wood as hard as he could. That wood seemed wonderfully deep and dark, fit to hide any fugitive. But it had acquired an extraordinary habit of moving further and further away. He had to exert his will so hard that his hand fairly trembled on his bridle rein. Yet he remained master of himself, and went on sitting the saddle in the slouchy attitude that he had adopted when he knew himself to be observed.

The wood was only three or four hundred yards away, when far to his left he saw several horsemen appear on a slope, and he was quite sure that their uniforms were blue. The distance to the wood was now so short that the temptation to gallop was powerful, but he still resisted. Pride, too, helped him and he did not increase the pace of his horse a particle. He saw the dark, cool shadow very near now, and he thought he heard one of the new horsemen on his left shout to him. But he would not look around. Preserving appearances to the last, he rode into the forest, and its heavy shadows enveloped him.

He stopped a moment under the trees and wiped the perspiration from his forehead. He was also seized with a violent fit of trembling, but it was over in a half minute, and then turning his horse from the path he rode into the densest part of the forest.

Harry felt an immense relief. He knew that he might be followed, but he did not consider it probable. It was more than likely that he passed for some countryman riding homeward. Martial law had not yet covered all the hills with a network of iron rules. So he rode on boldly, and he noticed with satisfaction that the forest seemed to be extensive and dense. Night, heavy with clouds, was coming, too, and soon he would be so well hidden that only chance would enable an enemy to find him.

In a half hour he stopped and took his bearings as best he could. It seemed to be a wild bit of country. He judged that it was ground cropped too much in early times, and left to grow into wilderness again. He was not likely to find anything in it save a hut or two of charcoal burners. It was a lonely region, very desolate now, with the night birds calling. The clouds grew heavier and he would have been glad of shelter, but he put down the wish, recalling to himself with a sort of fierceness that he was a soldier and must scorn such things. Moreover, it behooved him to make most of his journey in the night, and this forest, which ran almost to Washington, seemed to be provided for his approach.

He had fixed the direction of Washington firmly in his

mind, and having a good idea of location, he kept his horse going at a good walk toward his destination. As his eyes, naturally strong, grew used to the forest, and his horse was sure of foot, they were able to go through the bushes without much trouble. He stopped at intervals to listen for a possible enemy—or friend—but heard nothing except the ordinary sounds of the forest.

By and by a wind rose and blew all the clouds away. A shining moon and a multitude of brilliant stars sprang out. Just then Harry came to a hillock, clear of trees, with the ground dipping down beyond. He rode to the highest point of the hillock and looked toward the east into a vast open world, lighted by the moon and stars. Off there just under the horizon he caught a gleam of white and he knew instinctively what it was. It was the dome of the Capitol in that city which was now the capital of the North alone. It was miles away, but he saw it and his heart thrilled. He forgot, for the moment, that by his own choice it was no longer his own.

Harry sat on his horse and looked a long time at that far white glow, deep down under the horizon. There was the capital of his own country, the real capital. Somehow he could not divest himself of that idea, and he looked until mists and vapors began to float up from the lowlands, and the white gleam was lost behind them. Then he rode on slowly and thoughtfully, trying to think of a plan that would bring rich rewards for the cause for which he was going to fight.

He had discovered something already. He had seen the bayonets of a regiment marching to join the Northern army, and he had no doubt that he would see others. Perhaps they would consider themselves strong enough in a day or two to attack. It was for him to learn. He was back in the forest and he now turned his course more toward the east. By dawn he would be well in the rear of the Northern army, and he must judge then how to act.

But all his calculations were upset by a very simple thing, one of Nature's commonest occurrences—rain. The heavy clouds that had gathered early in the night were gone away merely for a time. Now they came back in battalions, heavier and more numerous than ever. The shining moon and the brilliant stars were blotted out as if they had never been. A strong wind moaned and a cold rain came pouring into his face. The blanket that he carried on his saddle, and which he now wrapped around him, could not protect him. The fierce rain drove through it and he was soaked and shivering. The darkness, too, was so great that he could see only a few yards before him, and he let the horse take his course.

Harry thought grimly that he was indeed well hidden in the forest. He was so well hidden that he was lost even to himself. In all that darkness and rain he could not retain the sense of direction, and he had no idea where he was. He rambled about for hours, now and then trying to find shelter behind massive tree trunks, and, after every failure, going on in the direction in which he thought Washington lay. His shivering became so strong that he was afraid it would turn into a real chill, and he resolved to seek a roof, if the forest should hold such a thing.

73

It was nearly dawn when he saw dimly the outlines of a cabin standing in a tiny clearing. He believed it to be the hut of a charcoal burner, and he was resolved to take any risk for the sake of its roof. He dismounted and beat heavily upon the door with the butt of a pistol. The answer was so long in coming that he began to believe the hut was empty, which would serve his purpose best of all, but at last a voice, thick with sleep, called: "Who's there?"

"I'm lost and I need shelter," Harry replied.

"Wait a minute," returned the voice.

Harry, despite the beat of the rain, heard a shuffling inside, and then, through a crack in the door, he saw a light spring up. He hoped the owner of the voice would hurry. The rain seemed to be beating harder than ever upon him and the cold was in his bones. Then the door was thrown back suddenly and an uncommonly sharp voice shouted:

"Drop the reins! Throw up your hands an' walk in, where I kin see what you are!"

Harry found himself looking into the muzzle of an old-fashioned long-barreled rifle. But the hammer was cocked, and it was held by a pair of large, calloused, and steady hands, belonging to a tall, thin man with powerful shoulders and a bearded face.

There was no help for it. The boy dropped the reins, raised his hands over his head, and walked into the hut, where the rain at least did not reach him. It was a rude place of a single room, with a fire-place at one end, a bed in a corner, a small pine table on which a candle burned, and clothing and dried herbs hanging from hooks on the wall. The man wore only a shirt and trousers, and he looked unkempt and wild, but he was a resolute figure.

"Stand over thar, close to the light, whar I kin see you," he said.

Harry moved over, and the muzzle of the rifle followed him. The man could look down the sights of his rifle and at the same time examine his visitor, which he did with thoroughness.

"Now, then, Johnny Reb," he said, "what are you doin' here this time o' night an' in such weather as this, wakin' honest citizens out o' their beds?"

"Nothing but stand before the muzzle of your rifle."

The man grinned. The answer seemed to appeal to him, and he lowered the weapon, although he did not relax his watchfulness.

"I got the drop on you, Johnny Reb; you're boun' to admit that," he said. "You didn't ketch Seth Perkins nappin'."

"I admit it. But why do you call me Johnny Reb?"

"Because that's what you are. You can't tell much about

the color of a man's coat after it's been through sech a big rain, but I know yourn is gray. I ain't takin' no part in this war. They've got to fight it as best they kin without me. I'm jest an innercent charcoal burner, 'bout the most innercent that ever lived, I guess, but atween you an' me, Johnny Reb, my feelin's lean the way my state, Old Virginny, leans, that is, to the South, which I reckon is lucky fur you."

Harry saw that the man had blue eyes and he saw, too, that they were twinkling. He knew with infallible instinct that he was honest and truthful.

"It's true," he said. "I'm a Southern soldier, and I'm in your hands."

"I see that you trust me, an' I think I kin trust you. Jest you wait 'til I put that hoss o' yourn in the lean-to behind the cabin."

He darted out of the door and returned in a minute shaking the water from his body.

"That hoss feels better already," he said, "an' you will, too, soon. Now, I shet this door, then I kindle up the fire ag'in, then you take off your clothes an' put them an' yo'self afore the blaze. In time you an' your clothes are all dry."

The man's manner was all kindness, and the poor little cabin had become a palace. He blew at the coals, threw on dry pine knots, and in a few minutes the flames roared up the chimney.

Harry took off his wet clothing, hung it on two cane chairs before the fire, and then proceeded to roast himself. Warmth poured back into his body and the cold left his bones. Despite his remonstrances, Perkins took a pot out of his cupboard and made coffee. Harry drank two cups of it, and he knew now that the danger of chill, to be followed by fever, was gone.

"Mr. Perkins," he said at length, "you are an angel."

Perkins laughed.

"Mebbe I air," he said, "but I 'low I don't look like one. Guess ef I went up an' tried to j'in the real angels Gabriel would say, 'Go back, Seth Perkins, an' improve yo'self fur four or five thousand years afore you try to keep comp'ny like ours.' But now, Johnny Reb, sence you're feelin' a heap better you might tell what you wuz tryin' to do, prowlin' roun' in these woods at sech a time."

"I meant to go behind the Yankee army, see what reinforcements were coming up, find out their plans, if I could, and report to our general."

Perkins whistled softly.

"Say," he said, "you look like a boy o' sense. What are you wastin' your time in little things fur? Couldn't you find somethin' bigger an' a heap more dangerous that would stir you up an' give you action?"

Harry laughed.

"I was set to do this task, Mr. Perkins," he said, "and I mean to do it."

"That shows good sperrit, but ef I wuz set to do it I wouldn't. Do you know whar you are an' what's around you, Johnny Reb?"

"No, I don't."

"Wa'al, you're right inside o' the Union lines. The armies o' Patterson an' McDowell hem in all this forest, an' I reckon mebbe it wuz a good thing fur you that the storm came up an' you got past in it. Wuz you expectin', Johnny Reb, to ride right into the Yankee pickets with that Confedrit uniform on?"

"I don't know exactly what I intended to do. I meant to see in the morning. I didn't know I was so far inside their lines."

"You know it now, an' if you're boun' to do what you say you're settin' out to do, then you've got to change clothes. Here, I'll take these an' hide 'em."

He snatched Harry's uniform from the chair, ran up a ladder into a little room under the eaves, and returned with some rough garments under his arm.

"These are my Sunday clothes," he said. "You're pow'ful big fur your years, an' they'll come purty nigh fittin' you. Leastways, they'll fit well enough fur sech times ez these. Now you wear 'em, ef you put any value on your life."

Harry hesitated. He wished to go as a scout, and not as a spy. Clothes could not change a man, but they could change his standing. Yet the words of Perkins were obviously true.

But he would not go back. He must do his task.

"I'll take your clothes on one condition, Mr. Perkins," he said, "you must let me pay for them."

"Will it make you feel better to do so?"

"A great deal better."

"All right, then."

Harry took from his saddle bags the purse which he had removed from his coat pocket when he undressed, and handed a ten dollar gold piece to the charcoal burner.

"What is it?" asked the charcoal burner.

"A gold eagle, ten dollars."

"I've heard of 'em, but it's the first I've ever seed. I'm bound to say I regard that shinin' coin with a pow'ful sight o' respeck. But if I take it I'm makin' three dollars. Them clothes o' mine jest cost seven dollars an' I've wore 'em four times."

"Count the three dollars in for shelter and gratitude and remember, you've made your promise."

Perkins took the coin, bit it, pitched it up two or three times, catching it as it fell, and then put it upon the hearth, where the blaze could gleam upon it.

"It's shorely a shiner," he said, "an' bein' that it's the first I've ever had, I reckon I'll take good care of it. Wait a minute."

He picked up the coin again, ran up the ladder into the dark eaves of the house, and came back without it.

"Now, Johnny Reb," he said, "put on my clothes and see how you feel."

Harry donned the uncouth garb, which fitted fairly well after he had rolled up the trousers a little.

"You'd pass for a farmer," said Perkins. "I fed your hoss when I put him up, an' as soon as the rain's over you kin start ag'in, a sight safer than you wuz when you wore that uniform. Ef you come back this way ag'in I'll give it to you. Now, you'd better take a nap. I'll call you when the rain stops."

Harry felt that he had indeed fallen into the hands of a friend, and stretching himself on a pallet which the charcoal burner spread in front of the fire, he soon fell asleep. He awoke when Perkins shook his shoulder and found that it was dawn.

"The rain's stopped, day's come, an' I guess you'd better be goin'" said the man. "I've got breakfast ready for you, an' I hope, boy, that you'll get through with a whole skin. I said that both sides would have to fight this war without my help, but I don't mind givin' a boy a hand when he needs it."

Washington - balloon view 1861[74]

Harry did not say much, but he was deeply grateful. After breakfast he mounted his horse, received careful directions from Perkins, and rode toward Washington. The whole forest was fresh and green after its heavy bath, and birds, rejoicing in the morning, sang in every bush. Harry's elation returned. Clothes impart a certain quality, and, dressed in a charcoal burner's Sunday best, he began to bear himself like one. He rode in a slouchy manner, and he transferred the pistols from his belt to the large inside pockets of his new coat. As he passed in an hour from the forest into a rolling open country, he saw that Perkins had advised him wisely. Dressed in the Confederate uniform he would certainly have had trouble before he made the first mile.

He saw the camps of troops both to right and left and he knew that these were the flank of the Northern army. Then from the crest of another hill he caught his second view of Washington. The gleam from the dome[2] of the Capitol was

[2] As noted earlier, the capitol's dome was not completed until 1863

much more vivid now, and he saw other white buildings amid the foliage. Since he had become technically a spy through the mere force of circumstances, Harry took a daring resolve. He would enter Washington itself. They were all one people, Yanks and Johnny Rebs, and no one could possibly know that he was from the Southern army. Only one question bothered him. He did not know what to do with the horse.

But he rode briskly ahead, trusting that the problem of the horse would solve itself, and, as he turned a field, several men in blue uniforms rode forward and ordered him to halt. Harry obeyed promptly.

"Where are you going?" asked the leading man, a minor officer.

"To Washin'ton," replied the boy in the uncouth language that he thought fitted his role.

"And what are you going to Washington for?"

"To sell this hoss," replied Harry, on the impulse of the moment. "I raised him myself, but he's too fine fur me to ride, specially when hosses are bringin' sech good prices."

"He is a fine animal," said the officer, looking at him longingly. "Do you want to sell him now?"

Harry shook his head.

"No," he replied. "I'm goin' to make one o' them big bugs in Washin'ton pay fur him an' pay fur him good."

The officer laughed.

"You're not such a simpleton as you look," he said. "You're right. They'll pay you more for him in the capital than I could. Ride on. They may pass you over Long Bridge or they may not. That part of it is not my business."

Harry went forward at a trot, glad enough to leave such dangerous company behind. But he saw that he was now in the very thick of mighty risks. He would encounter a menace at every turn. Had he realized fully the character of his undertaking when he was in the charcoal burner's hut he would have hesitated long. Now, there was nothing to do but go ahead and take his fate, whatever it might be.

Yet his tale of wishing to sell a horse served him well. After a few questions, it passed him by a half dozen interruptions, and he became so bold that he stopped and bought food for his noon-day meal at a little wayside tavern kept by a woman. Three or four countrymen were lounging about and all of them were gossips. But Harry found it worthwhile to listen to their gossip. It was their business to carry vegetables and other provisions into Washington for sale and they picked up much news. They said that the Northern government was pushing all its troops to the front. All the politicians and writers in Washington were clamoring for a battle. One blow and "Jeff Davis and Secession" would be smashed to atoms. Harry's young blood flamed at the contemptuous words, but he could not afford to show any resentment. Yet this was valuable information. He could confirm Beauregard's belief that an attack would soon be made in great force.

When Harry left them he turned again to the left, as he saw a stretch of country rolling and apparently wooded lying in that direction. Once, when a young boy, he had come to Washington with his father for a stay of several weeks, and he had a fair acquaintance with the region about the capital. He knew that forested hills lay ahead of him and beyond them the Potomac.

In another hour he was in the hills, which he found without people. Through every opening in the leaves he saw Washington and he could also discern long lines of redoubts on the Virginia side of the river.

Late in the afternoon he came to a small, abandoned log cabin. He inferred that its owner had moved away because of the war. As nearly as he could judge it had not been occupied for several weeks. Back of it was a small meadow enclosed with a rail fence, but everything else was deep woods. He turned his horse into the meadow and left his saddle, bridle, and saddle blanket in the house. He might not find anything when he returned, but he must take the risk.

Then he set off at a brisk pace through the woods, which opened out a little after dusk, and disclosed a great pillared white house, with surrounding outbuildings. He knew at once that this was Arlington, the home of one of the Southern generals, Lee, of whom he had heard his father speak well.

But he also saw, despite the dusk, blue uniforms and the

gleam of bayonets. And as he looked he saw, too, earthworks and the signs that many men were present. He lay long among the bushes until the night thickened and darkened and he resolved to inspect the earthworks thoroughly. No very strict watch seemed to be kept, and, in truth, it did not seem to be needed here so near to Washington, and so far away from the Southern army.

Before ten o'clock everything settled into quiet, and he cautiously climbed a great beech which was in full and deep foliage. The boughs were so many and the leaves so dense that one standing directly under him could not have seen him. But he went up as far as he could go, and, crouched there, made a comprehensive survey.

It was a fine moonlight night and he saw the earthworks stretching for a long distance, thorough and impregnable to anything except a great army. Beyond that was a silver band which was the Potomac, and beyond the river were the clustered roofs which were Washington. But he turned his eyes back to the earthworks, and he tried to fasten firmly in his mind their number and location. This, too, would be important news, most welcome to Beauregard.

The boy's elation grew. They had given him a delicate and dangerous task, but he was doing it. He had overcome every obstacle so far, and he would overcome them to the end. He was bound to enter that Washington which, in the distance, seemed to lie in such a close cluster.

He felt that he had lingered long enough at Arlington, and, descending, he made a great curve around the earthworks, coming to the river north of Arlington. His next problem was the passage of the Potomac. He did not dare to try Long Bridge, which he knew would be guarded strictly, but he thought he might find some boatman who would take him over. As the capital was so crowded, the farmers were continually crossing with loads of provisions, and now that an uncommonly hot July had come the night would be a favorite time for the passage.

A search up and down the bank brought its reward. A Virginian, who said his name was Grimes, had a heavy boat filled with vegetables, and Harry was welcome as a helper.

"It's a dollar for you," said Grimes, who did not trouble to ask the boy his name, "an' here are your oars."

The two, pulling strongly, shot the boat out into the stream, and then rowed in a diagonal line for the city, which rose up brilliant and great in the moonlight. Other boats were in the river, but they paid no attention to the barge, loaded with produce, and rowed by two innocent countrymen. They soon reached the Washington shore, and Grimes handed Harry a silver dollar.

"You're a strong young fellow," he said, "an' I guess you've earned the money. My farm is only four miles up the river an' thar's goin' to be a big market for all I kin raise. I need a good han' to help me work it. How'd you like to come with me an' take a good job, while them that don't know no better go ahead an' do the fightin'?"

"Thank you for your offer," replied Harry, "but I've got business to attend to in Washington."

He slipped the dollar into his pocket, because he had earned it honestly, and entered Washington, just as the rising sun began to gild domes and roofs. Coming from the boat, his appearance aroused no suspicion. People were pouring into Washington then as they were pouring into the Confederate capital at Richmond. One dressed as he, and looking as he, could enter or depart almost as he pleased, despite the ring of fortifications.

Up went the sun, and the full day came, extremely hot and clear. Harry turned into a little restaurant, and spent half of his well-earned dollar for breakfast. Neither proprietor nor waiter gave him more than a casual glance. Evidently they were used to serving countrymen. Harry, feeling refreshed and strong again, paid for his food and went outside.

The streets were thronged. He had expected nothing else, but there was a great air of excitement and expectancy as if something important were going to happen.

"What is it?" asked Harry of a man beside him.

"Don't you know what day this is?" asked the man.

"I've forgot," replied the boy in the slouchy speech and intonation of the hills. "I jest came in with dad this mornin', bringin' a wagon load of fresh vegetables."

"You look as foolish as you talk," said the man scornfully. "This is the Fourth of July, and the special session of Congress called by President Lincoln is to meet this morning and decide how to give the rebels the thrashing they need."

"I did hear somethin' about that," replied Harry, "but workin' in the field I furgot all about it. I 'low I'll stroll that way."

Washington, St Jarrets hotel[75]

He drifted on with the crowd toward the Capitol, which rose nobler and more imposing than ever, a great marble building, gleaming white in the sunshine. Harry's heart throbbed. He could not yet dissociate himself from the idea that he, as one of the nation, was a part owner of the Capitol. But, forgetting all danger, he persisted in his errand. A great event was about to occur, and he intended to see it.

There were soldiers everywhere. The streets blazed with uniforms, but the people were allowed to gather about the Capitol and many also entered. A friendly sentinel passed Harry, who stood for a few moments in the rotunda. He was careful to keep near other spectators, in order that he might not attract attention to himself.

All things that he saw cut sharply into his sensitive and eager mind. It was in truth an extraordinary situation for one who had come as he had come, and he waited, calm of face, but with every pulse beating. The comments of the other spectators told him who the famous men were as they entered. Here were Cameron and Wade of the lowering brows. There passed Taney, the venerable Chief Justice, and then dry and quiet Hamlin, the Vice-President, on his way to preside over the Senate, went by. A tall and magnificent figure in a general's uniform next attracted Harry's attention. He was an old man, but he held himself very erect and his head was crowned with splendid snowy hair.

Washington, Union troops, before Bull Run, 13 May 1861[76]

"Old Fuss and Feathers," said a man near Harry, and the boy knew that this was General Scott, the Virginian, who had led the famous and victorious march into the City of Mexico, and who was now in name, but in name only, commander of the Northern army. His father had served under him in those memorable battles and Harry looked at him with a certain veneration, as the old man passed on and disappeared in another room. Then came more, some famous and others destined to be so.

The atmosphere of the great building was surcharged. Harry and his comrades had heard that the North was discouraged, that the people would not fight, that they would "let the erring sisters go in peace." It did not seem so to him here. The talk was all of war and of invading the South, and he seemed to feel a tenacious spirit behind it.

He managed to secure entrance to the lobbies of both Senate and House, and he listened for a while to the debates. He discovered the same spirit there. He felt that he had a right to report not only on the forts of Washington and the movements of brigades, but also on the temper in the North. Resolution and tenacity, he now saw, were worth as much as cannon balls.

Harry did not leave the Capitol until the middle of the afternoon, when he drifted back to the restaurant at which he had obtained his breakfast, where he spent the other half of the dollar for luncheon. Then he resolved to escape from Washington that night. He had picked up by casual talk and observation together a fair knowledge of Washington's defenses. Above all he had learned that the North was pouring troops in an unbroken stream into the capital, and that the great advance on the line of Bull Run would take place very soon. He could scarcely expect to achieve more; he had already surpassed his hopes, and it was surely time to go.

He left the restaurant. The streets were still crowded, and he saw standing at the nearest corner a figure that seemed familiar. He took a long look, and then he was shaken with alarm. It was Shepard. He had seen him under such tense conditions that he could never forget the man. The turn of his shoulders, the movement of his head—all were familiar. And Harry had a great respect for the keenness and intelligence of Shepard. He could not forget how Shepard had talked to him that night in Montgomery. There was something uncanny about the man, and he had a sudden conviction that Shepard had seen him long since and was watching him. He thrust his hands into his capacious pockets. The pistols were still there, and he resolved that he would use them if need be.

He went at first toward the Potomac, and he did not look back for a long time, rambling about the streets in a manner apparently aimless. Now and then a quiver ran down his back, and he knew it was due to the mental fear that Shepard was pursuing. When he did look back at last he did not see him, and he felt immediate elation. It would not be long now until dark, and then he would make his escape across the river.

Time was slow, but it could not keep darkness back forever, and, as soon as it had come fully, he turned toward the north. Southern troops would not be looked for there, and egress would be easier in that direction. He passed on without interruption and soon was in the suburbs, which were then so shabby. Then he looked back, and cold fear plucked at the roots of his hair. A man was following him, and he could tell even in the dim light that it was Shepard.

A shudder shook him now. A rope was the fate for a spy. But he recovered himself and walked on faster than ever. The cabins thinned away, and he saw before him bushes. His keen hearing brought to him the soft sound of the pursuing footsteps. Now he took his resolution. There were few games at which two could not play.

He passed between two bushes, came around, and returned to the open. But he returned with one of the pistols cocked and levelled, his finger on the trigger. Shepard, pursuing swiftly, walked almost against the muzzle, and Harry laughed softly.

"Well, Mr. Shepard," he said, "you've followed me well, but as I've no mind to be hung for a spy or anything else, I must ask you to go back."

"You have the advantage at present, it is true," said Shepard, "but what makes you think I was going to shoot at you or have you seized?"

"Isn't it what one would naturally expect?"

"Yes—perhaps. But I could have given the alarm while you were still in the city. I speak the truth when I say I do not know just what I had in mind. But at all events the tables are turned. You hold me at the pistol's muzzle and I admit it."

He smiled and the boy could not keep from liking him.

"Mr. Shepard," said Harry, "what you told me at Montgomery was true. We of the South did not realize the numbers, power, and spirit of the North. I know now the truth of what you told me, but, on the other hand, you of the North do not realize the fire, courage, and devotion of the South."

"I understand it, but I'm afraid that not many of our people do so. Suppose we call it quits once more. Let this be Montgomery over again. You do not want to shoot me here anymore than I wanted to shoot you down there."

"I admit that also," said Harry.

"Then you are safe from me, if I'm safe from you."

"Agreed," said Harry, as he lowered the weapon.

"Good-bye," said Shepard.

"Good-bye."

But they did not offer to shake hands. Each turned his back on the other, and, when Harry stopped in the bushes, he saw only the dim outlines of Washington. At midnight he found a colored man who, for pay, rowed him across the Potomac. At dawn he found his horse peacefully grazing in the meadow, and at the next dawn he was once more within the southern lines.

Unidentified Confederate soldier, Virginia Volunteers[77]

15. BATTLE'S EVE

Harry found little change in the Southern army, except that more troops had come up from Richmond. It still rested upon Bull Run. The country here was old, having been cropped for many generations, the soil mostly clay and cut in deep ruts. There were many ravines and water courses, and hillocks were numerous. Colonel Talbot had told Harry a month before that it was not a bad place for a battle ground, and he remembered it now as he came back to it. He had not taken the time to return to the charcoal burner's hut for his uniform, and, when he approached his own lines he still wore the Sunday best of Perkins.

The sentinel who hailed him first doubted his claim that he was a member of the Invincibles, but he insisted so urgently, and called all its officers by name so readily that he was passed on. He dismounted, gave his horse to an orderly, and walked toward a clump of trees where he saw Colonel Talbot writing at a small table in the open. The colonel, engrossed in his work, did not look up, as the boy's footsteps made little sound on the turf. When Harry stood before him he saluted and said:

"I have returned to make my report, Colonel Talbot."

The colonel looked up, uttered a cry of pleasure, and seized Harry by both hands.

"Thank God, you've come back, my boy!" he said. "I hesitated to send your father's son on such an errand, but I thought that you would succeed. You have seen the enemy's forces?"

An Orderly; Edwin Forbes[78]

"I've been in Washington, itself," said Harry, some pride showing in his voice.

"Then we'll go at once to General Beauregard. He is in his tent now, conferring with some of his chief officers."

A great marquée stood in the shade of a grove, only two or three hundred yards away. Its sides were open, as the heat was great, and Harry saw the commander-in-chief within, talking earnestly with men in the uniform of generals. Longstreet, Early, Hill, and others were there. Harry was somewhat abashed, but he had the moral support of Colonel Talbot, and, after the first few moments of embarrassment, he told his story in a direct and incisive manner. The officers listened with attention.

"It confirms the other reports," said Beauregard.

"It goes further," said Longstreet. "Our young friend here is obviously a lad of intelligence and discernment and what he saw in Washington shows that the North is resolved to crush us. The battle that we are going to fight will not be the last battle by any means."

"Each side is too sanguine," said Hill.

"You have done well, Lieutenant Kenton," said Beauregard, "and now you can rejoin your regiment. You are to receive a promotion of one grade."

Harry was glad to leave the marquée and hurry toward the camp of the Invincibles. The first of his friends whom he saw was Happy Tom Langdon, bathing his face in a little stream that flowed into Young's Branch. He walked up and smote him joyously on the back. Langdon sprang to his feet in anger and exclaimed:

"Hey, you fellow, what do you mean by that?"

He saw before him a tall, gawky youth in ill-fitting clothes, his face a mask of dust. But this same dusty youth grinned and replied:

"I hit you once, and if you don't speak to me more politely I'll hit you twice."

Langdon stared. Then recognition came.

"Harry Kenton, by all that's wonderful!" he exclaimed. "And so you've come back! I was afraid you never would! What have you been doing, Harry?"

"I've been pretty busy. I drove in the right wing of the Yankee army, put to flight a couple of brigades in their center, then I went on to Washington and had a talk with Lincoln. I told him the North would have me to reckon with if he kept on with this war, but he said he believed he'd go ahead anyhow. I even mentioned your name to him, but the menace did no good."

Langdon called to St. Clair and soon Harry was surrounded by friends who gave him the warmest of greetings and who insisted upon the tale of his adventures, a part of which he was free to tell. Then a new uniform was brought to him, and, after a long and refreshing bath in a deep pool of the stream, he put it on. He felt now as if he had been entirely made over, and, as he strolled back to camp, a tall, thin man, black of hair and pallid of face, hailed him.

Harry took two glances before he recognized Arthur Travers in the Southern uniform. Then he grasped his hand eagerly and asked him when he had come.

"Only two days ago," replied Travers. "I'm in another regiment farther along Bull Run. I merely came over here to tell you that your father was well when I last heard from him. He is with the Western forces that are to be under Albert Sidney Johnston."

Harry did not care greatly for Travers, but it was pleasant to see anybody from the old home, and they talked some time. But Harry did not see him again soon, as the bonds of discipline were now tightened. Regiments were kept in ranks and the men were not permitted to wander from their places. Northern bands were continually in their front, and it was reported daily that the great army at Washington was about to move.

Yet the days passed, and no important event occurred. July advanced. The heat became more intense. The fields were bare, the vegetation trodden out by armies, and, when the wind rose, clouds of dust beat upon them. It was lucky for them that the country was cut by so many streams.

The Invincibles were moved about several times, but they stopped at last at a little plateau where a branch railroad joined the main stem, giving to the place the name Manassas Junction. Bull Run was near, flowing between high banks, but with crossings at two fords and two bridges. Beauregard had thrown up earthworks at the station, and strong batteries were hidden in the foliage at the fords. The Southern army, weary of waiting, was eager for battle. The Northern people, also weary of waiting, demanded that their own troops advance.

Confederate battery marches to the First Battle of Bull Run[79]

As Harry sat with his friends one hot night the word was passed that the Northern army was coming at last. The Southern scouts had reported that McDowell's whole force was already on the march and was drawing near. It would attempt the passage of Bull Run. A murmur ran through the camp of the Invincibles, but there was little talk. They had already tasted of battle at the fort in the valley, and it was not a thing to be taken lightly.

Harry resolved that he would sleep if he could, but there was no rest for the Invincibles just then. An order came from Beauregard, and, with Colonel Talbot at their head, they took up their arms, marching to one of the fords of Bull Run, where they lay down among trees near a battery. They were forbidden to talk, but they whispered, nevertheless. The ford before them was Blackburn's, and the heavy attack of the Northern army would be made there in the morning.

Harry and the Invincibles were at the very edge of the river. They had been under heavy fire before, but, nevertheless, everything they now saw or heard played upon their nerves. The murmur of the little river was multiplied thrice. Every time a bayonet or a saber rattled it smote with sharpness upon the ear. The neigh of a horse became a fierce, lingering note, and out of the darkness that covered the rolling country in front of them came many sounds, but few of which were real.

For a long time there was movement on their own side of the stream. Troops were continually coming up in the night and taking position. It required no acute mind to perceive that the Southern commander expected the main attack to be made here, and was massing his troops in force to receive it. Except at the ford itself the banks of the river were high, but those on the Northern side were higher. A skirt of forest lined the Southern bank, and Harry saw Longstreet and his men march into it, and lie there on their arms. Nearer to him among the trees were the powerful batteries of artillery. Beauregard himself had come and he now had with him seven brigades eager for the attack.

Fording a river; Edwin Forbes[80]

The night was hot and windless, save at distant intervals, when a slight breeze blew from the North. Then it brought dust with it, and Harry believed that it came from the dry soil, trod to powder by the marching feet of a great army, and the wheels of many cannon.

Comparative silence came after a while on his own side of the river. There was no sharp sound, only a low and almost continuous murmur made by the whispering, and restless movements which so many thousands of men could not avoid. But the sound was so steady that they heard above it the croak of frogs at the edge of the stream, and then another sound which Harry at first did not understand.

"What is it?" he whispered to St. Clair, who lay a little higher than he.

"It's a lot of our men crossing the ford. Raise up and you can see them walking in the water. I take it that the general is going to put a force in the bushes and trees on the other bank to sting the Northern army good and hard before it pushes home the main attack."

Standing up Harry saw men wading Bull Run in a long file, every one carrying a rifle on his shoulder. In the hot dim night they looked like lines of Indians advancing through the water to choose an ambush. They were crossing for half an hour, and then they melted away. He could not see one of the figures again, nor did any sound come from them, but he knew that the riflemen lay there in the bushes, and that many a man would fall before they waded Bull Run again.

"Do you think the attack is really coming this time?" whispered Langdon.

"I feel sure of it," replied Harry. "All the scouts have said so and you may laugh at me, Tom, but I tell you that when the wind blows our way I feel the dust raised by thirty thousand men marching toward us."

"I'm not laughing at you, Harry. Sometimes that instinct of yours tells when things are coming long before you can see or hear 'em. But while I'm no such wonder myself I can hear those bullfrogs croaking down there at the edge of the water. Think of their cheek, calmly singing their night songs between two armies of twenty or thirty thousand men each, who are going to fight tomorrow."

"But it's not their fight," said St. Clair, "and maybe they are croaking for a lot of us."

"Shut up, you bird of ill omen, you raven, you," said Happy Tom. "Everything is going to happen for the best, we are going to win the victory, and we three are going to come out of the battle all right."

St. Clair did not answer him. His was a serious nature and he foresaw a great struggle which would waver long in doubt. Harry had lain down on his blanket and was seeking sleep again.

"Stop talking," he said to the other two. "We've got to go to sleep if it's only for the sake of our nerves. We must be fresh and steady when we go into the battle in the morning."

"I suppose you are right," said Happy Tom, "but I find this overtaking slumber a long chase. Maybe you can form a habit of sleeping well before big battles, but I haven't had the chance to do so yet."

Harry did fall asleep after a while, but he awoke before dawn to find that there was already bustle and movement in the army about him. Fires were lighted further back, and an early but plentiful breakfast was cooked. All were up and ready when the sun rose over the Virginia fields.

"Another hot day," said Happy Tom. "See, the sun is as red as fire! And look how it burns on the water there."

"Yes, hot it will be," Harry said to himself. They had eaten their breakfast and lay once more among the trees. Harry searched with his eyes the bushes and thickets on the other side for their riflemen, but most of them were still invisible in the day. Then the Southern brigades were ordered to lie down, but after they lay there some time Harry felt that the film of dust on the edge of the wind was growing stronger, and presently they saw a great cloud of it rising above hills and trees and moving toward them.

"They're coming," said St. Clair. "In less than a half hour they'll be at the ford."

"But I doubt if they know what is waiting for them," said Harry.

The cloud of dust rapidly came nearer, and now they heard the beat of horses' feet and the clank of artillery. Harry began to breathe hard, and he and the other young officers walked up and down the lines of their company. All the Invincibles clearly saw that great plume of dust, and heard the ominous sounds that came with it. It was very near now, but suddenly the fringe of forest on the far side of the river burst into flame. The hidden riflemen had opened fire and were burning the front of the advancing army.

But the Northern men came steadily on, rousing the riflemen out of the bushes, and then they appeared among the trees on the north side of Bull Run—a New York brigade led by Tyler. The moment their faces showed there was a tremendous discharge from the Southern batteries masked in the wood. The crash was appalling, and Harry shut his eyes for a moment, in horror, as he saw the entire front rank of the Northern force go down. Then the Southern sharpshooters in hundreds, who lined the water's edge, opened with the rifle, and a storm of lead crashed into the ranks of the hapless New Yorkers.

"Up, Invincibles!" cried Colonel Talbot, and they began to fire, and load, and fire again into the attacking force which had walked into what was almost an ambush.

"They'll never reach the ford!" shouted Happy Tom.

"Never!" Harry shouted back.

The Southern generals, already trained in battles, pushed their advantages. A great force of Southern sharpshooters crossed the river and took the Northern brigade in flank. The New Yorkers, unable to stand the tremendous artillery and rifle fire in their front, and the new rifle fire on their side also, broke and retreated. But another brigade came up to their relief and they advanced again, sending a heavy return fire from their rifles, while the artillery on their flank replied to that of the South.

The combat now became fierce. The Invincibles in the very thick of it advanced to the water's edge, and fired as fast as they could load and reload. Huge volumes of smoke gathered over both sides of Bull Run, and men fell fast. There was also a rain of twigs and boughs as the bullets and shells cut them through, and the dense, heated air, shot through with smoke, burned the throats of blue and gray.

But the South had the advantage of position and numbers. Moreover, those riflemen on the flanks of the Northern troops burned them terribly and they were weary, too, with long marching in dust and heat. As the artillery and rifle fire converged upon them and became heavier and heavier they were forced to give way. They yielded ground slowly, until they were beyond range of the cannon, and then, brushing off the fierce swarm of sharpshooters on their flank, they retreated all the way back to the village, whence they had come.

The firing on the Southern side of Bull Run ceased suddenly, and the smoke began to drift away. The Invincibles, save those who had fallen to stay, stood up and shouted. They had won the greatest victory in the world, and they flung taunts in the direction of the retreating foe.

"Stop that!" shouted Colonel Talbot, striding up and down the line. "This is only a beginning. Wait until we have a real battle."

"This has happened for the best," said Happy Tom, "but I'd like to know what the colonel calls a real battle. The fire was so loud I couldn't hear myself speak, and I know at least a million men were engaged. Arthur, how can you be cool enough to bathe your face in that water?"

"It's to make it cool," replied St. Clair, who had stooped over Bull Run, and was laving his face. "I feel that dust and burned gunpowder are thick all over me."

He stood up, his face now clean, and began to arrange his uniform. Then he carefully dusted his coat and trousers.

"Hope you are all ready for another battle, Arthur," said Tom.

"Not yet," replied St. Clair laughing. "That will do me for quite a while."

St. Clair had his wish. The enemy seemed to have enough for the time. The hot, breathless day passed without any further advance. Now and then they heard the Northern bugles, and the scouts reported that the foe was still gathering heavily not far away, but the Invincibles, from their camp, saw nothing.

"I suppose the colonel was right," said Happy Tom, "and this must have been a sort of prologue. But if the prologue was so hot what's the play going to be?"

"Something hotter," said Harry.

"A vague but true answer," said Langdon.

Yet the delay was long. They lay all that day and all that night along the banks of Bull Run, and a hundred conflicting reports ran up and down their ranks. The Northern army would retreat, it would attack within a few hours; the Southern army would retreat, it would hold its present position; both sides would receive reinforcements, neither would receive any fresh troops. Every statement was immediately denied.

"I refuse to believe anything until it happens," said Harry, when night came. "I'm getting hardened to this sort of thing, and as soon as my time off duty comes I'm going to sleep."

Sleep he did in the shot-torn woods, and it was the heavy sleep of exhaustion. Nerves did not trouble him, as he slept without dreams and rose to another windless, burning day. The hours dragged on again, but in the night there was a tremendous shouting. Johnston, with eight thousand men, had slipped away from Patterson in the mountains, and the infantry had come by train directly to the plateau of Manassas, where they were now leaving the cars and taking their place in the line of battle. The artillery and cavalry were coming on behind over the dirt road. The Southern generals were already showing the energy and decision for which they were so remarkable in the first years of the war. Johnston was the senior, but since Beauregard had made the battlefield, he left him in command.

Flight of former slaves and Union soldiers from Hampton, Virginia, to Fort Monroe, Summer 1861 (after Bull Run)[81]

The Invincibles were moved off to the left along Bull Run, and were posted in front of a stone bridge, where other troops gathered, until twelve or thirteen thousand men were there. But Harry and his comrades were nearest to the bridge, and it seemed to him that the situation was almost exactly as it had been three nights before. Again they faced Bull Run and again they expected an attack in the morning. There was no change save the difference between a ford and a bridge. But the Invincibles, hardened by the three days of skirmishing and waiting, took things more easily now.

They lay in the woods near the steep banks, and the batteries commanded the entrance to the bridge. The night was once more hot and windless and they were so quiet that they could hear the murmur of the waters. Far across Bull Run they saw dim lights moving, and they knew that they were those of the Northern army.

"I think things have changed a lot in the last three days," said Harry. "Then the Yankees didn't know much about us. They charged almost blindfolded into our ambush. Now we don't know much about them. We don't know by any means where the attack is coming. It is they who are keeping us guessing."

"But there are only two fords and two bridges across Bull Run," said Langdon, "and they have got to choose one out of the lot."

"Which means that we've got to accumulate our forces at some one of four places, one guess out of four."

Harry did not speak at all in a tone of discouragement, but his intelligent mind saw that the Northern leaders had profited by their mistakes and that the Southern general did not really know where the great impact would come. The Northern scouts and skirmishers swarmed on the other side of Bull Run, and even in the darkness this cloud of wasps was so dense that Beauregard's own scouts could not get beyond them and tell what the greater mass behind was doing. Harry was summoned at midnight by Colonel Talbot. Behind a clump of trees some distance back of the bridge, Beauregard, Johnston, Evans, who was in direct command at the ford, Early, and several other important officers were in anxious consultation. Colonel Talbot told Harry that he would be wanted presently as a messenger, and he stood on one side while the others talked. It was then that he first heard Jubal Early swear with a richness, a spontaneity, and an unction that raised it almost to the dignity of a rite.

Harry gathered that they could not agree as to the point at

which the Northern attack would be delivered, but the balance of opinion inclined to the bridge, before which the command of Evans was encamped. Hence he was sent farther down the stream, with a message for a North Carolina regiment to move up and join Evans.

The regiment lay about a mile away, but Harry walked almost the whole distance among sleeping men. They lay on the grass by thousands, and exhausted by the movement and marching of recent days they slept heavily. In the moonlight they looked as if they were dead. It was so quiet now that some night birds in the trees uttered strange moaning cries. But far across Bull Run lights still moved and Harry had no doubt that the great battle, delayed so long, was really coming in the morning.

Joseph E Johnston HQ at the 1st Battle of Bull Run[82]

The North Carolina regiment rose sleepily and marched with him to the bridge, where it was incorporated into the force of Evans. Beauregard, Johnston and Early had gone to other points, and Harry knew that they were still anxious and of divided opinions. Colonel Talbot and Lieutenant-Colonel St. Hilaire, to whom he had to report, and who moved their own regiment down near Evans, did not conceal the fact from him.

"Harry," said the colonel, "we're all sure that we'll have to fight on the morrow, and it looks as if the battle would come in the greatest weight here at the bridge, but the Invincibles must be prepared for anything. You lads are fit and trim, and I hope that all of you will do your duty tomorrow. Remember that we have brave foes before us, and I know most of their officers. All who are of our age have been the comrades of Lieutenant-Colonel St. Hilaire and myself."

"It is true, and it is a melancholy phase of this war," said Hector St. Hilaire.

They walked away together and Harry rejoined those of his own age near the banks of Bull Run. But Langdon and St. Clair were sound asleep on their blankets, and so were all the rest of the Invincibles, save those who had been posted as sentinels. But Harry did not sleep that night. It was past midnight now, but he was never more awake in his life, and he felt that he must watch until day.

He had no duties to do, and he sat down with his back to a tree and waited. Far in his front, three or four miles, perhaps, he thought he saw lights signaling to each other, but he had no idea what they meant, and he watched them merely with an idle curiosity. Once he thought he heard the distant call of a trumpet, but he was not sure. Woods and fields were flooded with the brightness of moon and stars, but if anything was passing on the other side of Bull Run, it was too well hidden for him to see it. His senses were soothed and he sank into a state of peace and rest. In reality it was a physical relaxation coming after so much tension and activity, and the bodily ease became mental also.

Resting thus, motionless against the trunk of the tree, time passed easily for him. The warm air of the night blew now and then against his face and only soothed him to deeper rest. The last light far across Bull Run went out and the darker hours came. Nothing stirred now in the woods until the hot dawn came again, and the brazen sun leaped up in the sky.

Unidentified Confederate soldier, Virginia Militia[83]

16. BULL RUN

Harry rose to his feet and shook St. Clair and Langdon.

"Up, boys!" he said. "The enemy will soon be here. I can see their bayonets glittering on the hills."

The Invincibles sprang to their feet almost as one man, and soon all the troops of Evans were up and humming like bees. Food and coffee were served to them hastily, but, before the last cup was thrown down, a heavy crash came from one of the hills beyond Bull Run, and a shell, screaming over their heads, burst beyond them. It was quickly followed by another, and then the round shot and shells came in dozens from batteries which had been posted well in the night.

The Southern batteries replied with all their might and the riflemen supported them, sending the bullets in sheets across Bull Run. The battle flamed in fifteen minutes into extraordinary violence. Harry had never before heard such a continuous and terrific thunder. It seemed that the drums of his ears would be smashed in, but over his head he heard the continuous hissing and whirring of steel and lead. The Northern riflemen were at work, too, and it was fortunate for the Invincibles that they were able to lie down, as they poured their fire into the bushes and woods on the opposite bank.

The volume of smoke was so great that they could no longer see the position of the enemy, but Harry believed that so much metal must do great damage. Although he was a lieutenant he had snatched up a rifle dropped by some fallen soldier, and he loaded and fired it so often that the barrel grew hot to his hand. Lying so near the river, most of the hostile fire went over the heads of the Invincibles, but now and then a shell or a cluster of bullets struck among them, and Harry heard groans. But he quickly forgot these sounds as he watched the clouds of smoke and the blaze of fire on the other side of Bull Run.

"They are not trying to force the passage of the bridge! Everything is for the best!" shouted Langdon.

"No, they dare not," shouted St. Clair in reply. "No column could live on that bridge in face of our fire."

It seemed strange to Harry that the Northern troops made no attempt to cross. Why did all this tremendous fire go on so long, and yet not a foe set foot upon the bridge? It seemed to him that it had endured for hours. The sun was rising higher and higher and the day was growing hotter and hotter. It lay with the North to make the first movement to cross Bull Run, and yet no attempt was made.

Colonel Talbot came repeatedly along the line of the Invincibles, and Harry saw that he was growing uneasy. Such a great volume of fire, without any effort to take advantage of it, made the veteran suspicious. He knew that those old comrades of his on the other side of Bull Run would not waste their metal in a mere cannonade and long range rifle fire. There must be something behind it. Presently, with the consent of the commander, he drew the Invincibles back from the river, where they were permitted to cease firing, and to rest for a while on their arms.

But as they drew long breaths and tried to clear the smoke from their throats, a rumor ran down the lines. The attack at the bridge was but a feint. Only a minor portion of the hostile army was there. The greater mass had gone on and had already crossed the river in face of the weak left flank of the Southern army. Beauregard had been outwitted. The Yankees were now in great force on his own side of Bull Run, and it would be a pitched battle, face to face.

The whole line of the Invincibles quivered with

excitement, and then Harry saw that the rumor was true, or that their commander at least believed it to be so. The firing stopped entirely and the bugles blew the retreat. All the brigades gathered themselves up and, wild with anger and chagrin, slowly withdrew.

"Why are we retreating?" exclaimed Langdon, angrily. "Not a Yankee set his foot on the bridge! We're not whipped!"

"No," said Harry, "we're not whipped, but if we don't retreat we will be. If fifteen or twenty thousand Yankees struck us on the flank while those fellows are still in front everything would go."

Union advance at Bull Run, 2:00 p.m. 21 July 1861[84]

These were young troops, who considered a retreat equivalent to a beating, and fierce murmurs ran along the line. But the officers paid no attention, marching them steadily on, while the artillery rumbled by their side. Both to right and left they heard the sound of firing, and they saw the smoke floating against both horizons, but they paid little attention to it. They were wondering what was in store for them.

"Cheer up, you lads!" cried Colonel Talbot. "You'll get all the fighting you can stand, and it won't be long in coming, either."

They marched only half an hour and then the troops were drawn up on a hill, where the officers rapidly formed them into position. It was none too soon. A long blue line, bristling with cannon on either flank, appeared across the fields. It was Burnside with the bulk of the Northern army moving down upon them. Harry was standing beside Colonel Talbot, ready to carry his orders, and he heard the veteran say, between his teeth:

"The Yankees have fooled us, and this is the great battle at last."

The two forces looked at each other for a few moments. Elsewhere great guns and rifles were already at work, but the sounds came distantly. On the hill and in the fields there was silence, save for the steady tramp of the advancing Northern troops. Then from the rear of the marching lines suddenly came a burst of martial music. The Northern bands, by a queer inversion, were playing Dixie:

"In Dixie's land
I'll take my stand,
To live and die for Dixie.
Look away! Look away!
Down South in Dixie."

Harry's feet beat to the tune, the wild and thrilling air played for the first time to troops going into battle.

"We must answer that," he said to St. Clair.

"Here comes the answer," said St. Clair, and the Southern bands began to play "The Girl I Left Behind Me." The music entered Harry's veins. He could not look without a quiver upon the great mass of men bearing down upon them, but the strains of fife and drum put courage in him and told him to stand fast. He saw the face of Colonel Talbot grow darker and darker, and he had enough experience himself to know that the odds were heavily against them.

The intense burning sun poured down a flood of light, lighting up the opposing ranks of blue and gray, and gleaming along swords and bayonets. Nearer and nearer came the piercing notes of Dixie.

"They march well," murmured Colonel Talbot, "and they will fight well, too."

He did not know that McDowell himself, the Northern

commander, was now before them, driving on his men, but he did know that the courage and skill of his old comrades were for the present in the ascendant. Burnside was at the head of the division and it seemed long enough to wrap the whole Southern command in its folds and crush it.

Scattered rifle shots were heard on either flank, and the young Invincibles began to breathe heavily. Millions of black specks danced before them in the hot sunshine, and their nervous ears magnified every sound tenfold.

"I wish that tune the Yankees are playing was ours," said Tom Langdon. "I think I could fight battles by it."

"Then we'll have to capture it," said Harry.

Now the time for talking ceased. The rifle fire on the flanks was rising to a steady rattle, and then came the heavy boom of the cannon on either side. Once more the air was filled with the shriek of shells and the whistling of rifle bullets. Men were falling fast, and through the rising clouds of smoke Harry saw the blue lines still coming on. It seemed to him that they would be overwhelmed, trampled underfoot, routed, but he heard Colonel Talbot shouting:

"Steady, Invincibles! Steady!"

And Lieutenant-Colonel St. Hilaire, walking up and down the lines, also uttered the same shout. But the blue line never ceased coming. Harry could see the faces dark with sweat and dust and powder still pressing on. It was well for the Southerners that nearly all of them had been trained in the use of the rifle, and it was well for them, too, that most of their officers were men of skill and experience. Recruits, they stood fast nevertheless and their rifles sent the bullets in an unceasing bitter hail straight into the advancing ranks of blue. There was no sound from the bands now. If they were playing somewhere in the rear no one heard. The fire of the cannon and rifles was a steady roll, louder than thunder and more awful.

The Northern troops hesitated at last in face of such a resolute stand and such accurate firing. Then they retreated a little and a shout of triumph came from the Southern lines, but the respite was only for a moment. The men in blue came on again, walking over their dead and past their wounded.

"If they keep pressing in, and it looks as if they would, they will crush us," murmured Colonel Talbot, but he did not let the Invincibles hear him say it. He encouraged them with voice and example, and they bent forward somewhat to meet the second charge of the Northern army, which was now coming. The smoke lifted a little and Harry saw the green fields and the white house of the Widow Henry standing almost in the middle of the battlefield, but unharmed. Then his eyes came back to the hostile line, which, torn by shot and shell, had closed up, nevertheless, and was advancing again in overwhelming force.

Harry now had a sudden horrible fear that they would be trodden under foot. He looked at St. Clair and saw that his face was ghastly. Langdon had long since ceased to smile or utter words of happy philosophy.

"Open up and let the guns through!" someone suddenly cried, and a wild cheer of relief burst from the Invincibles as they made a path. The valiant Bee and Bartow, rushing to the sound of the great firing, had come with nearly three thousand men and a whole battery. Never were men more welcome. They formed instantly along the Southern front, and the battery opened at once with all its guns, while the three thousand men sent a new fire into the Northern ranks. Yet the Northern charge still came. McDowell, Burnside, and the others were pressing it home, seeking to drive the Southern army from its hill, while they were yet able to bring forces largely superior to bear upon it.

The thunder and crash of the terrible conflict rolled over all the hills and fields for miles. It told the other forces of either army that here was the center of the battle, and here was its crisis. The sounds reached an extraordinary young-old man, bearded and awkward, often laughed at, but never to be laughed at again, one of the most wonderful soldiers the world has ever produced, and instantly gathering up his troops he rushed them toward the very heart of the combat. Stonewall Jackson was about to receive his famous nickname.

Jackson's burning eyes swept proudly over the ranks of his tall Virginians, who mourned every second they lost from the battle. An officer retreating with his battery glanced at him, opened his mouth to speak, but closed it again without saying a word, and infused with new hope, turned his guns afresh toward the enemy. Already men were feeling the magnetic current of energy and resolution that flowed from Jackson like water from a fountain.

A message from Colonel Talbot, which he was to deliver to Jackson himself, sent Harry to the rear. He rode a borrowed horse and he galloped rapidly until he saw a long line of men marching forward at a swift but steady pace. At their head rode a man on a sorrel horse. His shoulders were stooped a little, and he leaned forward in the saddle, gazing intently at the vast bank of smoke and flame before him. Harry noticed that the hands upon the bridle reins did not twitch nor did the horseman seem at all excited. Only his burning eyes showed that every faculty was concentrated upon the task. Harry was conscious even then that he was in the presence of General Jackson.

The boy delivered his message. Jackson received it without comment, never taking his eyes from the battle, which was now raging so fiercely in front of them. Behind came his great brigade of Virginians, the smoke and flame of the battle entering their blood and making their hearts pound fast as they moved forward with increasing speed.

Harry rode back with the young officers of his staff, and now they saw men dash out of the smoke and run toward them. They cried that everything was lost. The lip of Jackson curled in contempt. The long line of his Virginians stopped the fugitives and drove them back to the battle. It was evident to Harry, young as he was, that Jackson would be just in time.

Then they saw a battery galloping from that bank of smoke and flame, and, its officer swearing violently, exclaimed that he had been left without support. The stern face and somber eyes of Jackson were turned upon him.

"Unlimber your guns at once," he said. "Here is your support."

Then the valiant Bee himself came, covered with dust, his clothes torn by bullets, his horse in a white lather. He, too, turned to that stern brown figure, as unflinching as death itself, and he cried that the enemy in overwhelming numbers were beating them back.

"Then," said Jackson, "we'll close up and give them the bayonet."

Continuing battle at Bull Run 21 July 1861, Currier & Ives[85]

His teeth shut down like a vise. Again the electric current leaped forth and sparkled through the veins of Bee, who turned and rode back into the Southern throng, the Virginians following swiftly. Then Jackson looked over the field with the eye and mind of genius, the eye that is able to see and the mind that is able to understand amid all the thunder and confusion and excitement of battle.

He saw a stretch of pines on the edge of the hill near the Henry house. He quickly marched his troops among the trees, covering their front with six cannon, while the great horseman, Stuart, plumed and eager, formed his cavalry upon the left. Harry felt instinctively that the battle was about to be restored for the time at least, and he turned back to Colonel Talbot and the Invincibles. A shell burst near him. A piece struck his horse in the chest, and Harry felt the animal quiver under him. Then the horse uttered a terrible neighing cry, but Harry, alert and agile, sprang clear, and ran back to his own command.

On the other side of Bull Run was the Northern command of Tyler, which had been rebuffed so fiercely three days before. It, too, heard the roar and crash of the battle, and sought a way across Bull Run, but for a time could find none. An officer named Sherman, also destined for a mighty fame, saw a Confederate trooper riding across the river further down, and instantly the whole command charged at the ford. It was defended by only two hundred Southern skirmishers whom they brushed out of the way. They were across in a few minutes, and then they advanced on a run to swell McDowell's army.

General Thomas J. "Stonewall" Jackson at Bull Run[86]

The forces on both sides were increasing and the battle was rising rapidly in volume. But in the face of repeated and furious attacks the Southern troops held fast to the little plateau. Young's Branch flowed on one side of it and protected them in a measure; but only the indomitable spirit of Jackson and Evans, of Bee and Bartow, and others kept them in line against those charges which threatened to shiver them to pieces.

"Look!" cried Bee to some of his men who were wavering. "Look at Jackson, standing there like a stone wall!"

The men ceased to waver and settled themselves anew for a fresh attack.

But in spite of everything the Northern army was gaining ground. Sherman at the very head of the fresh forces that had crossed Bull Run hurled himself upon the Southern army, his main attack falling directly upon the Invincibles. The young recruits reeled, but Colonel Talbot and Lieutenant-Colonel St. Hilaire still ran up and down the lines begging them to stand. They took fresh breath and planted their feet deep once more. Harry raised his rifle and took aim at a flitting figure in the smoke. Then he dropped the muzzle. Either it was reality or a powerful trick of the fancy. It was his own cousin, Dick Mason, but the smoke closed in again, and he did not see the face.

The rush of Sherman was met and repelled. Tie drew back only to come again, and along the whole line the battle closed in once more, fiercer and more deadly than ever. Upon all the combatants beat the fierce sun of July, and clouds of dust rose to mingle with the smoke of cannon and rifles.

The advantage now lay distinctly with the Northern army, won by its clever passage of Bull Run and surprise. But the courage and tenacity of the Southern troops averted defeat and rout in detail. Jackson, in his strong position near the Henry house, in the cellars of which women were hiding, refused to give an inch of ground. Beauregard, called by the cannon, arrived upon the field only an hour before noon, meeting on the way many fugitives, whom he and his officers drove back into the battle. Hampton's South Carolina Legion, which reached Richmond only that morning, came by train and landed directly upon the battlefield about noon. In five minutes it was in the thick of the battle, and it alone stemmed a terrific rush of Sherman, when all others gave way.

Noon had passed and the heart of McDowell swelled with exultation. The Northern troops were still gaining ground, and at many points the Southern line was crushed. Some of the recruits in gray, their nerves shaken horribly, were beginning to run. But fresh troops coming up met them and turned them back to the field. Beauregard and Johnston, the two senior generals, both experienced and calm, were reforming their ranks, seizing new and strong positions, and hurrying up every portion of their force. Johnston himself, after the first rally, hurried back for fresh regiments, while Jackson's men not only held their ground but began to drive the Northern troops before them.

The Invincibles had fallen back somewhat, leaving many dead behind them. Many more were wounded. Harry had received two bullets through his clothing, and St. Clair was nicked on the wrist. Colonel Talbot and Lieutenant-Colonel St. Hilaire were still unharmed, but a deep gloom had settled over the Invincibles. They had not been beaten, but certainly they were not winning. Their ranks were seamed and rent. From the place where they now stood they could see the place where they formerly stood, but Northern troops occupied it now. Tears ran down the faces of some of the youngest, streaking the dust and powder into hideous, grinning masks.

Harry threw himself upon the ground and lay there for a few moments, panting. He choked with heat and thirst, and his heart seemed to have swollen so much within him that it would be a relief to have it burst. His eyes burned with the dust and smoke, and all about him was a fearful reek. He could see from where he lay most of the battlefield. He saw the Northern batteries fire, move forward, and then fire again. He saw the Northern infantry creeping up, ever creeping, and far behind he beheld the flags of fresh regiments coming to their aid. The tears sprang to his eyes. It seemed in very truth that all was lost. In another part of the field the men in blue had seized the Robinson house, and from points near it their artillery was searching the Southern ranks. A sudden grim humor seized the boy.

"Tom," he shouted to Langdon, "what was that you said about sleeping in the White House at Washington with your boots on?"

"I said it," Langdon shouted back, "but I guess it's all off! For God's sake, Harry, give me a drink of water! I'll give anybody a million dollars and a half dozen states for a single drink!"

A soldier handed him a canteen, and he drank from it. The water was warm, but it was nectar, and when he handed it back, he said:

"I don't know you and you don't know me, but if I could I'd give you a whole lake in return for this. Harry, what are our chances?"

"I don't know. We've lost one battle, but we may have time to win another. Jackson and those Virginians of his seem able to stand anything. Up, boys, the battle is on us again!"

The charge swept almost to their feet, but it was driven back, and then came a momentary lull, not a cessation of the battle, but merely a sinking, as if the combatants were gathering themselves afresh for a new and greater effort. It was two o'clock in the afternoon, and the fierce July sun was at its zenith, pouring its burning rays upon both armies, alike upon the living and upon the dead who were now so numerous.

The lull was most welcome to the men in gray. Some fresh regiments sent by Johnston had come already, and they hoped for more, but whether they came or not, the army must stand. The brigades were massed heavily around the Henry house with that of Jackson standing stern and indomitable, the strongest wall against the foe. His fame and his spirit were spreading fast over the field.

The lull was brief, the whole Northern army, its lines reformed, swept forward in a half curve, and the Southern army sent forth a stream of shells and bullets to meet it. The brigades of Jackson and Sherman, indomitable foes, met face to face and swept back and forth over the ground, which was littered with their fallen. Everywhere the battle assumed a closer and fiercer phase. Hampton, who had come just in time with his guns, went down wounded badly. Beauregard himself was wounded slightly, and so was Jackson, hit in the hand. Many distinguished officers were killed.

Union retreat at First Bull Run[87]

The whole Northern army was driven back four times, and it came a fifth time to be repulsed once more. In the very height of the struggle Harry caught a glimpse in front of them of a long horizontal line of red, like a gleaming ribbon.

"It's those Zouaves!" cried Langdon. "Shoot their pants!"

He did not mean it as a jest. The words just jumped out, and true to their meaning the Invincibles fired straight at that long line of red, and then reloading fired again. The Zouaves were cut to pieces, the field was strewed with their brilliant uniforms. A few officers tried to bring on the scattered remnants, but two regiments of regulars, sweeping in between and bearing down on the Invincibles, saved them from extermination.

The Invincibles would have suffered the fate they had dealt out to the Zouaves, but fresh regiments came to their help and the regulars were driven back. Sherman and Jackson were still fighting face to face, and Sherman was unable to advance. Howard hurled a fresh force on the men in gray. Bee and Bartow, who had done such great deeds earlier in the day, were both killed. A Northern force under Heintzelman, converging for a flank attack, was set upon and routed by the Southerners, who put them all to flight, captured three guns and took the Robinson house.

Fortune, nevertheless, still seemed to favor the North. The Southerners had barely held their positions around the Henry house. Most of their cannon were dismounted. Hundreds had dropped from exhaustion. Some had died from heat and excessive exertion. The mortality among the officers was frightful. There were few hopeful hearts in the Southern army.

It was now three o'clock in the afternoon and Beauregard, through his glasses, saw a great column of dust rising above the tops of the trees. His experience told him that it must be made by marching troops, but what troops were they, Northern or Southern? In an agony of suspense he appealed to the generals around him, but they could tell nothing. He sent off aides at a gallop to see, but meanwhile he and his generals could only wait, while the column of dust grew broader and broader and higher and higher. His heart sank like a plummet in a pool. The cloud was on the Federal flank and everything indicated that it was the army of Patterson, marching from the Valley of Virginia.

Harry and his comrades had also seen the dust, and they regarded it anxiously. They knew as well as any general present that their fate lay within that cloud.

"It's coming fast, and it's growing faster," said Harry. "I've got so used to the roar of this battle that it seems to me alien sounds are detached from it, and are heard easily. I can hear the rumble of cannon wheels in that cloud."

"Then tell us, Harry," said Langdon, "is it a Northern rumble or a Southern rumble that you hear?"

Harry laughed.

"I'll admit it's a good deal of a fancy," he said.

Arthur St. Clair suddenly leaped high in the air, and uttered at the very top of his voice the wild note of the famous rebel yell.

"Look at the flags aloft in that cloud of dust! It's the Star and Bars! God bless the Bonnie Blue Flag! They are our own men coming, and coming in time!"

Now the battle flags appeared clearly through the dust, and the great rebel yell, swelling and triumphant, swept the whole Southern line. It was the remainder of Johnston's Army of the Shenandoah. It had slipped away from Patterson, and all through the burning day it had been marching steadily toward the battlefield, drummed on by the thudding guns. Johnston, the silent and alert, was himself with them now, and aflame with zeal they were advancing on the run straight for the heart of the Northern army.

Kirby Smith, one of Harry's own Kentucky generals, was in the very van of the relieving force. A man after Stonewall Jackson's own soul, he rushed forward with the leading regiments and they hurled themselves bodily upon the Northern flank.

The impact was terrible. Smith fell wounded, but his men rushed on and the men behind also threw themselves into the battle. Almost at the same instant Jubal Early, who had made a circuit with a strong force, hurled it upon the side of the Northern army. The brave troops in blue were exhausted by so many hours of fierce fighting and fierce heat. Their whole line broke and began to fall back. The Southern generals around the Henry house saw it and exulted. Swift orders were sent and the bugles blew the charge for the men who had stood so many long and bitter hours on the defense.

"Now, Invincibles, now!" cried Colonel Leonidas Talbot. "Charge home, just once, my boys, and the victory is ours!"

Covered with dust and grime, worn and bleeding with many wounds, but every heart beating triumphantly, what was left of the Invincibles rose up and followed their leader. Harry was conscious of a flame almost in his face and of whirling clouds of smoke and dust. Then the entire Southern army burst upon the confused Northern force and shattered it so completely that it fell to pieces.

The bravest battle ever fought by men, who, with few exceptions, had not smelled the powder of war before, was lost and won.

As the Southern cannon and rifles beat upon them, the Northern army, save for the regulars and the cavalry, dissolved. The generals could not stem the flood. They rushed forward in confused masses, seeking only to save themselves. Whole regiments dashed into the fords of Bull Run and emerged dripping on the other side. A bridge was covered with spectators come out from Washington to see the victory, many of them bringing with them baskets of lunch. Some were Members of Congress, but all joined in the panic and flight, carrying to the capital many untrue stories of disaster.

Ruins of Bull Run Bridge after the First Battle of Bull Run[88]

A huge mass of fleeing men emerged upon the Warrenton turnpike, throwing away their weapons and ammunition that they might run the faster. It was panic pure and simple, but panic for the day only. For hours they had fought as bravely as the veterans of twenty battles, but now, with weakened nerves, they thought that an overwhelming force was upon them. Every shell that the Southern guns sent among them urged them to greater speed. The cavalry and little force of regulars covered the rear, and with firm and unbroken ranks retreated slowly, ready to face the enemy if he tried pursuit.

But the men in gray made no real pursuit. They were so worn that they could not follow, and they yet scarcely believed in the magnitude of their own victory, snatched from the very jaws of defeat. Twenty-eight Northern cannon and ten flags were in their hands, but thousands of dead and wounded lay upon the field, and night was at hand again, close and hot.

Harry turned back to the little plateau where those that were left of the Invincibles were already kindling their cooking fires. He looked for his two comrades and recognized them both under their masks of dust and powder.

"Are you hurt, Tom?" he said to Langdon.

"No, and I'm going to sleep in the White House at Washington after all."

"And you, Arthur?"

"There's a red line across my wrist, where a bullet passed, but it's nothing. Listen, what do you think of that, boys?"

A Southern band had gathered in the edge of the wood and was playing a wild thrilling air, the words of which meant nothing, but the tune everything:

"In Dixie's land
I'll take my stand,
To live and die for Dixie.
Look away! Look away!
Look away down South in Dixie."

"So we have taken their tune from them and made it ours!" St. Clair exclaimed jubilantly. "After all, it really belonged to us! We'll play it through the streets of Washington."

But Colonel Leonidas Talbot, who stood close by, raised his hand warningly.

"Boys," he said, "this is only the beginning."

Unidentified woman holding photo of Confederate soldier[89]

About the editor (compiler of illustrations)

Ryan K Englund was first introduced to Altsheler's works by a dedicated elementary school librarian. Ryan has been a management consultant for more than three decades. In his writing and presentations for business he conveys principles through stories. His clients have earned several billion dollars with his counsel (ignoring, of course, one trillion-dollar misfortune). He has deep experience bringing peace in a world that seems to have more than a few bullies. Ryan also knows how it feels to fail and, with no power, how to get things done.

Business is his vocation; stories are his nature. Ryan and Mary, his wife of 41 years, participate as multiple characters in his semi-autobiographical novels. They also play roles in novels exploring historical turning points in which their ancestors engaged. Mary and Ryan are the parents of six children and 13 grandchildren. They have lived in California, Idaho, Maine, Massachusetts, Utah, Washington, and Wyoming.

ENDNOTES

As noted in the Introduction, unless otherwise indicated, illustrations for this edition are derived from images created during the U.S. Civil War period (1861-1865) and are in the public domain, according to the rights advisory for each image derived from the website of the Library of Congress.

To learn about an original image, query a web search engine by typing, firstly, "Library of Congress" and, secondly, the image number below with ".tif" or ".tiff" added immediately following the number. The link to the image should appear within the first few search results.

---

1 3b49684u

2 3b32191u and 3a37766u

3 35627u, this soldier is wearing a Private's uniform

4 3a02884u ; A Straggler, from *Harper's Weekly* 28 Mar 1863

5 21023u ; Spring on the railroad near Richmond, ca July 1862

6 3a49760u; "Head of the Knights of the Golden Circle," according to an 1865 publication by an unknown publisher

7 37165u

8 20680u.tif ; Potomac Creek bridge, Feb 1863

9 21023u

10 20753u; drawn about 1876 as part of *Life studies of the great army*

11 10900u

12 34506u

13 21552u

14 3b34242u, female secessionist in Baltimore, *Harper's* 7 Sep 1861

15 1s01816u

16 3c27613u

17 3c19751u

18 35457u

19 20648u; drawn 30 Sep 1863, after Chickamauga, of a Union soldier

20 31657u

21 20323u

22 1s02946u, photographs sometime 1861-1869

23 3b09844u

24 21660u

25 21107u

26 03007u, drawing actually made in 1863

27 33348u

---

[28] 23852u , Jefferson Davis, photographed 1858-1860 by Matthew Brady
[29] 10971u, Brierfield slave quarters, photographed 1860-1870?
[30] 3c32567u
[31] 20232u
[32] 20232u
[33] 3b32486u
[34] 31461u
[35] 00120u
[36] 35359u.tif; drawn ca 1864
[37] 35361u
[38] 31309u
[39] 32284u
[40] 35456u
[41] 3c29741u; 1st Regiment, South Carolina Infantry, Company D—also known as the Abbeville Volunteers—6 months in 1861
[42] 3a51675u, *Harper's* 24 Dec 1864
[43] 21772u
[44] 20211u
[45] 32624u
[46] 20229u, ca 1860-1865
[47] 20034u
[48] 32685u and 33441u
[49] 40604u
[50] 34643u
[51] 32684u
[52] 04792a
[53] 20623u; this drawing, made 25 Apr 1864, is of a fireplace in African-American hut
[54] 33306u
[55] 22525u; Homer's sketches were modified in *Harper's* 23 Nov 1861
[56] 3c00583u
[57] 3c38384u
[58] 37159u
[59] 32474u
[60] 21268u; Captain Ricketts Battery, Charleston VA, 10 Mar 1862
[61] *21536u*
[62] 20646u
[63] 20771u; drawn about 1876 as part of *Life studies of the great army*
[64] 22487u
[65] 20697u, drawn 12 May 1864 at Spotsylvania Courthouse
[66] 20768u; drawn about 1876 as part of *Life studies of the great army*
[67] 31553u
[68] 20665u; hut drawn near Fredericksburg
[69] 07545a
[70] 21554u
[71] 20744u; drawn about 1876 as part of *Life studies of the great army*

---

[72] 37149u
[73] 20605u; the drawing,20 May 1863, is of a soldier's hut, Falmouth, VA
[74] 3b30010u
[75] 21324u; drawing made Apr 1865
[76] 3b32809u
[77] 40691u
[78] 20759u; drawn about 1876 as part of *Life studies of the great army*
[79] 23159u
[80] 20770u; drawn about 1876 as part of Life studies of the great army
[81] 35556u; illustration shows African Americans, carrying their possessions, running along a river bank at night, toward a bridge that leads to Fort Monroe; there are some Union soldiers among them. Fort Monroe, Virginia, remained in Union hands throughout the War
[82] 20479u
[83] 37275u
[84] 3b27095u
[85] 3b52202u
[86] 3b49684u, 1st Battle of Bull Run; painted in 1900
[87] 00335u
[88] 32895u
[89] 31281u

Made in the USA
Charleston, SC
14 July 2015